Song of the Celtic Stones

Song of the Celtic Stones

Deborah L. Gonzalez

www.mascotbooks.com

Song of the Celtic Stones

Cover illustration by Paul Smith

For more information, please contact:
Mascot Books, an imprint of Amplify Publishing Group
620 Herndon Parkway, Suite 220
Herndon, VA 20170
info@mascotbooks.com

Library of Congress Number: 2025927278

CPSIA Code: PRV0126A

ISBN-13: 979-8-89138-757-7

Printed in the United States

I dedicate this book to my family—those who paved the way, those who walk with me, and those yet to be.

And to you, dear reader—thank you for finding this story.

CHAPTER 1

California Dreamin'

The warm, golden rays of the California sun streamed through my bedroom window, wrapping me in a cozy embrace as I turned off my relentless alarm. I stretched my arms luxuriously, savoring the moment. A pulse of excitement surged through me when I remembered what day it was. I was officially on vacation, bound for Spain in just a few hours. My heart fluttered at the thought of my destination: Zafra, a charming little town nestled in the province of Badajoz.

I could finally get away from the chaos of my love life and focus on me again for a while. Imagining myself on a plane sipping a mineral water and watching California get smaller and smaller was enough to spring me out of bed, and for the first time in a long time, I found myself singing out loud on the way to the shower.

Before Brian Golding, I'd always sung to myself.

Until recently, my life had felt perfectly aligned, thanks to him. He'd seemed like the ideal partner to begin with, with his sun-kissed blond hair, piercing blue eyes, and physique that could only belong to a quintessential California surfer. He's always been somewhat of an old-fashioned soul, but after the engagement, he became more protective, more controlling, and more decisive on mutual decisions, ones I should have had a say in. It seemed like he no longer appreciated a strong, independent woman. I had not changed. Brian was the one who had changed.

It's better this way, I told myself as I stood under the shower, blasting some cold water to distract myself from thinking about him.

It didn't work.

As I rinsed the shampoo from my hair, I couldn't help wishing that *we'd* worked. It turns out opposites may attract, but they don't always stick. Brian, born into affluence, had inherited a sprawling mansion in Germany and supported himself as an independent journalist, seeking stories in the most exotic corners of the globe. He was so different from me, and I thought that meant we'd complement one another. Wasn't that what people always said should happen? We did to start with. We used to have such fun together, that is, until we became engaged.

Then our relationship fell apart—when Brian changed.

I could feel some of my excitement waning as I slowly got dressed in the bathroom. I shouldn't be thinking about the past, not before an exciting trip. But I couldn't think about Brian without thinking of his marriage proposal, and I couldn't think about his marriage proposal without thinking about—

Mom.

I swallowed hard, trying to banish the picture in my mind of her pale, sunken face in the hospice bed.

Breast cancer was a cruel disease, taking away the person I loved most in the world and leaving an unfilled void in my heart.

My dad is another story. Mom always said he had a wild streak and a serious gambling problem. One day, just after my first birthday, he left the house, supposedly to run an errand, and he never returned home. He and my mom divorced soon thereafter. The next time I saw my dad was on my fourteenth birthday when he gifted me with a season of archery lessons with a well-renowned master archer. That was the last time I saw my dad. Mom did an incredible job raising me on her own, working two jobs to support us. From an early age, I learned the value of a dollar and how to budget to make ends meet. Growing up, I became very aware of the social and economic injustices in the world.

After graduating from college with a Bachelor of Arts in Education degree,

I took my first job as a substitute teacher. That position lasted about a year before I was hired as a full-time Spanish teacher for eighth-grade students. My goal was not just to educate children but to find solutions that would bridge the gap between students from affluent neighborhoods and those whose families relied on state assistance for affordable housing. Growing up without a father had motivated me to become a strong, independent woman who could succeed on her own, with or without a partner.

Mom would have been pleased to know I was going on a vacation to explore and paint the Spanish countryside of Zafra. It will help me feel closer to her. She always encouraged me to pursue my passions. In her final days, she'd urged me to follow my passion for painting rather than the stable path of a teacher. Her words struck me deeply, forcing me to reevaluate my priorities in life. I owed her that much; all she ever wanted was for me to be happy.

Brian and I were supposed to go on this vacation together, but work commitments pulled him away, and he abruptly canceled my airline ticket. Though I insisted on going solo, he voiced concerns about my safety. Fortunately, I snagged one of the last seats available on the plane.

Pilates, I told myself. That will keep me grounded and stop me from spiraling.

Hopefully.

After a refreshing session that energized my body, I whipped up a quick breakfast, my mind racing with anticipation.

A thrill coursed through me as I heard my Uber's engine outside. I checked my belongings—passport, art supplies, and a heart full of hope—before stepping out the door, ready to embrace whatever adventure awaited.

The Uber ride passed in a blur, and the airport buzzed with activity as I arrived with thirty minutes to spare. I freshened up in the ladies' room, taking a moment to breathe and center myself before the flight. Nerves danced in my stomach, but excitement overpowered them. I was ready for this new chapter.

As the aircraft ascended into the clear blue sky, I looked out the small window, watching the vibrant city of San Diego dwindle beneath me.

CHAPTER 2

Zafra, Spain

As I stepped off the bus in Zafra, I looked around in wonder at the sight of horses and carriages trotting down the main road, giving the town an enchanting, timeless quality. The charming little shops and eateries with their rustic facades felt like a scene from the mid-1970s. With some time to spare before my ride arrived, I wandered across the street to the Zafra market to gather some necessary groceries.

As I emerged from the market, my arms loaded with fresh produce and groceries, I spotted a handsome young man holding a sign that read "Maryann LeMaster." I waved and walked up to him.

"Hello, I'm Maryann LeMaster," I said. "Are you my driver?"

The man tipped his hat when he noticed the young woman waving at him with a broad grin. "Hello, Miss Maryann. I'm Bruno Pilato, the best driver in all of Zafra!" he declared, with laughter and merriment dancing in his eyes. "If you don't mind, miss, I'll be happy to stow your groceries and belongings in the back of my carriage."

"No, not at all, Bruno," I replied with a giggle, happy to have a driver with such a gregarious personality. As I stepped up to the carriage, I admired the vibrant red and green hand-painted sign on its side that read "Pilato's Fine Gypsy Wares" in both English and what I guessed was Romani.

The ride through town was bumpy but entertaining. Bruno's spirited stories about his family distracted me from any discomfort. Before I knew it, the carriage came to a halt. Looking out, I was struck by the sight of a picturesque stone cottage nestled at the foot of a mountain, utterly alone in its serene surroundings. Distracted by the breathtaking view, I was startled when Bruno opened the door and extended his hand to help me disembark.

"The steps are a bit steep. Allow me to help you down, Miss Maryann," he said, as he reached out and took my hand.

"Thank you, Bruno," I replied with a blush, deeply appreciating his kindness.

As we walked toward the cottage, the sweet scent of wild jasmine filled the air. Bruno trailed behind, carrying my bags with ease. I eagerly unlocked the door and stepped into the cozy entrance of the cottage, Bruno following closely behind. I smiled, thanked him, and handed him a generous tip.

"You are welcome," he replied in a pleasant Romani accent. "And thank you for the generous tip, Miss Maryann. If you ever need a ride to town, call me." He whipped out his business card. "I'm usually at the tavern a mile back up the road most evenings," he replied with a mischievous smile, "if you need some company."

Blushing and steering the conversation to a more serious question, I asked, "Bruno, I plan to do some oil painting during my vacation. Are there any fortresses or abandoned cottages nearby?"

His laughter rang out. "You'll find old buildings everywhere in Zafra. Just walk in any direction." With a playful grin and a wink, he added, "And remember, don't hesitate to reach out to me if you want company." In a slightly more serious tone, he said, "If there is anything you need, I'm close by." Tipping his hat, he strolled to his carriage whistling a happy tune.

I chuckled as his carriage rolled away into the distance. Bruno was quite a character, and I could easily see us becoming friends. Closing the front door, a wave of contentment washed over me as I surveyed the spacious, modern kitchen. The living room had a vintage charm. There was an old-fashioned love seat in the center, with a hand-quilted blanket draped over its back. A lovely Tiffany lamp illuminated the small space, while an old brick fireplace dominated one wall. My heart raced at the sight of a timeworn piano nestled in the corner. As I sat down to play a few notes, I was surprised to find it perfectly tuned.

The modest yet inviting bedroom boasted a plush, full-size bed with pristine white bedding and a beautifully crafted heirloom armoire. The bathroom, with its vintage clawfoot bathtub, took my breath away, enticing me to indulge in a long soak.

After a refreshing bath, I poured myself a glass of chilled chardonnay and lit the fireplace. Settling into the love seat and savoring the crackling heat of the fire, I soon fell into a blissful sleep.

CHAPTER 3

The Castle

It took me a few moments to work out where I was when I woke up the next morning to light pouring through my window. It felt good to wake up refreshed instead of achy and groggy. Excited to start the day, I jumped out of bed and stretched.

While waiting for the water to boil for my herbal tea, I made myself comfortable on the window bench, enjoying the warmth of the sun's rays on my skin. The soft sound of a running stream beside the cottage relaxed me as a slight breeze drifted through the window, causing a gentle draft to ripple the semitransparent curtains. Eager to explore, I dressed in light clothes, grabbed a breakfast bar and sketch pad, and ventured outside.

An inviting, well-traversed path up the mountain caught my eye. That would be a good starting point. Walking up the trail, I began humming a lovely, yet strange, haunting melody. I stopped when goose bumps suddenly erupted on my arms.

Where did that weird melody come from?

Thirty minutes later, my breath caught in my throat as I reached the mountain's high point and stumbled upon an ancient castle—its solid walls seemingly frozen in time. As I gazed at the castle, it seemed to beckon me with an unmistakable sense of déjà vu, despite my never having set foot on its grounds.

My feet glided along the cobblestone path with a curious familiarity.

I've been here before.

Where did that thought come from? My stomach fluttered, and I told myself I should have picked up more than just a breakfast bar to start the day with.

When I reached the entrance, two fierce-looking stone gargoyles flanked the massive wooden door as if guarding the castle. Their watchful eyes seemed to peer into my soul, sending a shiver down my spine. Just then, I heard footsteps approaching quickly from behind me. A young man appeared before me, looking like an aristocrat with old-world charm. He had a lean, muscular build, dark curly hair, and serious brown eyes that seemed to hold secrets.

"Welcome, Señorita. I am Francisco Ignacio Gutiérrez, and this is my home, Castillo de los Conquistadores," he said with a slight Spanish accent.

"It's nice to meet you, Francisco," I stammered. "My name is Maryann LeMaster, and I'm vacationing in the valley below. I stumbled upon your castle while exploring the area."

Studying the attractive young lady before him, his eyes brightened. "Miss Maryann, I am glad you found the castle. Would you care for some refreshments? You must be tired from your hike."

Despite my usual caution with strangers, an inexplicable curiosity nudged me to accept. As I stepped into the castle's grand foyer, my breath caught in my throat. On display was a full suit of armor alongside an impressive family crest and an assortment of old swords.

Francisco chuckled softly. "Please forgive me. We don't often have visitors, and I see these old relics daily. The parlor is just ahead. Please, follow me."

As I followed him into a room rich with history, he said, "Have a seat, and I'll be right back with some refreshments."

"Thank you," I replied, grateful for his kindness.

As I surveyed the room, the faded upholstery and worn tapestries spoke of a long-lost elegance. Antique-looking artwork adorned the walls, and that same déjà vu washed over me again.

A brief moment later, Francisco reappeared with a tray of assorted beverages. "Would you like some wine, lemonade, or water?"

"Lemonade would be great. Thank you," I replied.

Francisco handed me the cup of lemonade and made himself comfortable in a chair directly across from me, gazing at me with curiosity in his eyes. "Excuse me, Miss Maryann, if I may ask, where are you from?"

"I'm from San Diego, California," I replied. "I teach Spanish to junior high students, but my life feels mundane compared to yours. I'd love to hear about your family history and the origins of this castle, if you don't mind sharing." Curiosity and excitement filled my voice. Francisco's eyes sparkled. I'd hit on something he loved to talk about.

"Trust me, my life is anything but exciting, but I am passionate about the history of my ancestors," replied Francisco. "They built this castle in the mid- to late 1500s, and our family has lived here ever since. For many years, my ancestors hosted jousting tournaments and grand balls and entertained kings and queens. However, the celebrations dwindled in the mid- to late 1600s."

I sat forward, fascinated. "That's incredible, Francisco! What do you think caused the decline?" I asked, my curiosity piqued.

Francisco hesitated, a shadow crossing his face. "There are whispers of family secrets and scandals, but I don't lend much credence to them. While there have been challenges in maintaining the castle, I doubt curses played a role, despite what my ancestors believed."

Lost in thought, I barely noticed an older man approaching, leaning heavily on a cane. Francisco sprang to his feet. "Miss Maryann, allow me to introduce my father, Miguel Gutiérrez. Father, this is Miss Maryann LeMaster from America. She discovered our castle while exploring the area."

"It's nice to meet you, young lady," he said, smiling warmly. "We rarely receive visitors here anymore. It's a blessing that you found your way here. Please, don't be a stranger. We would love for you to visit often while you are here on vacation."

"It is wonderful to meet you too, Mr. Gutiérrez," I said, taking in the old-world-charm ambience of the castle. "Your home is exquisite."

Just then, a dark-haired older woman entered the room. She seemed to glow with an inner radiance, her eyes bright with intelligence and curiosity.

"Allow me to introduce my aunt Juanita," exclaimed Francisco, with pride. "Her revered mother supervised the castle staff when my grandfather was alive. Aunt Juanita holds the treasures of this castle's history. I honestly don't know what we'd do without her."

Juanita smiled as she came closer, and I felt an electric energy in the air. She reached out, we shook hands, and zap! Both of us felt an electric shock. Gasping, she took a step back and stared at me, and the moment seemed to drag on. I began to feel uncomfortable, and I felt like she wasn't just staring at me but through me and beyond.

"Is everything all right?" I asked, as my concern for her grew.

Her eyes instantly softened and returned to a focused clarity. "Yes—I'm sorry," she stammered. "We both seem to be holding electricity in our bodies. It just startled me." Laughing, she said, "Perhaps we'll have a chance to talk more when you visit again."

"Yes, I would like that." Suddenly, the room felt heavier, denser, and then a second later, everything felt as it had before. But the brief, strange interaction with Juanita still lingered in my mind.

Francisco began talking again as if nothing strange had happened. He was saying something about the great women healers and psychics in Juanita's lineage and that she was also Miguel's half-sister. I was half listening at that point, as I was still feeling a bit strange.

In an instant, the melancholy chime of the grandfather clock echoed through the space, reminding me of my need to return home before it became too dark. "My apologies, but I must take my leave," I said reluctantly. *Why do I feel so sad about leaving?* I tried to picture the quaint cottage to which I was returning. After all, I'd come here for quiet and solitude, hadn't I? But something about the feeling of this place made me want to stay. Or maybe I was just dreading being alone again.

"Miss Maryann, you're welcome to visit us anytime," stated Francisco, with confidence and assurance. "Honestly, it gets dreadfully dull in this old castle." He chuckled as he opened the towering front door.

"I'll certainly try to return tomorrow," I said, stepping out into the cool evening air. "Thank you once again for your hospitality. It was nice to meet you all!"

As I walked away, the castle loomed behind me, its silhouette like a wise sentinel watching over the secrets of the past.

CHAPTER 4

The Dream

Back at the cottage, I kindled a fire in the stone fireplace and made some scrambled eggs on toast. Settling into the cozy love seat, feeling full and content, I wrapped myself in a soft quilt and drifted off to sleep. In the predawn stillness, I awoke with a racing heart, freezing at a disturbing sound. A faint echo of the same haunting melody I'd been humming the day before.

My stomach knotted. As my eyes fluttered open, the enchanting tune faded into silence, vanishing like a whisper in the breeze.

What is it about that strange melody?

Too weary to ponder its meaning, I shuffled to bed and surrendered to a deep, dreamless sleep for the remainder of the night.

The following day dawned bright and inviting, filling me with eagerness to return to the castle. After a light breakfast of yogurt and fresh fruit, I found solace at the piano, and for some reason, every note I played reminded me of the castle.

What is it about that castle?

It would make a spectacular subject for my painting and a cherished memento of my vacation. Fueled by determination, I set off on a hike up the mountain, excited by the prospect of seeking Francisco's permission to paint his castle.

The bright sun illuminated the path walkway, and I reveled in the beauty around me. Upon reaching the castle, I spotted Francisco lounging on the patio, engrossed in a newspaper. He looked up and acknowledged me with a nod and waved me over.

"Miss Maryann! I'm delighted you've returned. I was just about to go inside and enjoy some coffee and sweet bread. Would you care to join me?"

Grinning, I accepted his kind offer. As we stepped inside, he gestured for me to have a seat while he fetched the refreshments. My gaze wandered to the portraits adorning the walls—those of Francisco's ancestors—each face strikingly similar and exuding a sense of history and pride.

Returning with a tray of sweet bread and a carafe of rich coffee, he poured me a cup, his eyes sparkling brightly. "I hope you're enjoying your vacation here in Zafra. Is there anything I can do to make your stay even more memorable?" he asked.

Taking a deep breath to summon my courage, I said, "Actually, there is, Francisco. I'm an amateur oil painter and would love to paint your castle."

His face lit up with enthusiasm. "Oh, wow! Consider my casa your casa!" he exclaimed.

"Wonderful, thank you!" I said, feeling a rush of excitement.

After Francisco proudly gave me a mini-tour of the castle, we enjoyed a light lunch on the terrace. The rest of the afternoon was spent conversing and getting to know each other better. From our seats, the view of the forest and valley below was breathtaking, further fueling my inspiration.

As the soft golden glow of the setting sun began to spread across the valley, I knew it was time to leave. "Francisco, thank you once again for the lovely day," I said, my voice filled with gratitude. "I plan to bring my painting supplies tomorrow. I can't wait to start on the painting!" Excitement bubbled up within me.

"Yes, it was a nice day, and I enjoyed your company, Miss Maryann," he replied, smiling. "See you tomorrow."

Waving goodbye, I walked away feeling a sense of purpose, and a sense of contentment washed over me as I leisurely made my way back to the cottage.

After indulging in a relaxing bath, I brewed a soothing cup of chamomile tea. It didn't take me long to get comfy after that, as I nestled into my favorite spot on the love seat, the warmth of the crackling fire wrapping around me like an embrace. As I gazed into the mesmerizing flames, my eyelids grew heavy, and my body melted with relaxation. I roused myself with a reluctant sigh and retreated to bed, soon slipping into a vivid, lucid dream.

She was beautiful, the woman in the dungeon. Soft hair and piercing eyes. Her name was Lady Magdalena Constanza.

How did I know that? *I wondered as I watched her from the shadows. She was weeping in despair, and my heart broke for her with every sob. She'd brought it on herself, something whispered in the back of my mind. She'd deceived the castle's lord, trapping him with false lies. The agony of loss enveloped her, and I closed my eyes tightly at the sudden images that pushed their way into my mind.*

The baby.

The silence.

I sensed the weight of her silent childbirth, the emptiness that followed—no cries, no sound, just an aching void. Though she was consumed by darkness and madness, Lord Rodrigo Gutiérrez still came to see her, I remembered, and he'd been painfully aware of her betrayal.

And then somehow, I was looking through her eyes. Seeing what she saw. Seeing him. Tall and striking, with bright green eyes that sparkled with a fierce intensity. At that moment, I felt the depth of her love for him, and the emotion surged through my heart. But the tide of emotion soon turned to bitter fury, and I was thrown from her mind as Lady Magdalena condemned him and his future descendants. Her body convulsed violently, and with her final breath, she unleashed a curse that lingered in the air like a chilling wind.

Awakening in a tangle of sweat-soaked sheets, I stumbled to the bathroom, splashing cold water on my face to ground myself. Nerves still buzzing from the vivid dream, I lingered in the quiet darkness until the remnants of fear faded before finally retreating to bed, hoping for a dreamless sleep.

CHAPTER 5

The Gold Locket

After arriving at the castle grounds early the following day with my painting supplies, I began exploring the castle's perimeter. I found the perfect spot to set up my easel in a cozy, tucked-away clearing surrounded by tall bushes and fragrant wildflowers, with a small trickling stream flowing along the inner edge of the clearing. A large willow tree provided ample shade, shielding me from anyone who might survey the area from outside. The only visible opening was in one section of the foliage, giving me a perfect view of the castle to paint.

I unpacked my supplies and eagerly set up my easel. Holding my paintbrush and ready to make the first stroke on the blank canvas, I closed my eyes and sent a thought to my mother.

This is for you, Mom.

I painted for several hours, losing track of time until the sound of my growling stomach interrupted my concentration. I was pleased with my progress. The basic outline of the castle and its surroundings was taking shape. It was getting late, so I covered the painting, packed away the supplies, and began the walk back home to the cottage.

Over the following week, I embraced a new routine, arriving at the castle just after the morning sun had climbed high in the sky. Francisco and I would share meals on the terrace, savoring the crisp air and the gorgeous view before I ventured off to my painting retreat.

One particular morning after we'd finished brunch, I turned to Francisco, bursting to ask him the question that had burned in my mind all morning. "Would it be possible to explore one of the chambers once occupied by your ancestors? Delving into the history of the castle and its past occupants might give me more ideas and inspiration for the painting."

Francisco's laughter rang out like music, accompanied by a mischievous glint in his eye. "Oh, Miss Maryann, we can do even better! Several rooms on the top floor still hold treasures from my ancestors. Would you like to see one right now?" His enthusiasm was infectious, and I couldn't contain my excitement.

"Yes! Please, lead the way!" I said, unable to hide my glee. As he escorted me up the worn staircase beside the kitchen, my heart raced, a childlike thrill coursing through me. It was like stepping into a forgotten adventure as we climbed to the castle's shadowy upper wing. Francisco produced an ancient skeleton key, pausing at a doorway along the long, dusty corridor. With a click and a gentle push, he opened the creaking door to reveal a room shrouded in secrets and neglected for decades.

I coughed as the dust made its way to my nostrils. An oversize antique chest rested on the floor, flanked by an antique bed and a dresser that had seen better days. The air was thick with the scent of history, and I was eager to uncover its secrets. A shiver ran down my spine.

"This chest belonged to an unknown woman who we believe was a guest at the castle sometime in the early seventeenth century," he said, a twinkle sparkling in his eyes. "Though her identity remains a mystery, I thought you might enjoy unraveling a mystery."

As he lifted the lid, a world of wonders spilled forth. Beautiful gowns, meticulously wrapped and nestled in linen, lay alongside quilts, miniature portraits, and other small items of interest. Among the treasures, a small gold locket caught my eye. I picked it up cautiously, opening it to reveal a tiny, faded portrait of a woman. She had long auburn ringlets adorned with a fancy feathered hat that complemented her emerald dress. The features of her face were blurred with age, leaving only shadows of her beauty.

My breath caught as I read the engraving: "To the lovely ML. With loving affection, RG."

"What a coincidence!" My heart raced. "My initials are ML. Who do you think RG was?"

Francisco pondered the engraving, a thoughtful expression crossing his face. "RG might stand for my ancestor, Lord Rodrigo Gutiérrez, the castle's lord in the early 1600s. Perhaps ML was his mistress."

As he spoke, a vivid recollection washed over me, and the room began to spin—my dream.

Lady Magdalena and Lord Rodrigo Gutiérrez.

A shiver coursed through my body as I held ML's locket, and a tingling sensation surged up my arm. When I opened my eyes, Francisco was looking at me with a concerned expression.

"Are you all right, Miss Maryann?" he asked, his voice laced with genuine worry. "You look a bit pale."

"I'm fine, Francisco," I answered reassuringly. "I think it's because of the lack of sleep due to the strange dreams I've been having. Thanks for showing me this room and indulging my curiosity. It was an exciting adventure!"

He chuckled as he helped me rise from the floor, and I carefully returned the locket to the chest. "We can explore other rooms another day if you like."

"Oh, that would be great! Thanks again, Francisco. I can't wait for our next exploration."

Francisco led me back downstairs and accompanied me to the front door. "See you soon, Miss Maryann," he said with a soft kiss to my hand, a gesture I found quaint and old-fashioned yet undeniably charming.

"Such a gentleman!" I said with a chuckle. After saying my goodbyes, I practically skipped down the mountain path, feeling happy to have had such a fun and intriguing day.

The day's events replayed in my mind as I lay in bed a few hours later. My thoughts lingered on the locket and the inexplicable connection I'd felt while holding it.

Did it all mean something, or was the stress of the past year finally getting to me?

CHAPTER 6

Portrait of Lord Rodrigo Gutiérrez

The next morning, Francisco and I shared a delicious breakfast on the terrace, the bright sun providing comforting warmth.

Francisco turned to me and cleared his throat. "Unfortunately, I'm going to be busy the rest of the day, Miss Maryann," he stated. "Is there anything you need before I leave?"

"There is," I admitted. "Would you mind if I spent a little time looking at your ancestral portraits before I start painting today?"

"Of course not. Make yourself at home here," he said with an encouraging nod. "Have a good day, Miss Maryann!"

"Thanks, Francisco. The same to you," I replied. With a sense of anticipation thrumming in my veins, I walked through the castle toward the gallery of ancestral portraits, driven by a singular desire: to find Lord Rodrigo Gutiérrez.

As I ventured closer, an inexplicable pull drew me to his portrait. I halted before the piece, my gaze fixating on the name plaque: Lord Rodrigo Manuel Gutiérrez (1576–1661). A deep breath steadied my racing heart as I slowly lifted my eyes to his likeness. I froze, struck by an overwhelming recognition.

The same man from my dream. The resemblance was hauntingly uncanny.

Overwhelmed, I spun on my heel and fled the gallery, my heart pounding in rhythm with my hurried footsteps. I didn't stop until I reached the sanctuary of my painting retreat, breathless and shaken.

I clutched my paintbrush like a lifeline as I sat before the canvas propped against the easel. Closing my eyes, I focused on calming my breathing to keep the panic at bay. When I finally opened my eyes again, the world disappeared as my brush glided across the canvas.

CHAPTER 7

Gypsy Wisdom

I ventured outside the cottage and settled onto the porch steps, thinking back on my day. As I looked up and took in the tapestry of stars in the night sky, my mind churned with the mysteries unfurling around me. Why had Lord Rodrigo Gutiérrez crept into my dreams? Was Lady Magdalena a figment of my imagination, or had she once walked the castle halls? Questions swirled around in my mind, elusive as the night breeze. I wanted to talk to someone about my strange dreams, but I wasn't comfortable with the idea of talking to Francisco. Then a thought struck me—I could talk to Bruno Pilato, the carriage driver! Something about him inspired trust, and I'd felt an odd spark of camaraderie with him. Wrapping myself in a thick shawl against the evening chill, I set off on foot toward the tavern.

A crooked sign swayed in front of the weathered Zafra Tavern. After entering, I found Bruno at the bar, and we moved to a quiet booth. Over a pitcher of beer, I shared my chance encounter with the castle, the strong sense of déjà vu, my strange interaction with Juanita, and the vivid seventeenth-century dream. I also mentioned the gold locket inscribed with ML and RG, which Francisco believed belonged to Lord Rodrigo Gutiérrez and his mysterious mistress.

By the time I paused for breath, I realized he was staring at me open-mouthed, but there was a spark of understanding in his eyes. He didn't think I was crazy. Some of the tension left my shoulders.

"Maryann," Bruno began thoughtfully, "as a Romani, I believe everything in life carries significance and meaning. These experiences you're having are happening for a reason. I'm confident you'll unravel their meaning when the time is right."

"I thought I was losing my mind!" I said with a chuckle. "I feel so much better now, Bruno."

After sharing a final toast, Bruno walked me home. When we reached the cottage, I turned to him, gratitude swelling in my chest. "Thanks again for listening, Bruno. Your advice means a lot. Have a good night!"

"Good night, Maryann," he replied, his signature grin brightening his face. As he waved goodbye and headed back to the tavern, a flicker of hope ignited within me—I felt more confident that my questions would eventually be answered, and our conversation had only strengthened my resolve. Now, I just needed to uncover the mysteries that had entwined my life with this Lord Rodrigo Gutiérrez fellow.

CHAPTER 8

The Woman in Green

I dedicated myself to painting for hours the following day, losing track of time until a wave of drowsiness washed over me. My eyes grew heavier with each brushstroke. *Had I been at the wine today?* I found myself wondering. Surely this wasn't normal. Was I coming down with something? Before I could answer my own musings, darkness engulfed me. Then, like a silent movie unfurling before my eyes, I could once again see the flickering images whispering secrets of the past.

He was there again, that striking man.

Lord Rodrigo Gutiérrez.

He strolled alongside that same enigmatic woman from the locket in the castle gardens. Her features were blurred yet her presence was magnetic, and I couldn't look away. Long auburn hair cascaded down her shoulders, and she wore a stunning green gown, just like she had on in the locket, with an elegant green hat perched atop her head. A whisper escaped her lips as she leaned closer to Lord Rodrigo Gutiérrez, prompting a delighted laugh from him.

Suddenly, Lady Magdalena's head emerged from behind a bush, her gaze a storm of love, jealousy, and resentment aimed squarely at the pair.

I awoke with a jump, bewildered, and almost knocked my paints to the ground, reminding me that I was still perched in front of my easel. My painting had evolved during my slumber, and a gasp escaped me as I stared at my work. The rough outline of the castle seemed to mirror its former grandeur, as if I had been painting in a trance, lost to the world. Feeling dizzy and disoriented, I carefully covered my canvas and secured my painting supplies before heading home.

Back at home, I poured myself a glass of wine, mindful of Bruno's words about remaining open to possibilities. My dreams were trying to convey a message I couldn't grasp, but it felt important. Exhausted, I nestled into bed early that evening, slipping into a deep, dreamless sleep.

The next morning, I awoke refreshed and clearheaded, but in the following days, I began wading through a surreal reality, alternating between active painting and episodes of lucid dreaming where I would continue to paint in a fugue-like state. Each time, I awoke to discover that I had painted whole sections of the castle, almost as if the spirit of the place were guiding my hand.

After my fourth bewildering experience, a surge of confusion overwhelmed me. I couldn't go on with this—not knowing what was happening to me. It was starting to scare me. There was only one thing for it.

I needed to confide in Francisco, and just thinking about it made me anxious.

CHAPTER 9

The Strange Kiss

I wandered through the castle gardens, intent on finding Francisco. Lost in my spiraling thoughts, I almost collided with him, my hands trembling. Seeing my distress, he led me to a nearby bench and gingerly took my hands, meeting my eyes in a confident manner that made me feel uneasy for some reason.

"Maryann," he whispered, a hint of longing in his voice, "do you realize the effect you have on me?"

Before I could respond, his lips met mine, and I froze. A whirlwind of conflicting emotions raced through my mind. But as his kiss deepened, everything became even more surreal.

Lord Rodrigo's face began to replace Francisco's in my mind's eye.

What was happening?

Something was making my body melt, and I allowed myself to surrender to the moment, losing myself in the thrill of it, forgetting the episodes that haunted me.

A cough shattered the spell. Francisco's father appeared with disapproval etched across his face. I felt a pang of guilt and embarrassment as I realized the impropriety of our actions. "Francisco," his father reprimanded, and without another word my companion rushed away, trailed by his father scolding him, their voices fading in the distance.

Embarrassment flooded over me as I left the bench, returning to the cottage with my thoughts in disarray. I sought solace at the piano, letting the notes quiet my turbulent mind.

CHAPTER 10

The Painting

I awoke the following day to an overcast sky that mirrored my somber mood. After preparing two scrambled eggs, a cup of yogurt with granola, and my morning tea, I set off hiking up the mountain to the castle. My goal was to find solace through painting and remain undisturbed for several days. I cared for Francisco as a good friend, and for the life of me, I couldn't fathom why I'd lost control or allowed myself to imagine him as Lord Rodrigo. The thought of encountering him and his father filled me with dread. A girl could only endure so much mortification.

Settling into my secluded retreat, I poised my paintbrush before the canvas, and memories of my recent fugue episodes came to the surface. I struggled to concentrate and decided to step away, seeking the gentle sounds of the stream just a few feet away. I closed my eyes and inhaled deeply, allowing the trickling water and the buzzing insects to relax me further.

Oh no. Not again. But at least you might get some answers this time, I told myself.

And there was Lady Magdalena.

She was lying in the corner of the same dungeon, weeping softly with her eyes turned upward. Was she looking at me?

She was just as captivating as ever, with long, thick black hair braided loosely, dressed in a flowing skirt and a loose peasant-style white blouse. Her brandy-colored eyes and flawless porcelain skin glowed.

As she looked toward the ceiling, it seemed she was speaking directly to me, and her murmur pierced the silence: "Lord Rodrigo and all of his future male descendants will pay for my agony."

A beautiful blue sky greeted me when I opened my eyes, and the leaves of a willow tree danced in the breeze above me. As I sat up, brushing away the fallen leaves and blades of grass from my skinny jeans, my eyes fell upon my painting. My stomach lurched, and my head spun so fast I thought I might faint.

It was complete.

The castle stood majestically against a backdrop of azure skies and lush green forests, perched atop a hill with a quaint town nestled in the valley below. My breath quickened as I scrutinized the scene. A couple stood in front of the castle, locked in an embrace.

Lord Rodrigo Gutiérrez and the lady in green.

Just a short distance away, Lady Magdalena appeared to be creeping up behind the lady in green. Her extended belly hinted that she was on the brink of childbirth. In her right hand, she clutched something that made my stomach lurch as I focused on it.

A knife.

The message was unmistakable: The woman in Lord Rodrigo's arms was in grave danger.

My chest tightened, and I began to fear for my sanity. How was I doing all of this? Maybe this whole thing was a dream, and I hadn't even left California yet. I pinched myself. It hurt. Definitely still in Spain.

In my haste to get away from the painting, I stumbled backward, landing near a large, partially buried stone pillar I had overlooked. It was impressive. At approximately eight feet long and two feet wide, its flat surface revealed intricate Celtic symbols carved into the stone. Looking around, I noticed another partially buried stone pillar just a few feet away.

The sight sparked a sense of awe. These ancient-looking pillars reminded me of Stonehenge in Wiltshire, England. What were they doing here in Spain? Why were they half-buried? I recalled tales of Stonehenge, rich with speculation about its origin—from ancient rituals to mysterious powers linked to time travel. Perhaps these pillars had once stood erect, holding a story of their own.

As I knelt between the stone pillars, I traced the elaborate carvings, feeling an unexplainable energy radiating from them. When I placed my hands on the stones, an odd vibration surged, ceasing as soon as I withdrew. Intrigued, I pressed my palms back onto the stones, only to feel the vibrations increase, pulling me into a whirlwind. Just before the world around me faded, a familiar haunting melody drifted through the air, resonating deep within my soul.

CHAPTER 11

Castillo de los Conquistadores

I found myself lying on a carpet of soft grass as I slowly regained consciousness, the world around me bathed in the silvery glow of a full moon. I faintly recalled a vibrant blue sky before everything had gone dark. How much time had slipped away? Disoriented and dizzy, I remained flat on the ground, the spinning world adding to my confusion before I could slowly prop myself up.

When the world finally stabilized, I scanned my surroundings, my heart sinking as I realized my painting, supplies, phone, and those partially buried stone pillars had vanished without a trace.

Curious, I pushed aside the lush foliage and stepped out of the clearing. The wildflowers were more abundant than I recalled, and the heady scent of wild jasmine intoxicated my senses. I adjusted my floppy hat and tucked my braids away as I followed the winding path toward the castle.

As I strolled closer, a flurry of colorful-clad children rushed toward me, one wide-eyed little girl pointing and exclaiming, "What strange clothes you are wearing!"

Before I could respond, a commanding voice echoed from behind me. "Get along, children, and leave the poor lad alone!"

Startled, I turned abruptly, and the breeze swept my hat away, causing my braids to cascade around my shoulders. Standing before me was a remarkably handsome man—tall and muscular, with brilliant green eyes. His light brown hair was tied back in a loose ponytail, and he wore a white shirt, leather vest, and fitted pants tucked neatly into tall leather boots.

The man stepped closer, and his intense gaze softened when he realized he was looking at a young woman, not a boy. "Señorita, please allow me to introduce myself," he said softly in Spanish, his voice smooth like silk. "I am Lord Rodrigo Gutiérrez, and this is my home, Castillo de los Conquistadores."

Panic surged through me, my heart racing at the realization—either I was trapped in yet another vivid dream, or I'd somehow traveled more than four centuries into the past. The first option seemed more probable, but my gut told me the unlikeliest thing had happened. As fear gripped me like a vise, my vision blurred, darkness crept in, and my legs buckled beneath me.

Lady Magdalena concealed herself behind a bush, unwavering in her determination to win Lord Rodrigo's heart. Her eyes fixed on the peculiar exchange between Lord Rodrigo and the strange young woman in fitted breeches. This wasn't good. A sense of foreboding grew in her belly, and a frown etched on her face at the sight of her beloved Rodrigo rushing to the woman's aid, his strong arms catching her. From her hidden vantage point, Lady Magdalena felt a surge of jealousy. Had her meticulous schemes over the past months been for nothing? All she'd wanted was to win Lord Rodrigo's heart, and now the alluring stranger threatened to shatter her carefully laid plans.

Placing a delicate hand over her slightly extended belly, she smirked, a sense of power coursing through her. Several months ago, Lord Rodrigo found himself in a compromising position next to her at a tavern, naked. It had been easy to convince him that he was the father of the child growing within her. Now, nothing would stand in her way of claiming her destiny as the lady of the castle.

CHAPTER 12

Seventeenth-Century Spain

My eyes fluttered open to the sight of a grand ceiling adorned with intricate frescoes. A wave of disorientation washed over me, and my stomach tightened. I was lying within the very castle I had painted, its beauty now tangible and overwhelming. Though I felt the pull of reality, I clung to the hope that it was just a dream, a fleeting illusion. Cautiously, I turned to look and met the intense green eyes of Lord Rodrigo Gutiérrez.

"Are you all right, my lady?" he inquired, concern lacing his voice. "Would you care for some food and drink?" Without waiting for my response, he clapped his hands, and within moments a servant materialized bearing a tray filled with snacks and a bottle of wine.

Accepting the wine, I took a fortifying sip, my nerves settling as I surveyed the lavish surroundings. The furnishings mirrored those in Francisco's castle, yet they sparkled in pristine condition. Lord Rodrigo looked at me, concern etched on his face. Surprisingly, instead of pressing me for details about my strange presence and attire, he launched into a tale of the castle's history. As he spoke, my mind raced to recall snippets of seventeenth-century Spain from history lessons. Still, the only thoughts that surfaced were the reigning monarchs—Philip III and Queen Margaret of Austria—and the grim realities of the Spanish Inquisition.

As he spoke, a narrative began to take shape within me, explaining my bizarre arrival here. When he paused for a sip of wine, I seized the moment to speak.

Speaking in Spanish, I said, "Lord Gutiérrez, I can't thank you enough for allowing me to rest before I continue my journey. I've faced considerable misfortune recently."

His eyebrow arched in curiosity. "I am eager to hear your story, but first, may I know your name, my lady?" he asked.

"Lady Maryann LeMaster," I replied. Thinking swiftly, I continued. "My companions and I were journeying from France to Madrid when tragedy struck—a sickness plagued our ship. Over half the passengers and crew fell ill, with many succumbing to the illness, including my dear friends. The captain believed I had met the same fate."

Lord Rodrigo's expression sobered. "How did you survive alone on such a treacherous voyage, Lady Maryann?" he asked, as he switched seamlessly from Spanish to French.

This switch alerted me that he might be testing me, although his concern for me appeared genuine. I replied in flawless French, "The ship's elderly cook feared for my safety, disguised me as a cabin boy, and kept me out of sight until we landed in Zafra."

Switching back to Spanish, I elaborated, "When we docked here, I seized the opportunity to leave the ship. I roamed the town for hours until a kind older woman advised me to seek refuge at the castle. On my way to the castle, a driver graciously stopped and gave me a ride the remainder of the way. I do not seek charity, sir. I am well educated and willing to earn my keep until I can move on."

Lord Rodrigo scrutinized the lovely woman, measuring his words carefully. "Lady LeMaster, I have a proposal for you. I would be honored if you would stay here as my guest for as long as you like. Would you consider taking on the role of castle manager? It would alleviate my burdens immensely. I will oversee the livestock, horses, and maintenance while you manage the castle's interior. You will have a private chamber, all the comforts needed, and generous compensation. Would this arrangement be agreeable to you?"

Relief flooded through me. "Yes, Lord Gutiérrez, that would be wonderful! I would be honored to assist you in whatever capacity I can. However, I've never managed a castle of this size. I may need your guidance at first." Though my exterior appeared calm, anxiety swirled within me at the prospect of being trapped in this time period. But perhaps I was experiencing an exceptionally vivid lucid dream. It seemed to be a new habit of mine, after all. With that thought, I decided to embrace the unfolding adventure while it was here. What else could I do? I was bound to wake up eventually.

Lord Rodrigo refilled our goblets, his demeanor brightening. "To our new partnership!" he proclaimed, raising his glass high.

With a genuine smile, I joined him in the toast, hoping this time the dream might last a little longer.

CHAPTER 13

What Is Real?

A deep sigh of appreciation mixed with a tinge of anxiety escaped me when I awoke to an elegantly furnished room the following day. A stunning tapestry depicting an enchanting forest took up an entire wall. I'd slept in a large canopy bed draped in silky curtains that could be closed for privacy. An armoire and a small writing desk stood in the corner of the room, and a beautiful divan and matching chair were positioned in front of the crackling fireplace, separated by a delicate table that held a large vase filled with fragrant roses. I walked over to the enormous window and pulled back the curtains, revealing a perfect view of the courtyard and the castle gardens.

Surely this wasn't my new reality? I gave myself a mental shake. There were worse places to travel to, whether via time travel or lucid dreams, and I had to admit that it was rather beautiful and enchanting.

The room was comfortable and warm, likely thanks to someone who had lit the fireplace while I slept. A tray of food, still warm, sat on the small table beside the bed, the delicious aroma making my stomach growl. I quickly devoured the porridge, sausage, and rolls, savoring every bite.

Just then, a gentle knock interrupted my reverie. The door opened and revealed a smiling young woman carrying a beautifully crafted gown.

"Hello, I'm Maria. I've brought a gown for you to wear. If it doesn't fit or suit you, I'd be happy to make adjustments or bring another gown," she said with a friendly smile as she studied the beautiful young woman who was a guest at the castle.

"It's wonderful to meet you, Maria. My name is Lady Maryann. Thank you for the beautiful gown," I replied, feeling gratitude and curiosity. "Did you make it yourself?"

"Yes, I did," she said with pride. "I work as a seamstress here at the castle. Allow me to help you into the gown. You look lovely, and the green color suits you beautifully, Lady Maryann." She fastened the dress from behind, and after giving me a reassuring nod, she excused herself, adding, "I hope to see you soon! Please let me know if you need anything."

"Thank you for your kindness, Maria," I called after her, admiring the gown's beauty and rich fabric.

CHAPTER 14

Lady Magdalena

Weeks seemed to pass by quickly, each day a learning adventure in the seventeenth century. Maria and Clara, the castle cook, became my close friends and guides, showing me the intricacies of castle life. By each day's end, I was so exhausted that grief for my old life had no space to creep in, though I often wondered what my twenty-first-century friends thought of my sudden disappearance. Were they worried? Was I on the news? Were there appeals on Facebook about my whereabouts?

Today marked my first lesson in baking bread, and as I kneaded the dough, Clara filled the air with cheerful chatter. "Lady Maryann," she said, playfully tapping her foot, "have you spent any time with Lady Magdalena since arriving?"

I paused, looking at her with curiosity. "What do you mean, Clara?" I asked.

"Oh, come on now! You know what I mean, Lady Maryann. Have you spoken to Lady Magdalena since she left that dead rodent in your room?" she teased, a mischievous glint in her eyes.

The memory sent a shiver down my spine. A few days earlier, I'd opened my door to find the dark-haired woman from my dreams holding a hat box.

"Hello," she had said, her voice dripping with false sweetness. "I am Lady Magdalena Constanza, Lord Gutiérrez's fiancée. I have a welcome gift." Handing me a medium-size box, she smiled. As she pivoted to leave, she glanced back with a haughty look before walking away, her beauty cold, alluring, and intimidating.

I felt chills after my brief encounter with Lady Magdalena. Her smile had looked more like a grimace. Slightly bewildered over her strange behavior, I had closed the door and carried the box over to the bed. But when I opened it, I was horror-struck—inside lay a giant dead rat, a noose around its neck, cruelly placed as a malicious message. Feeling anxious and nauseous, I'd been shocked by the cruel act. She'd sent me a message or a warning, but from what?

With a sigh, I pushed the dreadful memory aside. "Clara, it's clear Lady Magdalena despises me. I can't fathom what I did to offend her, but she's determined to make my life miserable. Her goal seems obvious—to frighten me away. But I refuse to be cowed."

Clara shook her head, a tiny smile tugging at her lips. "You know why she did it. She's jealous. Everyone can see how Lord Gutiérrez looks at you. With Lady Magdalena, he thinks of duty more than love. Haven't you heard the gossip around the castle?" she asked innocently.

"Clara, if you mean the talk about Lady Magdalena seducing Lord Gutiérrez and becoming pregnant, then yes, I've heard the whispers. I've also heard the absurd tale that every legitimate Gutiérrez male is born with a crescent moon birthmark behind his left ear. That sounds more far-fetched than the rumors about Lady Magdalena, don't you agree?" I said, my voice carrying a note of skepticism and sarcasm.

Just then, a deep, familiar voice chimed in. "Well, Lady LeMaster," quipped Lord Rodrigo with a chuckle, "the birthmarks are a fact, not mere gossip. I'd happily show you my birthmark as well as the Gutiérrez family's meticulously documented birth and baptismal records. As for the rumor of my alleged seduction by the hands of Lady Magdalena, I honestly don't know what to believe because I don't remember it."

Heat rushed to my face, a blush of embarrassment overtaking me as I realized I had stepped into a web of intrigue. "Truly, Lord Gutiérrez," I said, trying to keep my composure, "I would be thrilled to see your family's birth records." After a pause, I continued. "And I may even want to see your birthmark." As soon as the words left my mouth, I covered my face, shocked and embarrassed by my outburst. Gathering my courage, I slowly lowered my hands and met his gaze head-on.

A charming grin spread across his face. “Lady LeMaster, if you’re free this afternoon, I would be delighted to give you a tour of the castle gardens and the church after lunch.”

I couldn’t help but smile back, my heart leaping at the invitation. “I would be more than happy to join you,” I replied, my grin stretching even wider.

“Wonderful. I’ll see you soon,” he said, giving me a playful wink before striding out of the kitchen. I watched him go, caught up in the moment, only to be jolted back to reality when Clara cleared her throat, a knowing glimmer in her eye.

“Mm-hmm, just as I thought. You can’t hide it from me! Something is brewing between you two,” she teased, whistling as she placed fresh loaves of bread into the open hearth.

“Don’t be ridiculous, Clara. He’s simply a gracious host,” I replied, trying to sound dismissive, but I could feel the redness creeping up my cheeks. “I have work to do now, but I’ll see you later.” I walked away briskly, unable to suppress my excitement.

CHAPTER 15

Lord Rodrigo

Standing over Maria's shoulder, I eagerly watched her work her magic as she placed careful stitches in the lovely gown she was working on.

"Maria, your talent amazes me!" I exclaimed with excitement and admiration. "If you're not too busy later, do you think you could help me pick out a gown for this afternoon? Lord Gutiérrez has invited me to tour the gardens and the church after lunch."

"Your timing is impeccable, Lady Maryann," Maria responded with a grin. "Now, please stand over here."

"Why do you need me to stand there?" I frowned, puzzled.

With a playful grin, she said, "Silly, this gown is for you!"

My heart fluttered with excitement as she held up the beautiful gown for my inspection. "Oh, Maria, it's exquisite!" I gasped, overflowing with joy.

"Stay still a moment, Lady Maryann," she chuckled. "I just want to check if any adjustments are needed. All right, it should fit you perfectly. I'll bring it to your room shortly."

"You're the best, Maria. I hugged her tightly before practically skipping down the hall to my room.

Thirty minutes later, a soft knock on my door startled me from my thoughts. I opened it to find Maria, her face beaming, with several gowns draped over her arm.

"Please come in!" I said, excitement coursing through my veins. Maria stepped into the room carrying a stunning gown across her arms.

Maria helped me into the gown and then styled my hair. "All right. Keep your eyes closed," she instructed as she led me to the mirror. "Okay, you can open your eyes now!"

I slowly peeled my eyelids apart, and a happy squeal escaped my lips at my reflection. The delicate light blue gown with bright yellow sunflowers hugged my figure perfectly. My auburn hair was elegantly swept up, with ringlets cascading down my back. Tears of happiness filled my eyes as I turned to Maria and hugged her.

"I feel beautiful! Thank you for everything, my dear friend."

"You truly look lovely, Lady Maryann. Enjoy your stroll in the garden with Lord Gutiérrez," she said, her eyes twinkling.

Feeling confident and beautiful in my new gown, I descended the staircase and entered the dining room, surprised to find it empty. *I must be early*, I thought, settling into my seat. Just then, Lord Rodrigo strolled in, his gaze appreciative and direct.

"Lady LeMaster, you look lovely! It seems we're dining alone today. I hope you don't mind," said Lord Rodrigo, smiling appreciatively.

"Not at all, Lord Gutiérrez. What about Lady Constanza?" I asked. "Will she be joining us for lunch?

"She's with the seamstress in the valley for more gown fittings," he sighed. "She has to have her gowns altered frequently to make room for the growing baby."

One by one, the kitchen staff entered, carrying freshly baked bread, hearty stew, ripe fruit, and several bottles of wine. As soon as the table was set up, they discreetly exited, leaving us alone again.

"Lady LeMaster, are you finding your chamber satisfactory? Is there anything else you require to be comfortable?" he asked, his eyes earnestly searching mine.

"Everything is perfect, and thank you for your kindness, Lord Gutiérrez," I replied gratefully, as I nervously fiddled with the linen napkin on the table.

"I've been meaning to apologize for the excessive gossip you are exposed to," he added with a humble expression. "Believe me, I know firsthand how trivial, tedious, and overwhelming it can all be."

"Oh, it doesn't bother me," I said, grinning mischievously. "Would you care to enlighten me as to which rumors are true?"

Lord Rodrigo roared with laughter, and I couldn't help but join in. "Ah, Lady LeMaster, your wit and honesty are refreshing. I will be candid with you about Lady Constanza. She and I are engaged, though I do not plan on ever marrying her."

He paused, his expression shifting to one of regret. "I struggle to recall the night we were allegedly together—I had far too much to drink. When she'd announced she was pregnant six weeks later, I felt obligated to propose because of the off chance that the baby could be mine. Rumors of her infidelities reach my ears constantly, and I honestly don't know what to believe anymore. I plan to offer her a generous settlement—perhaps set her up in a château in France after the child is born. I vowed to myself long ago that I would only marry for love. That is why I will never marry Lady Constanza."

He leaned closer, his voice dropping to a conspiratorial whisper. "And I have to say that it pains me to see how poorly she treats you, Lady LeMaster. If you wish, I will intervene and speak with her on your behalf."

His words lingered in the air, heavy with possibility, as thoughts and emotions swirled in my mind. "Thank you. I deeply appreciate your concern and kind gesture, but I feel fairly confident that I can handle whatever Lady Constanza throws at me." With a pause and a grin, I added, "Without being too presumptuous, may I ask you a personal question, Lord Gutiérrez?"

"I assure you, Lady LeMaster, nothing you say could ever offend me. Please, ask away."

"All right, then, what will happen if Lady Constanza bears a son without the Gutiérrez birthmark?"

His expression changed, revealing a mixture of emotions. "Then I will know for certain that I am not the father. Regardless of bloodline, I would welcome the child into my life and foster it. Lady Constanza has indicated that she plans to hand her child over to a nursemaid, suggesting her ambitions lie elsewhere. I believe her goal is to marry me to become the lady of this castle, but I will never allow that."

"You find yourself in a difficult situation," I said softly, "and you're likely correct about her aspirations. I'm trying to be patient around her, but it is challenging most days."

"Lady Maryann, I can see that you strive to see the goodness in people—but Lady Constanza might be a lost cause. And please let me know if you change your mind. I would be happy to speak with her on your behalf."

"Thank you, Lord Gutiérrez. I'll manage things as best I can, but your offer is a kindness I sincerely appreciate."

He nodded, his handsome eyes never leaving mine. "Shall we take that walk now, Lady LeMaster?"

"That sounds lovely," I replied, following him through the kitchen side door and rolling my eyes at Clara's knowing smirk as we left.

CHAPTER 16

The Tour

Lord Rodrigo led the way along the scenic path that led to the castle gardens. The sky was clear and sunny, and the fragrant scent of flowers filled the air around us. He turned to me and said, "Lady LeMaster, I want to thank you for your outstanding work in managing the castle. You are doing a wonderful job, but I am concerned that you may be taking on too much. Please let me know if you ever feel overwhelmed. I will be happy to give you as many assistants as you need. I want you to feel at home here."

"That is incredibly kind of you, Lord Gutiérrez, but I'm enjoying the work and learning a lot about running a castle of this size. I appreciate the opportunity you've given me, and I feel very much at home here. I hope you don't mind, but may I ask you a question about your childhood, Lord Gutiérrez?"

"Of course. Ask anything you like, Lady LeMaster. I am an open book to you."

"What was it like growing up in a castle as a child?" I asked. "Did you enjoy a carefree childhood, or were you burdened with lessons and responsibilities at an early age to prepare you for the role of lord of Castillo de los Conquistadores?"

He paused and turned to face me, vulnerability in his eyes. "I was an only child and the heir," he replied, his voice tinged with sadness and melancholy. "My father was diligent in imparting our family's history. He taught me from an early age how to be the lord of the castle. Thankfully, I was given several hours of free time each day to escape my responsibilities. You would have liked my mother. She was graceful, refined, fiercely opinionated, and wonderfully outspoken—much like you."

"What happened to your parents, if you don't mind my asking?" I inquired, feeling hesitant and hoping I wasn't being too intrusive with my questions.

A shadow crossed his face. "They were traveling through the countryside when thieves attacked them. When the driver attempted to intervene, the horses panicked, and the carriage careened off the bridge, plunging into the lake. My parents were trapped inside and sadly did not survive. That fateful day, I became the castle's lord at just twelve years of age, marking the end of my carefree days."

I placed a comforting hand on his arm. "I'm so sorry for your loss, Lord Gutiérrez."

"Thank you, Lady LeMaster. Although it happened long ago, some moments feel as recent as yesterday. I'm sorry—I hoped our walk would be lighthearted."

"Please don't apologize. I'm having a wonderful time."

We wandered through the gardens as Lord Rodrigo pointed out various flowers and plants, and we eventually emerged into the courtyard. A massive pond graced the center, dominated by a majestic marble dragon, water gushing from its mouth. Surrounding the pond were artfully shaped hedges twisted into whimsical animal forms. As we continued, I noticed a small group of Romani children begging for food outside the castle, and my heart ached for them.

"Lord Gutiérrez, is it common for the children to beg?" I asked, feeling a heightened concern for their well-being.

His eyes softened with sorrow. "Unfortunately, yes. I do my best to support them. Clara regularly gives them leftover food and sweets, but I wish I could do more."

"Lord Gutiérrez," I said, my heart brimming with compassion and hope, "would you allow me to help? I'd love to host a playday for the children in the courtyard, and if Clara agrees, perhaps we could treat them to an unforgettable feast."

"That would be wonderful, Lady LeMaster. You have my full support. Please let me know how I can assist. The children are our future, and we must do all we can to help them."

"Yes, the children are our future," I replied, discreetly dabbing at my watery eyes.

"Would you like to see the church now, Lady LeMaster?" he asked, smiling as he gently squeezed my hand.

"Absolutely," I nodded, my heart fluttering with anticipation. "Please, lead the way, sir."

CHAPTER 17

The Church

As Lord Rodrigo and I approached the charming small white church surrounded by colorful wildflowers, I felt a calm sense of serenity. Upon entering the church, I noted the simple wooden pews lined on both sides of the room, inviting yet unpretentious. The sight of the stunning stained glass covering one side of the building took my breath away. Brilliantly illuminated by the sun, the colored glass depicted several vibrant biblical scenes.

"This is a beautiful church, Lord Gutiérrez. Do you come here often?" I asked, my voice barely above a whisper.

"Not so much since my parents passed," he replied, a sad, distant look clouding his striking features. He opened a locked cupboard behind the pulpit and retrieved a massive tome—the Gutiérrez family Bible. He carefully maneuvered the large book and turned to a marked page.

"Rodrigo Manuel Gutiérrez was born on March 5, 1576, with a crescent moon birthmark behind his left ear," he read aloud, his voice resonating with pride. He then grinned as he showed me the records of his ancestors, their births etched in time like a cherished legacy. I read the dates of his father's, grandfather's, and great-grandfather's births in turn: November 3, 1546. May 15, 1506. January 14, 1469.

"How incredible," I said, my curiosity piqued. "Would you mind very much showing me your birthmark?"

"Of course," he chuckled, leaning slightly toward me.

My breath caught as my fingers traced the outline of his birthmark, a perfect half-moon against his skin. "Fascinating!" I marveled, looking up into his stunning green eyes. He returned my look with a dazzling smile.

"The birthmarks may seem curious, but they are a proud heritage for the Gutiérrez men," he explained, returning the family Bible to its place before offering his arm. "Shall we head back to the castle?"

"Yes, it's been a wonderful afternoon," I replied, linking my arm through his as we walked toward the castle. "Thank you for lunch and this lovely day. I enjoyed myself."

With an affectionate nod, he bowed and kissed my hand. "Until later, Lady LeMaster," he said, leaving my heart racing in his wake.

As I entered the kitchen through the back door, I startled Clara and Maria, who were seated at the table. Excitement bubbled inside me as I sat down and shared my plan for the Romani children with them.

"What a wonderful idea!" exclaimed Clara. "I wonder why no one has thought to do this before! You truly are such a giving person, Lady Maryann. The children will be so excited!" Her eyes shined with excitement and joy.

Maria, just as excited, promised to spread the word among the Romani villagers. This was really happening!

CHAPTER 18

The Children

Only two days had passed since we'd discussed our impromptu plan for the Romani children, and today was the day! Nearly thirty Romani children gathered in the courtyard, their eyes wide with uncertainty and anticipation. With just a few gentle, persuasive words, they began to shed their inhibitions and let loose. Joyful laughter and excited chatter filled the air as they raced through the gardens, their happiness infectious. They dove into games of hide-and-seek and make-believe, and some of the older kids jumped into the pond to cool off, splashing and playing without a care in the world.

After several hours of play, we gathered the children around a large wooden table. Their eyes widened as they watched the staff deliver tray after tray of delectable food. Delicious aromas filled the air as the children waited patiently. The table was laden with several varieties of bread, an assortment of meats, colorful fresh fruit, steamed vegetables, and a wide selection of sugary treats. As soon as the servers finished setting up, the children sat down and eagerly dug in. Most had never seen so much food in one setting, and pure bliss shone on their happy faces as they thoroughly enjoyed the feast.

The day was a resounding success, thanks to the compassionate teamwork of all the volunteers. Holding back grateful tears, I thanked everyone who had made this special day possible. The success of the feast was a true testament to the power of community and compassion.

CHAPTER 19

The Lady in the Mirror

Maria let out a triumphant cheer when she finished the last stitch on the gorgeous green velour gown she had altered for me to wear to this evening's dinner. The gown was part of a stunning collection originally crafted for Lady Magdalena, but she had rejected them. The reason for her rejection shocked me to my core—her deep-seated prejudice against Romani people. Simply because of Maria's Romani heritage, the gowns were turned away. I had to wonder if something had happened to her in the past that fueled such feelings. Regardless, I was now the proud recipient of this beautiful collection of gowns, and I felt extremely grateful.

Maria helped me into the green gown and carefully adjusted the sleeves. Once she finished styling my hair, she led me over to the large standing mirror, and I gasped in surprise. The woman staring back at me resembled the woman in green from the miniature gold locket I had found while rummaging through an old chest with Francisco—it felt like a lifetime ago.

What could this mean?

Maria sensed the shift in my mood almost instantly. "Are you well, Lady Maryann?" she asked, concern evident in her voice.

"I'm fine, Maria," I replied, forcing a smile to mask my swirling emotions. "The gown is simply stunning."

"Your beauty makes it all the more special," she said, turning me around to ensure the gown's hem was even. "The gown comes with a lovely matching green feathered hat, but you obviously won't be wearing it to dinner. I hope you have a wonderful time, my friend."

I still could not believe it.

I am the mysterious lady in green.

Breathing deeply to calm my shaky nerves, I gracefully descended the stairs and entered the formal dining hall.

My stomach flipped when I saw Lord Rodrigo. It was getting worse, the way my body kept betraying me whenever I saw him. My feelings for him were growing stronger. Yep, I was falling for him.

But no one could know.

He was already seated at the head of the table, and Lady Magdalena was positioned at his right, as was customary as his fiancée. The large mahogany dining table displayed a tempting assortment of dishes. I moved to the empty chair on Lord Rodrigo's left and felt the weight of his eyes upon me. Taking a deep breath, I smiled and nodded to him and then to the other diners, pointedly ignoring Lady Magdalena, whose attention I wanted to avoid.

Suddenly, she slapped the table loudly, getting everyone's attention. Raising her venom-laced voice for all to hear, she said, "Lady Maryann, why would you bother to feed those pathetic beggar gypsy brats? They do not deserve it!"

My eyes locked onto hers, and I immediately regretted it. Her face was flushed red from too much wine, twisted with disdain and hate. As she continued her venomous tirade, she suddenly paused mid-speech, staring at the gown I was wearing.

"You're wearing the gown I discarded!" she declared, sneering. "I always disliked that green gown." Her words pierced through me like poison, igniting a surge of anger. "I bet you're grateful for any scraps of cloth you can manage to salvage, being so destitute and poor."

In a surge of indignation, I stood up. I was so upset my hands shook, but I willed myself to take a few calming breaths and reined in my wild emotions. Clearing my throat, I said, "Lady Magdalena, unlike you, I am grateful for any gift I may receive, and I do not judge people by their lineage, status in life, gender, or skin color. I choose to look beyond those superficial things and measure a person's character by their actions, by how they treat others," I declared, taking in another deep breath.

"I have some advice for you, and I hope you will take it to heart. I wish you could feel the pain you have caused others. If you could, you would likely want to change. I believe you have faced hardships in your life that have shaped you into the woman you are today. If you genuinely desire change, you can become a better version of yourself, Lady Magdalena."

With that, I glanced over at Lord Rodrigo, politely excused myself from the table, and walked out of the room with my head held high. I headed straight for Maria's door and knocked. As soon as she opened it, I rushed into her room and collapsed into a chair, overwhelmed with emotions as tears ran down my cheeks.

Shocked into action, Maria wasted no time in handing me a glass of wine. "What happened at dinner, Lady Maryann?" she asked gently.

"Lady Magdalena is the most insufferable person I've ever encountered," I exclaimed, my voice trembling. "First, she criticized my beautiful gown, and then she insulted the Romani children. I couldn't remain in her presence, but before I left, I gave her some good advice."

After sharing everything that had transpired with Maria, she just stared at me. Then, she cracked a smile, which quickly turned into laughter. Before long, we were both laughing so hard that we had difficulty stopping.

Maria wiped her eyes, still chuckling. "Oh, Lady Maryann, I'm so proud of you for standing up to that woman. What I find incredibly hilarious is how you delivered your message with grace and dignity, all while being brutally honest and insightful. Then, you offered her sincere advice! I must say, I have never heard anyone tell another person off in such a nice way. You are truly a jewel, my friend."

"Thank you, my friend," I replied, smiling at her rather accurate assessment. "But I have a bigger problem, Maria. I have fallen hard for Lord Gutiérrez, and I don't know what to do about it!"

Maria paused, carefully choosing her words. "Lady Maryann, you are not alone in your feelings. Lord Gutiérrez harbors strong affections for you as well, but he is an honorable man. Lady Magdalena knows this, which is why she concocted a scheme to trap him by claiming she is pregnant with his child."

I went very still, struggling to process the information, but a surge of joy pulsed through my veins at the thought that he might feel the same way I did. "Maria, I cannot fathom how any woman could so callously attempt to trap a man like Lord Gutiérrez! He has confided in me that he doubts the child is his." I sighed, frustration bubbling within me.

"Lord Gutiérrez is no fool," she replied. "Lady Magdalena's secrets will come to light. You two belong together, and I believe everything will eventually work out. Do not worry."

Maria's gentle voice seemed to calm my tumultuous thoughts. I thanked her again for the lovely gown and our great conversation. As I retreated to my chambers, I had to muffle my giggles; it had certainly been a crazy and emotional evening!

CHAPTER 20

The Library

When the next day dawned, I decided to avoid Lady Magdalena after the dinner drama. I briefly met with Clara and Maria, but all they wanted to discuss was my speech to Lady Magdalena. The entire castle was now aware of what had happened. I didn't want to talk about it anymore, so I spent the rest of the afternoon in my room.

After supper, I decided to stretch my legs. As I wandered down the hall, I noticed a soft light under one of the rooms, and the door was ajar. Unable to resist, I peeked inside. To my astonishment, I was looking at a grand library.

The library exuded a comforting atmosphere. Two oversize leather armchairs beckoned me to sink into their embrace. The animal rugs on the polished floor and the crackling fireplace only added to the cozy ambience of the room. A mesmerizing mural depicting a hunting scene adorned one of the walls, adding to the room's masculine charm. Excitedly, I wandered over to the built-in bookcases that contained an impressive array of leather-bound tomes and books. The collection ranged from religious texts and philosophical treatises to art volumes, history, warfare, poetry, and fiction in Spanish, French, and English. It was a true treasure trove, a sanctuary for the mind and soul. Why hadn't I discovered this library sooner?

I selected a poetry book from the shelf and sank into one of the oversize chairs with a sigh. The warmth of the fire relaxed me, and before long, sleep claimed me.

Rodrigo had just finished his dinner. As was his evening custom, he headed for the library seeking quiet, peace, and solace. He opened the door and paused at the sight before him: Lady Maryann slumbering peacefully in his favorite chair, a poetry book resting on her lap. Not wanting to disrupt her tranquility, he lowered himself as silently as possible into the opposite chair, captivated by her beauty. Her long hair cascaded over her shoulders, and a delicate scatter of freckles danced across her nose. A glimpse of her shapely calf peeked from beneath her robe, further igniting his yearning. *What a beauty*, he thought. With a gentle flutter, her eyelids gradually lifted, and he shifted his eyes to the crackling flames.

"Lord Gutiérrez," she murmured, breaking the heavy silence. "Have you been here long?"

"I arrived only moments ago, Lady LeMaster," he replied, smiling softly toward her. "I hesitated to wake you, for you looked so peaceful."

A blush crept across her cheeks. "I hope my presence here doesn't trouble you. The door was ajar, and I couldn't resist the allure of the books. I had no intention of dozing off."

"You are welcome in any corner of this castle, Lady LeMaster," he declared. His deep voice sent shivers down my back. "I'm delighted to see you here. I had no idea you were such an avid reader. I believe we may be the only souls in this castle who share this passion. About last night—your words to Lady Magdalena were . . . magnificent! There are no other words to describe it. Such insightful and wise words."

"Why, thank you, Lord Gutiérrez. You know, I have no idea where the courage or the words came from. I think I had just had it with her attitude. It was like a dam broke, and the words, like water, just flowed out of me. I hope she takes heed of some of the advice. I would offer my friendship if she ever gave me a chance," she added sheepishly.

"I know you would, Lady Maryann. I don't think I've ever met anyone like you. You are such a wonderfully unique, thoughtful, and empathetic woman."

"All right, Lord Gutiérrez, you do know that I value honesty the same as you do. I know something is weighing on your mind besides our entertaining evening last night. Please share what it is."

As he hesitated, a shadow of conflicted emotions came over him, and the words got caught in his throat. Was he really about to say this? "Lady LeMaster, feelings have begun to stir within me. I understand that my engagement to Lady Magdalena makes my declaration seem improper, but I cannot deny what I feel. When I stepped into this room and saw you looking so beautiful and at peace, I had the strongest urge to awaken you with a kiss. I will not act on these feelings, for I respect you deeply and never want to make you uncomfortable."

With those words, he rose, his legs slightly unsteady. Acutely aware of the gravity of his admission, he retreated toward the door, glancing only briefly at Lady Maryann's lovely face.

A whirlwind of emotions surged as I watched Lord Rodrigo walk toward the door. I'd been wrestling with my feelings for him all week, and the thought of suppressing them further felt unbearable. The chasm of societal expectations loomed large, yet my heart urged me to reach across it.

"Lord Gutiérrez," I called softly, my voice barely above a whisper. "Would it truly be so terrible if I confessed that I would welcome your kiss?" My heart clenched. Was I being reckless? Probably. But my heart was leading me, and I'd said it now. Too late to unsay it.

He froze, turning slowly to face me. Hope and desire flickered in his eyes, quickening my heartbeat. We stepped toward each other, drawn together like magnets, and our bodies collided in a tender embrace. Lord Rodrigo tilted my chin upward, and as his lips brushed against mine, time seemed to still. The world around us faded, leaving only the sensation of his lips on mine, igniting a fire within me that spread through my body.

Abruptly, he pulled back, still holding me by the shoulders, his breath ragged. "Please forgive me, my lady," he whispered with a hint of anguish. Without another word, he turned and vanished from the library, the door clicking shut behind him.

Left alone, I sank back into my chair, my mind racing and my heart pounding. What had just transpired was undeniable: Lord Rodrigo's kiss had been nothing short of transformative, as though the world had shifted out of alignment. A bittersweet disappointment settled over me. I'd allowed my desires to overpower my caution in this strange era. I should have known better.

A tumult of uncertainty clouded my thoughts. I felt adrift, torn between two worlds. But one truth emerged from the chaos: the kiss had kindled a yearning I could no longer ignore.

CHAPTER 21

Lady Magdalena

Rodrigo walked toward his chambers, his thoughts lingering on the magical kiss he and Maryann had just shared. His heart hammered wildly as he replayed it in his mind. Her soft lips. Those piercing eyes. The way her body had felt against his . . .

Before he knew what was happening, he collided unexpectedly with the last person he wanted to encounter.

Lady Magdalena.

Lady Magdalena's eyes flickered over his disheveled appearance, and her voice raised in volume as she began to throw accusations at him. "How dare you, Lord Gutiérrez! I see you wasted no time bedding Lady Maryann! You are my fiancé, you hypocrite! You had no reservations about impregnating me, yet now you spurn my advances and seek comfort in a woman you scarcely know?"

Rodrigo's hand shot out, gripping Lady Magdalena by the shoulders, fury igniting his voice. "You will not lay such accusations at my feet! Lady LeMaster and I have not crossed that line, but if we had, it is none of your concern. I will not tolerate your cruelty and schemes against her. Regardless of your pregnancy, should I uncover any betrayal, I will send you to the dungeon." Narrowing his eyes with a final glare, he released her shoulders and strode toward his chambers, slamming the door behind him with a thunderous crash, mumbling, "Damn my sense of honor!"

Rodrigo poured himself a generous glass of whiskey inside his secluded sanctuary, letting the fiery liquid wash over his throat as he pondered his choices. Why had he ever proposed to Lady Magdalena?

But he knew why, and his jaw tightened. Initially, it had been an act of obligation, a desperate hope that the child she carried was his. Rumors buzzed like flies, and then everything shifted with Lady Maryann's arrival. Now he knew what he wanted. What he craved.

A release from his engagement and a chance to chase his burgeoning feelings for that beautiful woman whose kiss had just melted his heart.

Lady Maryann.

CHAPTER 22

Passions and Secrets

Days later, we were strolling through the castle's corridors, chatting amicably, when we came upon Lord Rodrigo's ancestral portraits, and we stopped to admire them. The portraits fascinated me, probably because I'd been fortunate enough to have seen them in the seventeenth century, as well as the twenty-first century. Lord Rodrigo could not hide his palpable pride in his lineage whenever he studied the portraits. I don't believe he was aware that his body seemed to stand just a bit taller, and his shoulders would roll back just enough to cause his chest to puff out a bit every time he gazed upon the portraits. I thoroughly enjoyed the display.

As I was studying the superior quality of the portrait paintings, the words just slipped out in an unguarded moment. "It would be so nice to paint again."

I must have broken his concentration, because he immediately turned toward me, astonishment softening his handsome features. "Are you a painter, Lady Maryann?"

"Well, I wouldn't say that I'm as skilled as some of the artists who painted these portraits, but yes, I love to paint," I confessed, thrilled that I had let the cat out of the bag.

"I will see what I can do to procure some painting supplies for you. But tell me, Lady Maryann, are there any other hidden artistic talents or secrets you wish to share?"

His mischievous, teasing grin initially ignited a spark of desire within me, until I felt the panic in my chest. The word "secrets" sent my pulse racing with the weight of my hidden truth.

What would he think if he knew mine?

How could I even begin to reveal my true origins as a time traveler from the future? The very notion sent chills down my spine. I suppressed my dread and forced my attention back to Rodrigo, but the moment felt awkward. Before I could collect my thoughts, I excused myself, claiming that pressing matters begged my attention.

As I retreated to the safety of my chamber, I shut the door and leaned against it as if it could provide the safety and security I sought. My breath came in unsteady gasps, the fear of exposure causing severe anxiety. How would he react if I told him? The thought of being labeled a witch, or worse, falling victim to the relentless grasp of the Spanish Inquisition, tightened like a band of steel around my chest. No. I shook my head. It couldn't happen. As long as I remained in seventeenth-century Spain, my true identity would remain secret, hidden away in the shadows of time.

CHAPTER 23

The Schoolhouse

One evening, as Lord Rodrigo and I were sharing a quiet evening, I opened up about my passion and love for teaching children. Tripping over my words in my rush to get them out, I described the joy I always felt when guiding young minds and helping them learn and grow.

Lord Rodrigo listened intently. With a thoughtful gleam and hint of mischief in his eyes, he said, “I have an idea, though I won’t say much more just yet.”

Several more days passed, and one afternoon Lord Rodrigo surprised me with an extraordinary gesture that left me nearly speechless. Without my knowledge, he’d gathered a group of skilled craftsmen who had worked day and night to construct a modest yet beautiful schoolhouse in a lovely area between the castle and the valley. As I stepped inside and allowed my eyes to absorb the simple, rustic, moderately sized room, my heart filled with gratitude. Every detail of the schoolhouse reflected Lord Rodrigo’s thoughtfulness and my dreams. It was perfect.

For the next several days, I threw myself into preparing for the first day of school. I could almost hear the excited chatter and laughter of the children who would soon fill this space where friendships would grow and learning would blossom. I couldn’t stop smiling at the thought.

I finally felt like I had a purpose here in this century.

CHAPTER 24

The First Day of School

The first day of school dawned bright and clear. Twenty children gathered in the little classroom, their faces filled with curiosity and nerves. "Good morning, students! Welcome to Zafra School!" I declared, smiling encouragingly. "To help you get to know each other, I want you all to sit by someone you're not well acquainted with. We'll change seats each week so everyone can make new friends."

As the children settled into their seats, I noticed an invisible line dividing them—Romani children on one side of the room and Spanish children on the other. The Romani children, many with worn clothes and tired faces, sat cautiously apart from the Spanish children, whose confident postures only highlighted the contrast. A renewed determination pulled at me. I needed to find a solution to bridge this divide. I felt so fortunate to have this opportunity to teach children in this century. And I wanted to make my childhood dream of finding a way to bridge the gap between the two social classes a reality. I was determined to find a solution.

"All right, everyone, let's introduce ourselves," I declared in a calm but authoritative voice. "My name is Lady Maryann LeMaster, but you may call me Miss Maryann if you wish."

As each child shared their name, I learned more about them, including their primary languages. To my delight, most of them understood basic English, which would allow me to teach primarily in English, with support in

Spanish or Romani as needed.

With introductions complete, I turned to the sizable wooden-backed easel and wrote the English alphabet in bold strokes. "Now, I'd like everyone to copy these letters," I instructed, watching as older students eagerly dipped quills into ink. At the same time, the younger children traced letters on trays of soft clay, using small wooden tools to form each letter carefully.

When they finished, I invited a few students to come forward and share a word they knew for each letter. Their responses gave me insight into their different reading levels and helped me arrange them into groups so each child could progress at their own pace.

Just before lunch, Clara appeared with a few helpers, each carrying baskets filled with fresh bread, fruit, and cheeses. We gathered outside to enjoy the meal. Laughter, squeals, and lively conversation filled the air as the children played and became acquainted with one another. After a brief playtime, I rang the school bell, calling everyone back in for the afternoon session. The day was moving along at a good pace. I could feel my shoulders relax a little more every moment.

We spent the afternoon exploring basic math concepts, and then we finished the day with a discussion about Spanish and Romani customs. The children shared pieces of their daily lives, sparking curiosity and understanding across the room. As the day drew to a close, my deep sense of fulfillment grew stronger.

"Thank you all for a wonderful first day," I said, my heart full as they filed out, waving goodbye with bright smiles. "I'll see you all again the day after tomorrow!"

CHAPTER 25

Lord Rodrigo

As the students began filing out the door, I began tidying up the classroom, and I noticed Lord Rodrigo standing outside. When he met my gaze, his eyes were full of warmth and admiration, igniting the butterflies in my stomach. After the last child left, he stepped inside, his voice low and sincere.

"Lady LeMaster," he began, "people have tried to bridge the divide between the Spanish and Romani communities for centuries, but it appears that you may have found the solution. By teaching the children the similarities between their cultures, customs, and daily lives, it encourages them to grow up together—as friends, partners, and perhaps family someday." He paused, his eyes tender. "Your kindness, your patience, and your insight—they are a rare gift. How could I not fall in love with you?"

His words surprised me, and a thrill of joy surged through me, but I still felt a trace of unease. Yes, I had fallen for Lord Rodrigo—I could feel it in every look, every gesture, every moment we shared. Yet with Lady Magdalena still present and my secrets lingering between us, how could we ever find solid ground? As my pulse quickened, I cast my eyes down, fearing they might reveal too much.

"Lord Gutiérrez," I murmured, my voice trembling slightly, "would you join me outside for a moment? I need some air." I could feel my cheeks reddening and forced myself to look away. What was I doing?

Concern flooded his face, his touch steady and gentle as he guided me out. “I hope I haven’t caused you distress,” he said, his sincerity unmistakable.

There was a gentle breeze outside, refreshing and soothing, and it seemed to calm my lingering anxieties. When our eyes met, the rest of the world seemed to fall away. At that moment, the air was thick with unspoken understanding. Lord Rodrigo leaned closer, and time seemed to slow. Just as our lips drew near, a sudden eruption of clapping and giggles from a nearby group of children broke the spell, snapping us back to the present.

My heart felt both light and weighted at the same time, full of hope yet uncertain. Lord Rodrigo’s words lingered, a balm and a thrill, yet I knew the questions hovering between us couldn’t be answered with an easy fix.

Some things weren’t meant to be simple.

CHAPTER 26

Pedro

Two older students in my classroom stood out for reasons beyond their age. The older student was Pedro Velasco, a reserved fifteen-year-old with light brown hair and sad gray eyes. The other student was Amalia Portola, a radiantly beautiful Romani girl who was fourteen.

Pedro was polite and always respectful, but he carried a quiet sadness that made it difficult for him to make new friends. My heart ached for him because he seemed to have difficulty relating to the other children and was often by himself. One afternoon, unable to shake my concern, I invited Pedro to join me on the school bench outside.

"Pedro, is everything all right? You seem distant, as though something is weighing on you. Is there anything I can do to help?"

He looked away, visibly tense, and then, blushing deeply, he finally spoke. "Miss Maryann, adjusting to life here in the valley and living with my aunt has been difficult. I miss my father, my home, and my horse." He took a shaky breath, his voice low with emotion. "I used to live in a small castle with my family. My father is Lord Felipe Velasco, and my mother is Lady Fátima. God rest her soul." His voice cracked, and he paused to steady himself. "When my mother passed away, my father remarried quickly. It seemed like he rushed into his new marriage without taking the time to grieve my mother. Lady Elena, his new wife, soon moved into the castle with her two children, Tomás, who was seventeen, and Teresa, who was ten. Tomás never liked me, but Teresa and

I became friends. We'd play outside, running wild over the estate pretending to be warriors."

A fleeting, sad smile crossed Pedro's face as he remembered those carefree days, but it faded quickly. "One day, Tomás came across us wrestling in the field. I suppose it looked improper to him. He rushed home and told our parents that I had attacked Teresa." Pedro's face tightened, his fists clenched, and he struggled to hold back tears. "My father wouldn't listen to me. I had to leave home and move in with my aunt here in the valley."

I squeezed his hand to reassure him. "Pedro, I believe you. I know you would never have knowingly hurt anyone, especially someone you cared about."

Pedro's shoulders relaxed, and he looked up, gratitude softening his troubled eyes. "Thank you, Miss Maryann."

"I'm so sorry, Pedro. Sometimes people make mistakes. Perhaps your father was still grieving your mother's passing and wasn't thinking clearly. You don't know what was in his heart, what caused him to take those actions. Hold on to hope, Pedro. There is no room for bitterness. Keep your heart open to hope and love, and with a little patience mixed in, the possibilities are infinite."

Pedro's face softened with a glimmer of hope. "Thank you, Miss Maryann. You've given me hope." He stood, his resilience shining through, and smiled gratefully. "I should get home before my aunt worries. See you in a few days!"

CHAPTER 27

Amalia

Amalia Portola was special and beautiful inside and out, with expressive, almond-shaped brown eyes and long, wavy brunette hair. She was always thoughtful and generous, with a joyful exuberance that seemed to uplift everyone around her. I'll never forget the first time she spoke with Pedro—his eyes widened, and a deep blush crept across his cheeks. At that moment, he was utterly captivated, and before long the two became inseparable friends.

One afternoon after school while I was tidying up the classroom, I noticed Amalia standing by the door looking at me. Narrowing my eyes, I approached her. "Amalia, is everything all right?"

She hesitated and looked at me with concern. "I'm fine, Miss Maryann. It's you I'm worried about."

I flinched. "Me? Whatever do you mean?"

"My aunt Maria says you can feel love and sorrow simultaneously," she replied, tilting her head as if trying to understand her words. "Sometimes I think I see both in your eyes." Her gaze was steady, revealing a surprising wisdom for her age.

I smiled softly, touched by her observation. "Your aunt is a wise woman, Amalia. Sometimes I do feel both—love and sorrow can be complicated."

Her expression brightened slightly, and she leaned closer. "Miss Maryann, could I come to visit the castle someday?"

"Of course, Amalia," I replied with an encouraging grin. "How about I walk you home so we can ask for your mother's permission. If she approves, you can come home with me."

"Oh, that would be wonderful, Miss Maryann! I can hardly wait to get home now!" she declared exuberantly.

CHAPTER 28

Grandmama

When we arrived at Amalia's home, I was overwhelmed by a sudden sense of déjà vu. Was this real? This cottage sat in the exact spot as the Airbnb cottage I had rented in the twenty-first century, and the memory sent my heart racing. I struggled to steady my nerves as a woman approached us, her presence at once calm and welcoming.

"Greetings! I'm Esmeralda Portola, Amalia's mother," she said, as she smiled shyly. "She talks about you constantly, Lady Maryann. She loves school!"

"I'm so glad she loves school," I replied, feeling touched by her kind words. "It's wonderful to meet you, Mistress Esmeralda. I walked here with Amalia to ask your permission for her to visit the castle as my guest. I'm sure her Aunt Maria will be overjoyed as well. Would that be all right with you?"

Esmeralda's eyes brightened, though a slight furrow of worry appeared on her brow. "Of course, I'm sure she would be thrilled. But what if Lord Gutiérrez disapproves?"

"Please don't worry," I reassured her. "Lord Gutiérrez adores children and would gladly welcome Amalia with open arms."

Seeing her daughter's excitement, Esmeralda immediately gave her blessing and permission to go, and Amalia rushed inside the cottage to pack. While we waited outside, Esmeralda invited me to sit with her on a weathered wooden bench. We exchanged stories of our families and dreams, and I went very still when a familiar haunting melody drifted through the air, catching me off guard.

Esmeralda suddenly quieted and studied me thoughtfully. “Do you often hear the Song of the Celtic Stones?” she asked, her eyes locked onto mine with surprising intensity.

Startled by the question, I nodded. “Yes, I’ve heard it several times. Do you hear it too?” I breathed, my heart quickening.

A knowing look crossed her face, and she turned, calling into the cottage, “Grandmama! We have a guest! Please come out and join us!”

Moments later, an older woman appeared in the doorway, leaning on a cane as she shuffled outside. Her face lit up as soon as our eyes met, and though her years were evident on her weathered and wrinkled face, her expression was full of kindness, life, and wisdom. She took my hand, examining it as though reading something only she could see, her touch comforting and reassuring.

“My lady, you are special,” she murmured with awe and wonder. “I am the guardian of the stones of this land at this time. You are special because you are among the few who can hear the Song of the Celtic Stones. You, dear one, are destined to walk the paths of time.” She looked deeply into my eyes, her gaze both gentle and piercing. “Your journey has only just begun, and you will tread several paths. Whatever path you choose will shape your destiny and that of your descendants. Remember this—your role in your family’s lineage is as powerful as it is essential.” The wisdom in her words both captivated and bewildered me.

With an intense and all-knowing look, she gave my hand a final squeeze, and, without another word, she smiled and then turned back toward the cottage, while I struggled to understand the deep meaning of her message.

Amalia giggled as she returned with a small bundle, looking every bit the young girl again. “Lady Maryann, close your mouth, or you’ll catch a bug!” she teased, throwing a playful grin my way, echoing the same lighthearted reminder I often gave my students when I caught them daydreaming.

With a chuckle, I thanked Mistress Esmeralda for her hospitality and the unexpected visit from her grandmother. “Your grandmother is lovely,” I said, still feeling the weight of her words.

“Thank you,” replied Mistress Esmeralda. “Grandmama is getting up there in age. We love her, and she is extremely wise."

"I would have to agree," I replied. "I'm happy to have finally met you. Amalia will be fine. She will be well cared for at the castle."

After saying our goodbyes, we headed up the trail to the castle. I could still hear echoes of my unusual conversation with Esmeralda's grandmother still ringing in my ears.

Guardian of the stones.

What did it all mean?

CHAPTER 29

The Guest

As soon as Maria spotted us, she came running out of the castle, her excitement palpable, and rushed to her niece, enveloping her in a comforting embrace.

"What brings you here, my sweet Amalia?" she asked, her voice filled with joy and lightness. "It's been far too long! Come on, you two, let's go inside."

Amalia's eyes sparkled with happiness. "Lady Maryann invited me to be a guest at the castle! Are you happy to see me, Auntie?"

Maria chuckled softly. "Do you see an unhappy face? I've missed you dearly, niece!"

Maria turned to me with a huge grin, as her face lit up in delight. "Only you could orchestrate such a delightful surprise, my dear friend. Does Lord Gutiérrez know you've arrived?"

Before I could respond, Lord Rodrigo strolled in, feigning a stern demeanor. "What mischief has the vixen stirred now?"

Amalia dropped to the ground, her arms spread wide in a dramatic display. Not knowing Lord Rodrigo was jesting, she cried out, "Oh, Lord Gutiérrez, please don't punish Lady Maryann! She's blameless!"

Laughter erupted from Lord Rodrigo as he helped Amalia to her feet. "Young lady, if Lady Maryann has invited you here, consider yourself a cherished guest. You are welcome to stay as long as you wish. I'd be delighted if you and your aunt would join us for dinner tonight." Winking, he nodded to the ladies before departing.

As Amalia watched him leave, she couldn't help but exclaim, "Oh, Miss Maryann, I can see why you have such affection for him!" Her hands immediately flew to her mouth in shock, clearly realizing her faux pas.

Maria raised an eyebrow, a knowing smile playing at the corners of her lips. "Dear girl, the first lesson you must learn is to keep your thoughts to yourself," she teased in a mock-serious tone.

"I promise to do better, Auntie! Just don't send me away yet!" Amalia implored, her wide eyes filled with sincerity.

Maria cast a fond glance in my direction. "You've been a positive influence on Lord Gutiérrez, fostering more compassion in him for the Romani people, you know."

I returned her grin. "Lord Gutiérrez has always had a big heart for the Romani. What do you think about Amalia staying in your adjoining room? The connecting door will allow you privacy and the ability to be together whenever you wish. It would also be a wonderful opportunity for Amalia to see what you do here in the castle."

"Indeed, that could certainly work to my advantage," Maria replied, winking at her niece. "Now come along, Amalia. We have much to do!"

"Oh, and don't forget about dinner tonight, ladies," I said.

Amalia's curiosity was piqued. "Why would Lord Gutiérrez invite us to dinner and allow us to wear fancy clothes?" she queried, her brow wrinkling.

Maria shrugged, her expression thoughtful. "Do not question, dear Amalia. Just follow what I do," she replied with an enigmatic grin. "Now, come help me finish my tasks, and then we'll hunt for the perfect gowns. We don't want to disappoint Lady Maryann, do we?"

CHAPTER 30

Clandestine Meeting

Shrouded in a dark, hooded cloak, Lady Magdalena stealthily slipped out of the castle, her heart racing with fierce determination. All she needed to do was reach the Catholic church, just over a mile away. The journey seemed to take forever, and her frustration grew with every step. With each moment she wasted, Lord Rodrigo was becoming more and more infatuated with Lady Maryann. It was obvious to see, and her chest tightened with bitterness and frustration. She needed to put a stop to this if she were to ever get what she wanted. She had to eliminate the threat Lady Maryann posed to her future.

She was still angry with Lady Maryann for her speech the other night. *Humph . . . does she think she's better than me? Who does she think she is, doling out unsolicited advice to me of all people!* To be honest, she had not listened to anything Lady Maryann had said. Instead, she had only focused on the smirks and snide looks from the other guests. *I'll show Lady Maryann—nobody makes a fool of me!* Her resolve solidified as she marched on toward the church.

As Father Santiago opened the heavy doors of the church, surprise flickered across his face at the sight of Lady Magdalena Constanza, the soon-to-be lady of the castle. "Lady Constanza, please come in," he gestured.

She entered and sat at the edge of a pew, her posture projecting urgency and anxiety. "Father, I believe there is a heretic within the castle's walls," she murmured, her voice barely above a whisper.

"Calm yourself, my dear. Please feel free to speak your fears," the priest urged in his stern and attentive tone.

With a practiced tremor, Lady Magdalena spun her tale. "Not long ago, a strange woman arrived at the castle—Lady Maryann LeMaster. From the instant she arrived, she snubbed her nose at propriety and tradition, arriving wearing formfitting men's breeches. She has captivated the attention of my fiancé, even influencing him to construct a schoolhouse where she flagrantly teaches Romani and Spanish children together in one room!" A dramatic sigh escaped her lips as she wiped away her nonexistent tears. "Now, she aims to steal my fiancé by salacious methods! Father, I fear for my fiancé's soul."

Father Santiago's eyes widened, an involuntary flicker of arousal crossing his features at the mention of a woman in breeches. He smoothed his cassock, momentarily distracted, before regaining his composure and fixing her with a steady gaze. "Thank you, my dear, for bringing this important matter to my attention. Your vigilance is commendable, Lady Constanza," he replied solemnly.

Lady Magdalena demurely thanked the priest and took her leave. Stepping outside, she took a huge lungful of fresh air, relieved to be away from the pompous priest. She had begun to feel nauseous and faint from his intimidating presence. As soon as she reached an acceptable distance from the church, she picked up her pace, hoping to sneak back into the castle unnoticed.

She was almost there! As she turned the last corner of one of the outbuildings, she collided with Matilda, the milkmaid, which caused the buckets of milk Matilda was carrying to fly. Lady Magdalena fell backward, landing on her backside, her face, clothes, and hair dripping with milk.

"You imbecile! Why were you not looking where you were going? Now I need to bathe again, or I will smell like spoiled milk!" she yelled, glaring at Matilda with a murderous look.

Matilda covered her mouth, clearly trying her best not to laugh at Lady Magdalena, who looked ridiculous with milk dripping from her hair and face. But it was a lost cause, and Matilda erupted in uncontrollable laughter. She laughed so hard that she failed to notice Lady Magdalena sneaking up on her until a resounding slap filled the air. Gasping in shock, Matilda gingerly touched her tender face, pivoted, and fled the scene as fast as her short, chubby legs would carry her.

CHAPTER 31

The Scheme

Freshly bathed and feeling revitalized and unburdened, Lady Magdalena began to weave her final, cunning scheme, a plan to secure her future as the lady of the castle.

After dipping the goose quill pen into the ink jar, she meticulously began crafting invitations to influential friends and business associates of Lord Gutiérrez, inviting them to the grand weeklong festivities in celebration of the upcoming wedding of her and Lord Rodrigo Gutiérrez.

The weeklong celebration would be a spectacle of grandeur, showcasing a grand ball, sporting games, and a jousting tournament, all leading up to a wedding that would be gossiped about for years to come. Folding the envelope, she pressed Lord Rodrigo's stolen ring seal into the wax to seal the last invitation.

Chuckling softly, she tried to imagine Lord Rodrigo's reaction when he discovered her betrayal. Undoubtedly, he would be furious, but Lady Magdalena knew him well. He possessed integrity. Morals. At the very least, he wouldn't want to bring his family name into disrepute. He would proceed with the wedding to preserve his honor. With a sense of deep satisfaction, she leaned back in her chair, massaging the tension in her lower back. "He will soon be mine," she whispered to the shadows, the anticipation of the grand event palpable in the air.

CHAPTER 32

The Priest

Excitement coursed through my veins as I dressed for dinner, happy and grateful to Lord Rodrigo for inviting Maria and Amalia. I'd chosen a bright red gown that clung to me in all the right places, and I wore my hair down in loose curls around my shoulders.

As I made my grand entrance through the double doors of the formal dining hall, a palpable silence filled the air as all eyes turned toward me. Locking eyes with Lord Rodrigo, seated at the far end of the long table, I noticed how he stood, his eyes glinting with appreciation and desire. A server clearing his throat broke the spell, bringing his attention back to the room.

Lord Rodrigo stepped forward and helped me into the empty chair to his right. My heart fluttered when he murmured in my ear, "You look ravishing, my dear."

But then a moment later, reality struck like a thunderclap—as Lord Rodrigo's fiancée, Lady Magdalena, was meant to be seated to his right. My cheeks flushed as I realized the gravity of the faux pas. But it was too late to change seats, because Lady Magdalena chose that moment to enter the room, adorned in a shapeless blue gown with an oversize white collar. I couldn't help but wonder why she'd chosen such an unflattering gown to wear when I noticed the priest walking beside her, rigidly stiff in his black habit, scanning the room as if searching for a way to judge us all.

The priest's expression turned icy as he caught sight of me, and his face drained of color. Not wasting a moment, he aggressively pointed his finger at me and yelled, "Woman! How dare you flaunt your body in such whorish attire! Why are you wearing your hair down in such a disrespectful manner? A proper lady never lets her hair down in public! And look at you sitting in Lady Magdalena's seat—what disrespect is this? Who do you think you are, Mistress?"

I flinched, and my whole body went cold with shock. Then, a humiliated heat traveled up from my toes to my face, and my eyes stung with unshed tears. I had to get out of there! I sprang to my feet, nearly toppling my chair. Lady Magdalena seized that moment to push me out of her way, and I stumbled and lost my balance. Lord Rodrigo rushed forward, his strong hands steadying me before I could fall, and sat me down in his chair.

Standing tall, Lord Rodrigo faced Father Santiago, his voice low but filled with righteous anger. "Father, I have the utmost respect for the church," he began, each word like a warning shot, "but no one has the right to enter my home and insult my guests. Lady LeMaster is not only my special guest, but she also manages the castle. I see nothing indecent about her attire or lovely hair. She outshines every woman in this room with her radiant beauty!"

A collective gasp echoed around the room, tension building around us as Lord Rodrigo turned his fierce attention toward Lady Magdalena. "You, madam, may sit to my left or leave this dining hall immediately. I will see you banished if you ever disrespect Lady LeMaster again."

Lady Magdalena rose slowly, fists clenched, yet retained her composure as she returned to the priest's side. "I feel a bit ill, darling," she said, her voice cold and arrogant. "There's no need for you to accompany us. I can escort Father Santiago out. Good evening."

Wild emotions swirled within me. Despite the horror of the situation, my body reacted with pleasure at the sight of Lord Rodrigo defending my honor with such passion.

Father Santiago turned and sent me one last withering glare before he and Lady Magdalena left. *Was that a threat in his eyes, or my imagination?*

CHAPTER 33

The Aftermath

After Father Santiago and Lady Magdalena had left, the room fell into a heavy silence, tension almost thick enough to cut. Yet sweet young Amalia attempted to lighten the mood.

"Lord Gutiérrez, your home is beautiful, and my aunt and I are grateful for the dinner invitation," she quipped in a sweet voice.

"It was my pleasure, Amalia," Lord Rodrigo replied with a sigh. "I would like you and your aunt to join us for dinner every evening."

Maria nearly choked on her wine at his words. After delicately wiping her mouth, she responded, "Lord Gutiérrez, you may not understand the implications of what you're suggesting. It would be inappropriate for someone of my standing to dine at your table every evening."

"Nonsense, Maria," Lord Rodrigo replied with an audible sigh. "I will no longer heed the opinions of others about what is proper and what is not. From now on, I am going to make my own rules!"

A delighted grin lit up Amalia's face, and I couldn't help but giggle in approval. My heart swelled with gratitude for the man who had defended my honor. I needed all the support I could get, after all. My fear of the Inquisition coming for me could now become a reality since I'd inadvertently made an enemy of Father Santiago. At least I knew which side Lord Rodrigo was on.

Maria and Amalia said good night, leaving Lord Rodrigo and me alone in the large dining room. The remainder of the evening unfolded like a captivating dream. As the wine flowed, so did my resolve. The barriers I'd built between us seemed to crumble away.

We wandered over to the music room where a lone harpist played, the pure, angelic notes weaving several beautiful and heartfelt melodies together. We were both seated on a comfortable settee, listening to the lovely, mesmerizing music. I closed my eyes, surrendering to the blissful notes that wrapped around me. As the final note rang out, I slowly opened my eyes to a pair of vibrant green eyes looking at me just inches away. I then realized that my head was resting on his shoulder. The devastatingly handsome man disarmed me completely when he leaned over and softly kissed my forehead.

"Thank you for such a beautiful evening," I said softly as I gazed into his gorgeous eyes. As I got up to leave, he reached out and clasped my hand.

"Please don't go, Lady Maryann. The night is still young," he urged, his voice a silky caress to my senses.

"I must, but I am grateful for the wonderful evening and your fine company," I said softly. "It was also a very unforgettable dinner, don't you agree?"

"Lady Maryann," he replied, wiggling his eyebrows mischievously, his eyes sparkling with humor. "I agree. I also feel surprisingly uplifted after my enlightening chat with Father Santiago and Lady Magdalena."

"Your speech was nothing short of impressive, Lord Rodrigo. However, I must admit to feeling a bit uneasy around Father Santiago after the intense vitriol he threw at me," I confessed. "The good father seems to find me wanton, controversial, and completely improper. You know, if I didn't have your support, I would be very frightened of him."

"Lady Maryann, you never have to fear anything from Father Santiago. I will never allow that man to harm you. I vow to protect you at any cost!" he said, determination and love shining through his eyes.

I leaned over and planted a light kiss on his cheek. "Good night, Lord Rodrigo, and thank you again for such a lovely evening."

He nodded, smiling. "Good night, Lady Maryann. I hope you have pleasant dreams."

From the comfort of my bed, I stared at the frescoed ceiling, the unpleasant events from dinner replaying over and over in my mind. I couldn't forget the unsettling glare from Father Santiago just before he left. When he'd locked eyes with me, I'd detected a glimmer of darkness—and a disturbing mixture of desire and disdain. Despite the reassurances of protection from Lord Rodrigo, I still felt a cold wave of fear wash over me. What would Father Santiago do if he ever uncovered my true origins? Would Lord Rodrigo be able to protect me if the Catholic church learned of my secrets? The air grew cold, sending a shiver racing down my spine. It was some time before I was finally able to fall asleep.

CHAPTER 34

Missing Person

In twenty-first-century California, Brian Golding paced the floor, anxiety gnawing at him. Maryann, a diligent teacher and planner, had missed her return flight home, and his calls had gone unanswered.

His stomach churned, and his chest tightened. Something was wrong. She always prepared for every new semester at least a week beforehand.

He couldn't wait around any longer. With trembling hands, he opened his laptop and searched for the next available flight to Mérida, Spain, and his finger hovered over the button to book it.

Was he being ridiculous? After all, they weren't even together anymore. But he knew in his gut that she needed him. Driven by a restless need to find her, he booked the flight and requested time off work, completely unaware of just how much his life was about to change.

Francisco couldn't stop thinking about Maryann, and his concern for her grew, filling the halls of Castillo de los Conquistadores. It had been a week since Francisco had alerted the local authorities after discovering Maryann's haunting painting, an eerie reminder of her mysterious absence. As he studied Maryann's painting, he was struck by its vivid portrayal of the castle as it might have looked centuries ago, almost as if she had tapped into a forgotten history.

His family gathered for dinner that evening in the dimly lit dining room, a rare occurrence given the years that had passed since they had all shared a meal. Maryann's painting hung prominently on the wall, a centerpiece that sparked a whirlwind of questions among them.

"Father," Francisco began, his brow furrowing, "what do you make of the enigmatic lady in green in the painting? She bears an uncanny resemblance to the woman in the locket I showed you. I mentioned to Miss Maryann that the inscription from RG might refer to Lord Rodrigo Gutiérrez. Do you think this is all somehow linked?"

Miguel sighed, the lines on his face deepening with bewilderment. "I don't understand it at all, son. Why would Miss Maryann paint a pregnant Lady Magdalena stalking the woman in Lord Gutiérrez's arms?"

"That's the crux of it, Father! I never shared with her any portraits of Lady Magdalena Constanza or the tragic tale of her and Lord Gutiérrez's affair," Francisco replied, bewilderment creeping into his voice.

Turning to his aunt Juanita, Francisco asked, "What do you think could have become of Miss Maryann? They've stopped searching for her because they've exhausted all leads and have limited resources. They are hoping that she's sightseeing or visiting a friend."

Juanita's eyes sparkled with an unspoken intuition. "I have a feeling that she is safe. But how and why she painted Lord Rodrigo Gutiérrez, Lady Constanza, and the mysterious lady in green into her artwork—that's the true mystery here." With a playful smirk, she added, "Perhaps Miss Maryann possesses some hidden psychic abilities!"

CHAPTER 35

Bruno Pilato

Bruno Pilato whistled as he made his way along the bumpy, muddy road to visit his sister, niece, and nephew. It had rained heavily recently, but so far the dirt road was passable. As he guided the carriage slowly forward, he spotted a problem up ahead. The road was gone, replaced by a river of water. Frustrated but determined, he glanced around the area and noticed a dirt road off to the side. Although he wasn't familiar with this road and it appeared to be narrower than he liked, he had no choice. He had to take this alternate route because there was not enough room to turn the carriage around.

Once on the alternate road, the carriage moved forward at a good pace, and Bruno's thoughts went to Maryann. Just a week before, he'd visited her cottage, but she was nowhere to be found. After peering through the window, he'd caught a glimpse of a moldy loaf of bread sitting on the kitchen counter. Concern had gnawed at him, prompting him to enter the cottage. The unsettling sight of her unopened purse on the bed worried him. Praying she would forgive him, he'd rummaged through her things, hoping to find a clue as to her whereabouts. Judging by the advanced state of mold on the bread and fruit, Bruno was convinced she'd been gone for some time. Concerned for her safety and whereabouts, he'd rushed to town to alert the authorities, but Francisco Gutiérrez had already reported her disappearance. At that moment, he'd felt a chill creep up his spine. Where on earth could she have vanished to?

Snapping his attention back to the road, the horses came to a jarring halt without warning. Puzzled, Bruno leaped from the carriage and immediately spotted the problem. A tree had fallen and was blocking the road. Bruno unfastened the ropes from the carriage and secured them around the fallen tree. Then he guided and coaxed the horses as they pulled the log off to the side. After giving the horses a well-deserved treat, he reattached the ropes to the carriage. They traveled approximately another hundred yards when the horses began whinnying anxiously, visibly shaken by something unseen. Bruno could see no obstacles, so he flicked the reins and shouted encouragement to the horses. They inched forward slowly, clearly still feeling unease. As the carriage creaked ahead another ten feet, something caught his eye—two stone pillars half buried in the earth. Suddenly, the ground trembled beneath him. Panic gripped his stomach as the world around him seemed to spiral out of control. All he heard were the distant, desperate cries of the horses, and just before darkness swallowed him, a faint, haunting melody floated through the air, like a ghostly whisper in his mind.

As Bruno slowly blinked his eyes open, he realized that he must have blacked out and fallen out of the carriage. Luckily, he'd landed on soft grass. Shaking his head to clear the fog of disorientation in his mind, he tried to force his mind to focus, and all he could remember was the horses whinnying anxiously just before the ground began trembling. Was it an earthquake? The horses seemed calm at the moment, but he was not. Grabbing his decanter, he drank a healthy splash of whiskey, feeling its warmth travel down his body, calming his frayed nerves. The horses, now calm, obediently trotted forward at Bruno's command. Looking behind, he noticed that the stone pillars were now curiously gone.

Having no idea where he was, Bruno carefully guided his carriage around the next bend in the road. His eyes widened in surprise as a quaint stone cottage revealed itself amid the trees. Drawn by curiosity as well as a need to obtain directions, he stopped the carriage. A lovely Romani woman stood next to the road with long, wavy black hair. She had beautiful brown, almond-shaped eyes that sparkled with curiosity. As she stepped forward to greet him, Bruno found himself momentarily at a loss for words.

"Hello, sir. My name is Esmeralda Portola. Are you related to Stefan Pilato?" she asked, her eyes thoughtfully tracing the colorful sign on his carriage.

Finally able to find his voice and regain his composure, he replied, "I'm not sure, ma'am. He could be a distant relative. My name is Bruno Pilato, and it's a pleasure to meet you, Mistress Portola. I was on my way to visit my sister and her children when I got lost. Then I somehow lost consciousness and fell out of my carriage. I could have sworn there was an earthquake."

Her brow furrowed. "Are you all right, Mr. Bruno? I felt no earth tremors here. Perhaps you should come inside and rest for a bit. I can offer you fresh-baked apple pie and mead," she added, with a shy smile.

"Yes, Mistress Portola. I would like that very much, thank you," he replied. Following her into the small cottage, he felt a wave of anticipation wash over him. The scent of apples and cinnamon filled the air as he took a seat in the small kitchen. Esmeralda served him a generous slice of pie and handed him a mug of beer, the rich foam spilling over the rim. The warmth of the cottage and the delicious aromas in the room wrapped around him like a comforting blanket.

"This is the best pie I've ever tasted!" he exclaimed, savoring each bite slowly. "And the drink is delicious—did you brew it yourself, Mistress Portola?"

Esmeralda laughed softly. "You may call me Mistress Esmeralda, Mr. Bruno. I appreciate your kind words, but it's just a simple recipe. And yes, I do brew my own mead."

"I'm still baffled how I got lost," he said, leaning back. "I thought I knew every road around here. I don't know what came over me when I thought I'd experienced an earthquake. Perhaps I imagined the whole thing. I probably need to get more sleep."

"Do you have a family, Mr. Bruno?" she asked, curiosity dancing in her eyes.

"Yes, Mistress Esmeralda. I have a sister, a niece, and a nephew, but no wife yet," he chuckled. "I haven't found the right woman yet. How about you?"

"I am a widow, blessed with a lovely daughter," she replied, a hint of pride in her voice.

As Bruno gazed at the woman, he was puzzled as to why he had not met her before. He would never have forgotten someone as exquisite as she. "Mistress Esmeralda, an acquaintance of mine has gone missing, and several people are worried about her. Do you happen to know Miss Maryann LeMaster?" he asked, concern creeping into his voice.

Esmeralda's expression shifted to one of calm assurance. "Yes, Mr. Bruno. Lady Maryann is a guest at Lord Gutiérrez's castle. I saw her the other day, and she seemed in good health and spirits."

Bruno felt immense relief at the news. "Mistress Esmeralda, may I visit you again? I've thoroughly enjoyed our conversation and your delicious pie."

A delicate blush crept across Esmeralda's cheeks. "Yes, of course. I would gladly welcome another visit," she replied softly, her shyness only enhancing her charm.

As sunlight filtered through the cottage window, it seemed to illuminate Esmeralda's ethereal beauty, and Bruno's heart stilled as he gazed upon her, recognizing that this was no ordinary encounter. "I hope to see you soon, Mistress Esmeralda." Tipping his hat to her, he got up to leave just as an older woman with a walking cane hobbled out from the bedroom.

As soon as their eyes met, the woman's wrinkled face transformed into a breathtaking smile. *Was that recognition in her eyes?* "Hello, young man," she said. "I see that you have traveled a long distance. Your great-aunt was right when she said you were special. I can see it too. We'll be seeing each other again soon, young man."

Shocked and stunned into momentary silence, it felt like an eternity before Bruno seemed to snap out of it. "Uh, yes, ma'am," he stuttered. "I plan to visit soon. It was nice to meet you." He tipped his cap and turned to walk out the door, smiling at Mistress Esmeralda and glancing at the old woman one last time. *Wait, did she just wink at me?* Shaking his head, he briskly walked to his carriage, wondering if he had hallucinated the strange encounter with the old woman, when suddenly she stuck her head out the door and yelled, "Drive safely, young man. Don't anger your relative."

At this point, Bruno couldn't get out of there fast enough as he proceeded to guide his carriage up the narrow, winding road that appeared to lead to the mountaintop. After navigating the last bend in the road, a majestic castle suddenly loomed into view, and Bruno nearly lost control of the carriage, his heart racing, sweat beading down his back. This castle, while reminiscent of Francisco's, was newer and grander, with a vibrant Gutiérrez coat of arms flag waving proudly from its battlements, and surrounding the castle were several unfamiliar buildings.

Out of the corner of his eye, Bruno noticed a gathering of Romani people alongside several nearby colorful caravans. The women wore skirts and blouses splashed with colors from another era, and the men donned loose-fitting knickers that swayed with their movements. Was the castle hosting a historical reenactment? Why hadn't he been told about it? As he scanned the eclectic scene, one particular carriage caught his eye, sending a chill down his spine. It had a hand-painted sign in bright reds and greens that read "Pilato's Merchandise—the Best for Miles Around!"

Jerking the reins sharply, he brought the horses to a sudden halt and leaped from the seat. Leaning against a nearby tree, he almost passed out. He knew of no other Pilato relatives in Spain in the twenty-first century. *What was going on?*

Panic raced through him as he suddenly recalled a story from his childhood, spun by his great-aunt—a tale of magical ancient Celtic stones said to transport chosen souls across time, only available to those who could hear the Song of the Celtic Stones. He'd dismissed it as bedtime lore for all of these years, but she'd called him to her side just before passing and told him he was special, foretelling that the stones would summon him one day.

Wait, didn't Mistress Esmeralda's grandmother say that my great-aunt was right, that I was special?

How did she know about my great-aunt?

Bruno rewound the encounter with Mistress Esmeralda's grandmother in his mind as he took in his surroundings, and an inexplicable feeling of calm and acceptance enveloped him. He was experiencing an onslaught of emotions—excitement, fear, and determination. Drawing a deep breath, he collected himself and climbed back onto his carriage seat. Determined, he steered the horses toward a particular carriage, bracing himself for a confrontation with the hostile-looking man standing rigidly next to the *other* Pilato carriage. Out of the corner of his eye, a woman frantically waving her arms suddenly caught his attention. She looked to be in distress, so Bruno pivoted his carriage toward her. Confrontation with his angry ancestor would have to wait.

CHAPTER 36

A Trip to the Seamstress

Lady Magdalena was increasingly anxious as she waited for her driver, who was already ten minutes late. As she scanned the area, she noticed a striking young Romani driver whose carriage bore the name Pilato. Just then, he turned toward a cluster of carriages, one of which displayed the same surname. Leaning against it was a handsome man, glaring at the approaching driver. Sensing the brewing storm of a family feud, Lady Magdalena waved her arms in an attempt to thwart a possible altercation and to get the driver's attention because she needed passage.

"Driver Pilato, come back!" she shouted, her voice cutting through the tension. The man instantly turned his carriage around and approached her.

"Ma'am, are you all right? I saw you waving. Do you need assistance?"

"No, driver. I'm quite well, thank you. But I could use a ride to the seamstress in the valley."

Bruno nodded in agreement, his demeanor softening. "Let me assist you into the carriage, ma'am."

"Thank you," she replied, settling comfortably inside. "The seamstress is located on the main street."

Just before they reached their destination, Lady Magdalena began to flirt shamelessly and grew a little disappointed at the driver's lukewarm reaction. His heart was clearly elsewhere—was he thinking about another woman? When they arrived at the seamstress's shop, he jumped out to assist.

As she handed him a few coins, she looked at him thoughtfully. "Keep the peace with your family, driver. You don't want to stir up trouble in this village."

CHAPTER 37

Mail and Betrayal

Lord Rodrigo was in his study when the butler arrived, balancing a tray filled with letters. Rodrigo's curiosity was piqued because he rarely received more than a few missives. As he opened the first letter and read its contents, his pulse quickened with rage. After reading several more identical letters, he became so furious that he sent the tray crashing to the floor, scattering the letters like fallen leaves. To calm himself, he poured a generous dollop of brandy and drank it down in one gulp.

The identical letters were responses to wedding invitations that someone had sent from the castle.

What upcoming wedding?

There was no question about who had sent them. He had gravely underestimated Lady Magdalena's cunning ability to scheme. The shock of her betrayal cut deep, leaving a bitter taste in his mouth. Gritting his teeth against a surge of anger and frustration, he jumped to his feet and stormed out of his study, making his way toward the garden bordering the nearby forest in search of solace and solitude.

Regret gnawed at Rodrigo. He should have finalized a settlement with Lady Magdalena some time ago instead of being distracted by the allure of a captivating auburn-haired woman. Suddenly, small hands encircled his waist from behind, followed by a hard belly pressing against his back. Knowing instantly who it was, he pulled away from her embrace and turned to confront her, fury blazing in his eyes. "Are you insane, Lady Magdalena?" he seethed in a trembling voice. "What possessed you to send out those wedding invitations?"

Lady Magdalena's sensuous gaze swept over his form, her eyes glimmering with desire. "My love," she purred as she reached to grab his arm. With a seductive whisper, she calmly replied, "Why are you so angry, Lord Rodrigo? We are engaged after all. I just wanted to hurry things along a bit. I am impatient for this baby to be born and eager to be intimate with you again."

Lord Rodrigo recoiled and stepped back out of her reach. "Madam, I will never make love to you. Furthermore, I no longer believe your lies—we've never slept together! You shall answer for your betrayal, Lady Magdalena. That child you carry will be better off without you." He shot her one last glare before turning away and stalking back to the castle, the weight of betrayal heavy on his heart.

CHAPTER 38

The Wedding Planner

Alone in my room with my thoughts, memories of Lord Rodrigo's distraught face replayed in my mind after he'd revealed Lady Magdalena's betrayal. His look of shock, disbelief, anger, and helplessness was almost too much for me to bear. The wedding festivities were just a week away! Anxiety churned within me. How could this have happened? How could she have done this? I had hoped that Lady Magdalena would turn her life around or at least try to better herself. What she had done to Lord Rodrigo was unfathomable and went beyond mere betrayal. Had she done this for security and prestige, or was there love involved?

Sighing, I wondered if I needed a reality check. After all, people in the twenty-first century often act this way. Was I being naïve, clinging to dreams of a world where love, kindness, and goodness prevailed? My mother always told me I was too much of a "Pollyanna." I suppose she was right because I believed in optimism and tried to find good in everything.

To take my mind off the upcoming wedding, I impulsively offered to manage the wedding preparations, encouraging Lord Rodrigo to let me stay busy to stave off my despair. His initial response was a resounding no, but I convinced him that keeping occupied would be a welcome distraction.

My role would involve overseeing the guests' comfort within the castle, while he would plan the games and tournaments and hire extra hands. It felt like a paradoxical situation. We would be laboring to plan a week full of wedding festivities for one person—Lady Magdalena—the very person who had orchestrated this charade and caused all the emotional turmoil.

I spent the entire day preparing the rooms for the upcoming wedding guests. While not extravagant, the guest rooms were both comfortable and modern for the time. Each room featured functional wooden chests and armoires for clothing, modest beds, and fireplaces to keep the spaces cozy and warm. Private garderobes and privacy screens adorned the chambers, and mirrors made in Venice added a touch of elegance.

The grand hall would serve as the central gathering place. Beautiful tapestries were draped across the walls, bringing depth, elegance, and vibrant colors to the space. Artfully woven rugs, lovingly crafted by local Romani artisans, were strategically placed throughout the floors.

I was on my way to meet Clara to discuss meal planning for the upcoming festivities. As I approached the kitchen, I was shocked to find it in complete disarray, with pots and pans scattered everywhere. Clara stood at her worktable, her hands covered in flour, looking frazzled and stressed.

"Clara, I don't want you to overwork yourself!" I exclaimed. "Lord Gutiérrez said you could hire as many women from the valley as you need. Clara . . . you look so pale—are you all right?"

"Lady Maryann, please don't worry about me. I can get organized in no time. I should be asking how you are holding up," she replied, her tone filled with concern. "Word has spread throughout the castle about . . ." Sighing and twisting a dish towel in frustration, Clara declared, "It's scandalous how Lady Magdalena orchestrated this wedding for her gain. We were all hoping you would wed Lord Gutiérrez. Now there's a dark cloud hanging over the castle, and honestly, I'm not sure how any of us will get through this!" Tears welled in her eyes.

"Oh, Clara, I'm so sorry. I'm not happy about this situation either. But to be honest, I'm trying to stay busy so I don't have time to dwell on it! Lord

Gutiérrez is the real victim in this tragic tale," I said, my voice trembling with emotion. "He has been backed into a corner, and there seems to be no solution in sight."

"Yes, I understand all too well, Lady Maryann. If staying busy helps you, then I'd better get this kitchen organized. I'll be fine—don't worry about me," she replied, offering a smile that didn't quite reach her eyes.

"Together, we will find our strength, Clara," I said firmly.

All it would take was a little courage—and maybe a lot of wine.

CHAPTER 39

Wedding Guests

It was Sunday, and guests had begun arriving that afternoon from nearby provinces, with some even traveling from Mérida. They were expecting between forty and fifty guests in total. The servants and hired helpers had worked diligently all week, cleaning and preparing the castle for the upcoming events. Lord Rodrigo was already mingling with the guests in the grand hall. Wine, mead, and beautifully arranged platters of tempting meats, cheeses, fruits, and a variety of desserts were artfully displayed on a large table that sat flush against one of the walls.

Pedro's father, Lord Felipe Velasco, and his stepmother, Lady Elena, had just arrived and were making their entrance. Lord Velasco was a striking man, tall and muscular like Pedro, with gray eyes that sparkled with humor and chestnut brown hair sprinkled with silver. In contrast, Lady Elena was petite, with golden hair and icy blue eyes, but her pinched expression gave her an air of perpetual irritation.

With a broad grin, Lord Rodrigo approached the couple. Happy to see his old friend, he exclaimed, "Felipe, you look well! I'm so delighted to see you again! I trust you're ready for the jousting tournament—we'll be facing off against each other for the finale." A hint of mischief danced in his eyes as he added, "You know you're the only man who stands a chance of unseating me!" He laughed and patted his friend on the shoulder.

Felipe embraced Rodrigo, clapping him on the back. "My good friend, I can hardly believe you're getting married! I can sense a story brewing and can't wait to hear all about it." Turning to his wife, he said, "Lord Rodrigo, allow me to introduce my wife, Lady Elena. Elena, this is my good friend, Lord Rodrigo Gutiérrez."

Lord Rodrigo bowed with a flourish. "Lady Elena, it's a pleasure to make your acquaintance. I hope you enjoy the festivities this week."

"Lord Gutiérrez, it's lovely to meet you as well, and congratulations! But tell me, where is the bride-to-be? Is she hiding away?" she inquired, a hint of curiosity in her voice.

"Lady Magdalena has not been feeling well and is currently resting in her chambers. You'll have the pleasure of meeting her in the coming days," he replied smoothly. "If there is anything you need to make your stay more comfortable, please let me know. Better yet, I will introduce you to Lady LeMaster. She will ensure that you have everything you need." As he looked around the room, he spotted Lady Maryann in the doorway and waved her over.

As I stood in the doorway, observing the lively scene, I noticed Lord Rodrigo looking my way and waving to get my attention. When our eyes met, he gestured for me to come over. My body responded obediently, drawn to him like a magnet. As I approached his side, I became aware of the couple standing near him.

"Lord and Lady Velasco, allow me to present Lady Maryann LeMaster," he stated, his words laced with pride and warmth. "Lady LeMaster recently moved here from France and has been incredibly proficient in managing the castle. Everyone here adores her, and honestly, I can't imagine life without her."

I wished I could vanish. Rodrigo's affection for me was painfully clear, and my embarrassment escalated. With a practiced smile, I curtsied. "It's a pleasure to meet you both." I immediately recognized an older version of Pedro in his father, their resemblance remarkable. As I turned to address Lady Elena, I sensed her disapproval of Rodrigo's familiarity toward me. Pivoting, I chose to address her husband instead.

"Lord Velasco, I know your son, Pedro, quite well. He's not only one of my best students, but he's also an extraordinarily kind, intelligent, and polite young man. I'm sure you're proud of him."

The sudden frown that crossed Lord Velasco's face and the narrowing of Lady Elena's eyes immediately alerted me that I had crossed into dangerous territory. Realizing my faux pas, I quickly sought an escape. "I'm sorry to cut our conversation short, but I still have much to prepare for the wedding. It was lovely meeting you both." I curtsied again, pivoting on my heel, and headed toward the empty parlor, where I planned to collect my scattered thoughts.

Yet my moment of respite was short-lived. Lady Elena had followed me, catching me off guard. Seizing my arm, she rather rudely pulled me over to a nearby settee.

"Lady Maryann, I must apologize for my husband's rudeness," she began, her voice dripping with insincerity. "You see, Pedro is a sensitive topic for us. My husband intends to consult with Lord Gutiérrez while we're here about disinheriting him in favor of my son, Tomás. I can't fully blame Pedro for his behavior; he is very much his mother's son. What's that saying? Ah, yes, the apple doesn't fall far from the tree. His mother was never deemed worthy in my husband's eyes."

A rush of heat crept up my neck at her callous words. How dare she speak of Pedro and his deceased mother with such contempt? If I didn't leave immediately, I feared I might say something regrettably inappropriate, and the last thing I wanted was to tarnish Lord Rodrigo's reputation. Despite my anger, I forced myself to smile, swallowed my words, and curtsied again before hurrying out of the parlor, leaving Lady Elena's voice behind me.

Lady Magdalena emerged from the kitchen, her arms laden with an enticing assortment of bread and cheese she'd discreetly gathered, which she planned to devour in the privacy of her room. Just as she stepped into the corridor, Lady Maryann hurried past her, a storm of distress written on her face. As the heavy door of the kitchen swung shut, Lady Magdalena paused, glancing both ways. Curiosity piqued, she pressed her ear against the door, hoping to hear what had unsettled Lady Maryann.

"Lady Maryann, what's wrong? You look upset," Lady Magdalena heard Clara say through the door.

"Oh, Clara." Lady Maryann's voice was bursting with frustration. "It's Lady Elena, Pedro's stepmother. She was utterly disrespectful, spewing venomous words about Pedro and his late mother. It's unbearable! He's such a kindhearted young man. He doesn't deserve this wretched fate of being disinherited."

Clara's voice lowered but was still discernible to Lady Magdalena. "Lady Maryann, you care too much about everybody. Why do you torture yourself with other people's problems?"

"I can't just sit back and do nothing. Pedro needs someone to stand by him! Not only was he banished from his home, but according to his stepmother, he is soon to be disinherited. I believe her to be behind this because her son, Tomás, would benefit from Pedro's disinheritance," Maryann declared with passion.

"What about your troubles, Lady Maryann?" Clara pressed. "Doesn't it bother you that Lady Magdalena constantly treats you with disdain? What do you plan to do about that?"

Curious, Lady Magdalena leaned closer to the door, eager to catch every word of Lady Maryann's response.

"Oh, Clara," Maryann sighed. "Lady Magdalena has her reasons for disliking me. I believe she must have been mistreated in the past, which would explain why she's always on the offensive. She just needs to believe in herself. Anyone can change for the better, but it takes desire, commitment, and determination. I know from my own experience. In the meantime, I will continue to be respectful and kind to her. Perhaps one day she'll accept me as a friend."

"Your kindness is a double-edged sword, Lady Maryann. I worry about you because you wear your heart on your sleeve," Clara exclaimed. "If Lady Magdalena only knew what a good friend she could have in you! Just promise me that you will take care of yourself, my friend. Sometimes you need to guard your heart to protect it," she added with a warm smile.

Lady Magdalena shook her head, unable to comprehend what she had just heard. As she walked back to her chamber, a whirlwind of thoughts, questions, and emotions swirled in her mind. Lady Maryann's compassion and kindness confused her. *She would be my friend?* Regret gnawed at her. Perhaps seeking out Father Santiago had been a hasty decision, but now there was no stopping him. He was like a trained hunting dog, relentlessly pursuing his prey.

CHAPTER 40

The Squire

Pedro was in the stables feeding an apple to Macho, Lord Gutiérrez's horse. Anxiety bit at his heels as he thought about his upcoming interview with Lord Gutiérrez regarding the squire position. With several minutes to spare before the interview, he leaned against the outside stall, closed his eyes, and took a moment to calm his nerves. He found himself daydreaming about Amalia.

"Ah, excuse me, young man. Am I interrupting something?" Lord Rodrigo asked with a grin. "Are you perchance daydreaming about a particular young lady?"

Startled by Lord Gutiérrez's voice, Pedro quickly straightened his posture and turned to face him.

"No, sir. You haven't interrupted me, but I must admit, I was daydreaming a bit," he replied sheepishly.

"It's quite normal to daydream, young man," replied Lord Rodrigo, patting him on the shoulder before continuing. "It is my understanding that you are interested in the squire position. Is that correct?"

"Yes, sir," Pedro replied.

"Excellent. If you are hired for this position, you will need to work hard. The duties will include caring for my horse, running important errands for me, and ensuring that my weaponry and armor are clean, polished, and ready to wear. I'm happy to see that you and Macho are already well acquainted. If there is ever a battle, you will need to accompany me. Thus, you'll need to learn the skill of wielding a sword proficiently. Eventually, you will have an opportunity to become a knight if that is your desire. What say you, Pedro? The job is yours if you want it."

A rush of adrenaline coursed through Pedro as he stood before Lord Gutiérrez. He straightened his posture and raised his head proudly. His face reflected determination and resolve as he lifted his chin and confidently met Lord Gutiérrez's gaze. With each word carefully chosen and articulated, he replied, "My lord, I am deeply grateful for this opportunity." He continued, voice steady but laced with excitement. "It would be a tremendous honor to serve as your squire. I vow to dedicate myself fully to mastering the art of swordsmanship. I will strive to do my best to fulfill all of my obligations, and I promise to uphold your values and remain unwaveringly loyal to you, Lord Gutiérrez."

Lord Rodrigo peered at Pedro with admiration in his eyes, and his expression softened. Had he heard whispers about his father disowning him?

"Pedro, I believe we have reached an understanding. You are now my official squire." His tone was authoritative yet kind. "Each morning, your first task of the day will be to make sure Macho has water, food, and clean hay in his stall. After breakfast each day, we'll review your duties for the day. You'll have a chamber in the castle, as well as an allowance for clothing, food, and other necessities. Does that sound acceptable to you, young man?"

Overwhelmed with gratitude, Pedro nodded fervently and bowed deeply. His voice trembled with emotion as he replied, "Yes. Thank you, Lord Gutiérrez. That sounds wonderful."

CHAPTER 41

Lord Velasco and Pedro

After donning his riding gear, Lord Velasco entered the stables, invigorated by the crisp morning air. He heard a familiar voice murmuring to one of the horses, which piqued his curiosity. As he approached his horse's stall, the voice faded, and he spotted a young man brushing Macho.

Recognizing his son Pedro's tone, Felipe frowned. Pedro was supposed to be with his aunt Angelina in the village. A wave of guilt washed over Felipe as he listened to his son speak softly to the horse. Unable to contain his emotions, he stepped outside and sat on a nearby bench to clear his head, memories of Pedro's banishment rushing back to him.

He had married Elena to provide Pedro with a mother figure, hoping it would ease his grief. Although he didn't love Elena, he'd been fond of her during their brief affair after Fátima's death. He had loved his first wife dearly and greatly missed her.

After Elena and her children moved into the small castle, she immediately made changes to fit her preferences. Felipe had tried to remain optimistic, but he hadn't cared for the sudden changes. Pedro was always respectful to Elena, but she excluded him from the start, and her son, Tomás, followed suit, making Pedro feel like a third wheel. He was away on business for the first month and didn't realize the extent of the escalating situation until his return. By then, the only person Pedro connected with was Elena's ten-year-old daughter, Teresa.

He was immediately prompted to cancel all trips for the next month in a desperate effort to bring the family together. Felipe took the boys on a week-long hunting trip, hoping they would bond, but it turned out to be a disaster. While he and Pedro enjoyed themselves, Tomás struggled. He had no hunting skills and didn't know how to use a bow. He seemed resentful and uninterested, making a half-hearted attempt to participate. Frustrated, Felipe realized he didn't want to be there at all.

After that, Felipe decided to take the whole family on field outings, picnics, and trips to town. Then he encouraged eating together as a family for every meal. By the time the month was up, Felipe was exhausted and frustrated and could barely stand being around Elena. She was fine when they were away from home—she played the part of good stepmother and loving wife well. But at home, she was her true self and didn't seem to mind when he'd witnessed her unfair treatment of Pedro. Felipe was completely at a loss to fix the situation.

The morning of the banishment began as every other morning. As usual, Pedro sat at the other end of the table, away from Lady Elena and Tomás. When Teresa entered the room, she sat down next to Pedro. When she leaned over and said something to him, they both began laughing. Felipe remembered thinking at that time that it was so nice to hear laughter in the house for a change. At the other end of the table, where he sat with Elena and Tomás, there were no conversations, no laughter, just cold silence.

After breakfast, Teresa and Pedro went outside to play. About an hour later, Tomás burst into the house, exclaiming, "Pedro is hurting my sister!"

Felipe nearly called him a liar. "You're mistaken, Tomás. Pedro would never do that!"

Elena rushed in and, upon hearing Tomás, shouted, "I knew I couldn't trust that boy! Felipe, if you don't banish him, I'll tell the authorities!"

Panic set in as Felipe realized the gravity of the situation. He feared the scandal would ruin Pedro's life. He could face imprisonment. The only solution he could think of was to send him to his sister's house. It wasn't meant to be a banishment.

Felipe was frustrated and still furious at Elena when he found Pedro and Teresa outside, and he wasn't thinking clearly. Felipe told Pedro, "You're almost a man. Why are you rolling around on the ground with little girls? Appearances matter! You must go live with Aunt Angelina. Pack your bags now!"

At the time, Felipe thought he'd made the right decision by sending him away. The weight of shame bore down on him, especially when Elena threatened to leave months later if he didn't disinherit Pedro in favor of her son, Tomás. The very thought of it twisted his stomach. Felipe never explicitly told Elena no, but he also never agreed. He should have been more assertive.

Then, when Lady Maryann spoke so highly of Pedro, her words resonated with Felipe and prompted him to confront his mistakes.

Taking a deep breath, Felipe steeled himself and made his way to the back of the stables, determined to make amends.

Lost in his thoughts, Pedro didn't hear his father call out to him. When he finally turned around, his eyes widened in surprise at the sight of his father standing there.

"My son," Felipe began, his voice serious, "I owe you an apology for my unforgivable actions. I acted rashly to protect you from potential imprisonment because your stepmother threatened to go to the authorities. I should have been more frank with you. Can you ever find it in your heart to forgive me?"

Pedro's initial shock melted into a soft expression. "Father, I accept your apology. I understood that you had a difficult decision to make at the time."

Felipe pulled his son toward him and embraced him tightly instead. "I promise you, things will change. No one will come between us again. Once the wedding is over, I want you to return to the castle and reclaim your rightful place beside me."

As Pedro pulled away from his father with an earnest expression, he said, "There was a time when that was my greatest wish. However, I am now Lord Gutiérrez's squire, and I wish to forge my own path. I want you to know that I take great pride in being your son, Father."

Felipe stared at him, surprised yet proud at the man his son had become. The independence and determination in Pedro's eyes filled him with a new sense of pride and respect for his son.

"Father, there's something I must share," Pedro continued, his voice a mixture of hope and hesitation. "I am in love with a Romani girl, Amalia. We're young, but I envision a future with her. I don't concern myself with others' opinions, but I worry about Amalia facing criticism. Your support would mean the world to us."

Felipe inhaled deeply, contemplating the weight of Pedro's request. "I would be honored to welcome Amalia into our family," he replied, his voice filled with sincerity and affection. "I am so proud of you, son. If you ever need guidance or support, know that I am here. Your legacy and wealth will remain secure, ready for you when you claim it."

As they stood together, a newfound bond began to form, bridging the gap that had once separated them.

CHAPTER 42

Amalia and Pedro

Amalia stood outside, hanging freshly laundered clothes on the line, savoring the cool breeze that grazed her skin. After days of being confined within the castle, working alongside her aunt to alter garments, the refreshing scent of the outdoors felt like a magical escape. As she reached for the empty basket to collect more laundry, a sudden jolt from behind nearly knocked her over.

Regaining her balance, she was ready to reprimand the culprit when she turned to see Pedro, his face lit with a playful grin.

"Have you lost your mind, Pedro?" Amalia laughed, surprise evident in her voice. "What are you doing here, and why do you have that silly grin on your face?"

"Amalia, I have the most incredible news!" he exclaimed excitedly, his eyes sparkling. "I'm now Lord Gutiérrez's new squire!" His grin widened. "I even saw my father, and he apologized to me! Oh, I need to find Lady Maryann and thank her for encouraging me to apply for the squire position." His excitement filled the air with anticipation.

With a wink and generous smile, Pedro dashed off, leaving Amalia in a whirlwind of exhilaration and disbelief. She sighed but couldn't contain the grin that spread across her face as she stood there, processing his joyful news. Shaking her head in disbelief, she picked up the empty basket, her thoughts dancing along with the fluttering linens.

CHAPTER 43

Courtship

Esmeralda stood in the kitchen, her fingers deftly peeling onions, while her mind wandered to Bruno. Was she really thinking about another man? It had been so long since she felt this way, and she found herself humming as she continued preparing the meal. Since her husband's death seven years ago, she had closed her heart to the idea of love. The loss left her feeling isolated and lonely, and she had resigned herself to a life of solitude. So it was disarming when an unexpected spark ignited between her and Bruno, a man she had known for only a short time.

A glance out the window sent her pulse racing as she spotted Bruno's carriage approaching the castle. Abandoning her apron, she told Clara she was stepping outside for a moment. Smoothing her wayward curls and trying to appear calm, she strolled toward him, pushing down the excitement bubbling within her.

"Mister Bruno, what a delightful surprise! Here on business, I presume?" she called out, her voice light.

Bruno removed his cap and bowed as he gently kissed her hand. "Mistress Esmeralda, I'm here to check on Lady LeMaster. Do you happen to know where she is?"

A flicker of disappointment washed over her. "Yes, she's busy discussing the wedding festivities with Clara, the cook."

Bruno's eyes followed her gesture, relief washing over him like a gentle wave. He nodded and weighed his words carefully, as if they held greater significance. “I can see that Lady LeMaster is well, so I suppose I could delay our talk for a moment,” he said. Holding his hat in both hands, he looked into Esmeralda’s beautiful eyes and gave her his heartwarming signature smile. “Have I mentioned how lovely you look today, Mistress Esmeralda?”

Heat rushed to Esmeralda’s cheeks, and she laughed, a youthful spark igniting within her. “Oh, there’s no need for flattery, Mr. Bruno. I may have been beautiful once, but I’m just a widow past her prime now. Still, it is nice to hear kind words from a man as handsome as you.”

Bruno’s eyes bulged, and he shook his head in disbelief. “Past your prime? Surely you jest, Mistress Esmeralda! You are a stunningly beautiful woman, and I wish to court you.”

Esmeralda’s heart skipped a beat. Her eyes prickled with tears at his bold declaration. “You cannot be serious,” she replied softly. “Are you truly interested in someone like me?”

Bruno’s eyes held an unwavering sincerity as he straightened his shoulders and looked at her seriously and affectionately. “I must tell you of my feelings, Mistress Esmeralda. I never expected to feel such strong emotions toward any woman, but I do. I know we have only recently met, but I know without a doubt that we are meant to be together. Will you allow me to court you properly, Mistress Esmeralda?”

Stunned but giddy with excitement, Esmeralda couldn’t suppress her happiness. “I would be delighted to accept your courtship, Mister Bruno.”

“Then let us see where this leads, Mistress Esmeralda. Who knows? There may soon be another wedding!”

CHAPTER 44

Stefan Pilato

Around ten Romani men approached Bruno's carriage, their expressions dark and menacing. Bruno stiffened as their leader—Stefan Pilato—stood tall with crossed arms, glaring at Bruno. The air crackled with tension and the weight of the impending confrontation.

"Bruno Pilato," he called out, his voice booming like thunder. "What right do you have to use my family name among the gringos?" He spat on the ground, a clear sign of his disdain. "I have no family beyond my brother, Dorian, and I've not heard from him in thirty years!"

Bruno, whose quick wit usually saw him through any tricky confrontation, stepped in front of Esmeralda, chin raised defiantly. "I am Bruno Pilato, your brother's son," he stammered in halting Romani. "After my father died, a kind gringo couple took us in. That's why I wrote my sign in Romani and English."

Stefan scrutinized Bruno for what felt like an eternity. Slowly, his fierce demeanor softened. "Bruno, it is a pleasure to meet you," he said, a sly grin appearing. "You must be a true Pilato. All the men in our family resemble one another and have an undeniable charm. I'm your Uncle Stefan, and these are my comrades."

Relief washed over him. Bruno turned back to Esmeralda, her surprise evident as she stood by. "Uncle, this is Mistress Esmeralda Portola," he said with a hint of pride.

Esmeralda stepped forward, her voice steady. "Sir Stefan, I have long admired your family. I assure you, Bruno is a man of honor—one you will proudly claim as your own. Bruno and I are now officially courting, and I hope to become a member of your family," she stated, smiling shyly.

As Stefan's gaze locked onto Esmeralda's, a huge grin broke across his face. "Mistress Portola," he began, his tone light yet sincere, "it would truly be an honor to welcome you into our family. Should my nephew Bruno ever give you any trouble, you know where to find me," he added playfully, winking at her.

Bruno chuckled, a surge of unexpected joy swelling in his chest. Is this what it felt like to be part of a wider clan? The feeling of family kinship enveloped him, filling the void he hadn't even realized was there. At that moment, standing beside his beloved and surrounded by newfound kin, an unmistakable sense of belonging overwhelmed him. Amid this revelation, a flicker of wonder ignited in his mind. How had fate drawn him into this enchanting moment through the magic of stones?

CHAPTER 45

Lord Gutiérrez and Lord Velasco

Lord Rodrigo stood in the stables deftly saddling his horse when Lord Velasco strolled in casually. "Rodrigo, it seems great minds think alike," he quipped, a hint of mischief in his tone. "Do you mind if I join you for a ride?"

"Felipe, your company would be most welcome," Rodrigo replied, though a shadow flickered across his brow. "But I must warn you, I carry a burden that may not lend itself to pleasant conversation."

Mounted on their horses, the two rode out at a leisurely pace. As they ventured deeper into the forest, Rodrigo slowed Macho and veered down a secluded trail that led to a small clearing next to a lake. They dismounted beneath the graceful arch of a sizable evergreen tree, the sound of water lapping at the shore.

"All right, Rodrigo, spill it. What's bothering you?" Felipe prodded. "Is it by chance the charming auburn-haired beauty you're conflicted over?"

Rodrigo heaved a sigh, his eyes drifting toward the shimmering water. "Oh, my friend, you know me well. I never planned to marry Lady Magdalena. Our night together was a blur, lost in a haze of wine. Six weeks later, she announced she was with child. Out of a sense of honor, I asked for her hand despite the whispers of her infidelities reaching my ears. When I met Lady Maryann, everything changed. I intended to end my engagement with Lady Magdalena and offer her a generous settlement—a château in France, perhaps."

He paused, a flush creeping over his cheeks. "But I hesitated, and impatience seemed to have taken hold of Lady Magdalena. She forged the wedding invitations using my stolen ring seal. She didn't stop there. She invited my business acquaintances and esteemed contacts, and now I find myself trapped in a sham wedding with a woman I can barely tolerate."

Silence fell between them, each man grappling with the heavy weight of Rodrigo's predicament. After a long pause, Felipe spoke, his voice laced with sincerity. "Rodrigo, I'm at a loss for words. And though you're far too honorable to stoop to underhanded tactics, allow me twenty-four hours to devise a plan. Will you promise to consider my suggestion?"

"Felipe," Rodrigo replied, desperation creeping into his tone, "I will listen to your suggestion, as I feel like a condemned man."

"Wonderful, my friend. I just spoke with Pedro and took steps to mend our rift. I refuse to bend to my wife's demands any longer. Lady Elena was so sweet and docile when she was my mistress, but once we wed, the sweetness faded, leaving only schemes and nagging. I won't allow you to fall into the same trap."

Rodrigo nodded, grateful for his friend's support. "I pray you can devise a solution to end this nightmare. My reputation may take a hit, but what terrifies me more is the potential fallout of my business relationships. I cannot allow the village of Zafra to suffer because of my missteps. Let us return to the castle, shall we, Felipe?"

CHAPTER 46

The Tryst

Lord Felipe's mind whirled as he made his way to his wife's chambers. He knew what he needed to do, but it wasn't going to be easy. He needed to inform her that he'd changed his mind—he would not be disinheriting Pedro. His wife would be livid, and he could already picture the fury on her face. All she wanted was for her son, Tomás, to inherit the entire Velasco fortune, and she wouldn't be expecting this announcement.

Just as Felipe was about to pass an impressively sized chamber, his eyes flitted to his left, taking in the sight of the intriguingly beautiful woman leaning sensually against the door frame.

In a seductive voice, the woman purred, "Pardon me, Señor, I am Lady Magdalena Constanza. I thought I knew all of the guests, yet I do not recall seeing your handsome face before."

Was that desire dancing in her eyes? She definitely looked amused.

Felipe cleared his throat. "Lady Constanza, I am pleased to meet you. I am Lord Felipe Velasco," he said as he bowed and kissed her lightly perfumed hand.

Lady Magdalena glanced down the hall in both directions. Satisfied that it was empty, she pulled him into her room. Felipe stifled a startled gasp but went in quite willingly. Leaning into him, she stood on tiptoe and softly whispered, "Lord Velasco, I hunger for you, but I must warn you, sir, my appetite is ravenous. Would you care to meet me in the attic loft in two hours?"

All the air left Felipe's lungs. He felt as if his whole body was on fire with desire. He bowed again and kissed her hand slowly and deliberately. "My lady, I would be very pleased to join you in two hours."

CHAPTER 47

Lady Elena

After his tryst with Lady Magdalena, Felipe shook his head to try and dislodge the memories of what he'd just done. He couldn't deny that he'd had fun, but if his wife learned of his betrayal, he didn't dare imagine how she might retaliate. He resolutely approached her chamber, and when he reached the door, Lady Elena stepped out into the hallway, blocking the doorway.

"Felipe, where have you been?" she whined. "Have you met with Lord Gutiérrez yet?"

Felipe let out a long breath. "I canceled the meeting with Lord Gutiérrez after I spoke with Pedro this afternoon. After I asked for his forgiveness, I assured him that he would always be the only heir to the Velasco holdings." He braced himself for Lady Elena's reaction but felt a sense of lightness from revealing the truth. Sometimes, the truth does set you free.

Shock and fury burned in Lady Elena's eyes as she slapped him without thinking of the consequences. Her hands shook as she stared into her husband's furious expression, and she paled, realizing too late that she had gone too far.

Felipe had put up with her tantrums, outbursts, and possessiveness since they married, and he had finally had enough.

"Your meddlesome ways have gone unchecked for too long, Elena," he said in a low voice, trembling with rage. "If you continue to act like this, I will—I'll put an end to our marriage." He dropped her hands, spun on his heels, and stomped away.

CHAPTER 48

Grand Ball Fittings

Lady Magdalena cast her garments to the ground in a fit of despair. The village seamstress, Alana, had recently put the finishing touches on the gown for the ball, but it clung to her in all the wrong places. She peered at herself from each angle in the mirror, becoming more dissatisfied with her reflection at every turn. The bodice strained against her curves, and the sleeves, meant to billow gracefully, constricted her arms so tightly that she feared her circulation was at risk. A flood of tears escaped her eyes. She hadn't wept like this since she was jilted by the stable boy in favor of a barmaid's daughter.

Lady Magdalena's devoted maid, Elisa, paused her ironing at the sight of her mistress's anguish. "Your Ladyship, please don't despair. You look exquisite, and no one will suspect your condition. It's natural to feel vulnerable during times like this."

"Oh, Elisa, I've stumbled down a dark path," Lady Magdalena whispered, her voice raw with regret. "For too long, I've acted selfishly, and now that I can see clearly, I yearn to reverse the harm I've caused. Lord Rodrigo despises me now—and honestly, I can't blame him. I've been unkind to Lady Maryann, who has only ever shown me kindness." With that, she collapsed onto the bed, helpless sobs racking her body as grief poured from her soul, a torrent she felt powerless to stop.

Elisa rushed to her side, sitting carefully on the edge of the bed so as not to startle her. "My lady, this cloud will pass. When your baby arrives, you will find yourself again. But for now, you must rest. Tomorrow's ball awaits, and I will be by your side if you need anything."

Rafael stood nearby, ready to assist Lord Rodrigo with any final adjustments as he donned his attire for the grand ball. Everything seemed to fit perfectly, and Rafael imagined the usual flurry of admiration surrounding his lord during such events. After a decade of service, he knew Lord Rodrigo well. Yet a gnawing concern lingered in his thoughts. Marrying Lady Magdalena Constanza felt like a sacrifice—a forfeiture of a chance at genuine happiness with Lady Maryann.

"May I speak candidly, sir?" asked Rafael.

Rodrigo paused, intrigued, as he poured brandy into two cups and handed one to Rafael. He said, "Rafael, please share your thoughts. Your honesty is valued, and nothing you say will offend me."

Rafael took a fortifying sip and set the glass down. "Sir, marrying Lady Constanza would be a grave mistake. You're not suited for one another, and I assure you, the castle staff agrees. In contrast, Lady Maryann is a perfect match for you. What you two share is evident to everyone."

"Rafael, if I could get out of this upcoming wedding, I would. But until I have a reason to cancel the wedding, I'm stuck. Believe me, I wish with all my heart that it were Lady Maryann I was marrying instead of Lady Magdalena."

"I'm sorry, sir," Rafael replied, his tone heavy with sympathy. "If only I could alleviate your suffering. Should you discover a path forward, know I am here, ready to assist."

"Thank you, Rafael," Rodrigo sighed, looking overwhelmed. "Your friendship and support mean the world to me. I doubt I could bear this burden alone."

CHAPTER 49

Lady Maryann

Tonight was the grand ball, the prelude to the wedding everyone had been buzzing about. Lord Gutiérrez was set to marry Lady Constanza by the end of the week. Every time I thought about it, a wave of despair crashed over me. I sat on my bed, grappling with the reality that I couldn't witness their vows—or remain in the castle after their marriage. An idea tugged at me. Maybe it was time to find a way back to my own century. The thought made my stomach knot. I didn't want to leave Lord Rodrigo. My old life felt almost like a dream and seemed so long ago now.

Just then, a gentle knock interrupted my thoughts. I opened the door to find Maria cradling the exquisite gown she had lovingly crafted for me to wear to the ball.

With a knowing expression, she placed the gown on the bed and settled beside me. "Lady Maryann, what's troubling you? Why the long face?" she asked, concern etched on her features.

"Lord Rodrigo and Lady Magdalena are getting married at the end of the week," I confessed, anguish heavy in my voice. "I need to leave this place before the wedding!" Maria enveloped me in a warm embrace, allowing me to release the emotions I had bottled up. After what felt like an eternity, I drew back and wiped my tears. "Maria, is there truly nothing I can do?"

"Lady Maryann, do you not believe in miracles? True love can defy even the most daunting circumstances. Lord Gutiérrez cares for you—don't underestimate his resolve to escape this wedding. If you turn your back now, Lady Magdalena wins by default. You must be brave and trust in the love you share. Now dry those eyes, and let's prepare for the ball. You deserve to enjoy this night!" Her words were a beacon of hope amid the storm of my despair.

"Oh, Maria, your unwavering optimism can be exhausting," I said, a hint of a small smile breaking through my sorrow. Suddenly, memories of my mom flooded my mind.

Mom, full of grace, love, and courage up to the very end.

I can be brave and strong like my mom.

"I will go to the ball and find joy now, even if I have to wrestle with it," I said with conviction as I dried my tears, my heart feeling lighter.

With Maria by my side, along with memories of my brave mother, a flicker of hope ignited amid the shadows of uncertainty.

CHAPTER 50

The Grand Ball

The ballroom was a vibrant sea of elegance, with women gliding gracefully across the polished floor in their exquisite gowns. Couples moved in perfect harmony to the enchanting strains of Baroque music. An opulent table filled with sumptuous dishes lined the wall, and servants wove through the crowd, offering guests spiced wine and honeyed mead.

I couldn't shake the feeling of being out of place as I descended the staircase. When I finally reached the bottom and stepped into the ballroom, a large, gilded mirror caught my eye, and I barely recognized my reflection. The silk lavender gown hugged my figure just right, perfectly complemented by the matching amethyst necklace and earrings that Rodrigo had gifted me. Maria had styled my hair in a graceful updo, soft tendrils cascading down my back.

I overheard someone nearby murmur, "Who is she? She is easily the most beautiful woman in the room." Just then, a servant passed, offering me a glass of wine. Gratefully accepting it, I turned toward the staircase, only to see Lord Rodrigo making his entrance. His very presence was magnetic. Dressed impeccably in black, he looked devastatingly handsome as he strode confidently into the ballroom, radiating strength and elegance.

As he mingled with the guests, his gaze suddenly locked onto mine, eyes widening with admiration. Ignoring the others around us, he walked toward me with purposeful strides. When he reached my side, he extended his hand and said, "Lady LeMaster, you look stunning. I'm delighted to see you wearing the necklace and earrings I gave you. May I claim the first dance with you?"

My heart soared. I was giddy with excitement as I placed my hand in his. He led me to the dance floor, and as the orchestra began a romantic waltz, I stepped beside him, our movements perfectly synchronized. We lost ourselves in our world, oblivious to the crowd around us as one melody seamlessly flowed into another.

Without warning, the music halted, and all eyes turned to the staircase. Lady Magdalena stood there, gripping the railing, her face a mask of rage and envy aimed squarely at Lord Rodrigo and me. Though her empire dress concealed her pregnant belly, it clung unflatteringly to her figure. A twinge of sympathy pulled at me. Why had she declined Maria's offer to craft a more elegant gown for her?

Rodrigo reluctantly stepped away from me and ascended the stairs to assist her. Confused murmurs rippled through the gathering as guests exchanged glances between Lady Magdalena and me. Then it struck me. Many attendees hadn't yet met Lady Magdalena and had likely assumed I was the object of their scrutiny. After all, how else could they interpret the sight of Rodrigo and me dancing so closely, our eyes locked in an intimate embrace?

A sudden wave of unease washed over me, and I swiftly made my way to a side exit, feeling out of place. Spotting a cloak abandoned on a nearby chair, I draped it over my shoulders and slipped out of the room unnoticed.

I hurried past the kitchen and into my room, where I discovered a glass of leftover wine that Maria had left earlier. Without hesitation, I drank it down, seeking solace and amnesia. Feeling embarrassed, miserable, and emotionally exhausted, I quickly removed my gown and plopped on the bed face-first. My eyelids felt so heavy, they closed of their own accord, and soon I drifted off to sleep, my tears staining my cheeks.

CHAPTER 51

Lord Rodrigo and Lady Maryann

Secluded in my room, I fixed my hair at my dressing table and desperately prayed that the guests would forget the scandal that had unfolded at the ball last night. A resounding knock on my door abruptly shattered my wishful thinking. My heart raced as I silently pleaded for the intruder to disappear, but the persistent banging grew louder.

"Lady LeMaster, please open the door!" Lord Rodrigo's voice called out, urgency woven into every word. "I must speak with you!"

I creaked the door open just enough to see him. His face was flushed, his eyes wide with concern.

I swallowed hard. The last thing we needed was for someone to see him come to my chamber. "Lord Gutiérrez, I'm afraid I'm not ready for a conversation right now. Can we speak later?"

Yet his determination was unyielding. He pushed the door open, stepped inside, and shut it firmly behind him.

"I'm truly sorry for barging in," he panted as if he'd sprinted down the hall. "I've been tormented by guilt all night. I was thoughtless and selfish. You were so beautiful. Then, when Lady Magdalena appeared, the reality of the situation crashed down on me." He paused, swallowed hard, and continued. "I should have considered how this would affect you. I can't bear the thought of you being the subject of gossip. Will you ever find it in your heart to forgive me?"

"Lord Rodrigo," I replied, my voice trembling. "It's not your fault. I, too, was swept away by the enchantment of the evening. It was beautiful, if only for a moment."

He took my hands, his gaze piercing through the air between us. "Lady Maryann, I cannot marry her. It's you I love," he declared with such unwavering sincerity that I felt the ground shift beneath me.

I searched his steadfast eyes, my heart echoing his sentiment. "And I feel the same way, but I cannot ignore the pain we've caused Lady Magdalena. I'd never want to see her hurt further. You mustn't call off the wedding without cause."

"I understand," he said, his voice gentle yet bleak. "But I am working on a solution. Please don't give up on us. The jousting tournament is this afternoon. It would be good for you to attend, though I'll understand if you choose not to." He leaned down, his lips brushing softly against my forehead before slipping away.

When he left, I sank into the chair by the window, burying my face in my hands. A whirlwind of emotions spiraled inside me—laughter dancing with tears. Lord Rodrigo loved me. He hadn't abandoned hope, so why should I? Yet the reality of our situation loomed large, and I found no clear path forward. I was torn between my love for him and my guilt toward Lady Magdalena.

Moments later, another knock at my door pulled me from my thoughts. I opened it to find a flurry of servants bustling in, their arms laden with buckets of steaming water, swiftly filling the wooden tub. Maria followed, her arms overflowing with vibrant day dresses and hats.

After indulging in a rejuvenating bath, hope flickered back to life. Maria had a knack for lifting my spirits, and she reveled in pampering me with new gowns. From the two she presented, I chose a lovely sage-colored dress paired with a matching hat. It felt like a fresh start.

If Lord Rodrigo had not given up on us, neither would I.

CHAPTER 52

The Jousting Tournament

The small jousting arena buzzed with excitement as the stands began to fill with eager spectators jostling for the best seats in the arena. Just days prior, a local blacksmith had been commissioned to forge a dozen blunt, hollowed-out lances, ensuring the knights' safety while satisfying the competition's thrill. Ten skilled knights would face off with one another in the tournament, culminating in a highly anticipated final round between Lord Gutiérrez and Lord Velasco.

The crowd's energy washed over me as I arrived, thrilling and overwhelming. A castle guard located a coveted spot in the front row, and I took my place. A large hat adorned with green ribbons and feathers concealed my hair, and my large fan obscured my face, allowing me to blend seamlessly into the enthusiastic crowd. My palms grew clammy as I scanned the crowd for any sign of Lady Magdalena. The thought of facing her filled me with dread.

Suddenly, two page boys burst into the arena, one blowing a trumpet while the other announced the first two contestants from a nearby village. The knights mounted their mighty steeds, the tension thick in the air as they lined up for battle.

With a swift signal, they charged forward, determination etched on their faces. A two-and-a-half-foot barrier separated them as they lowered their lances, urging their horses to gallop faster. Instantly, one of the knights was struck down and thrown off his horse. The knights had performed in a spectacular display of skill as cheers erupted for the victorious contender.

The next three matches unfolded with similar intensity, the crowd gasping at a close encounter that resulted in an injury to one of the knights during the third joust.

Then, the moment we had all been waiting for arrived—the final match. Lord Gutiérrez and Lord Velasco, both resplendent in their gleaming armor, entered the arena. Lord Gutiérrez, astride his magnificent black steed Macho, was a sight to behold. His black vest, adorned with the gold-colored Gutiérrez family crest, shimmered in the sunlight, adding to the anticipation of the impending battle.

He looked up at the stands, caught sight of me, and signaled to the page boy for a pause. Galloping to the front, he bowed elegantly and flashed me a heart-stopping grin. "My lady," he said with a charming flair, "would you honor me with one of your green ribbons as a token of good luck?"

Gasps rippled through the nearby ladies, but I could only grin back, my heart racing as I offered him a ribbon from my hat. He tied it around his arm before returning to his position, the energy in the air electrifying.

With bated breath, I watched the horses thundering forward, both knights displaying breathtaking skill and agility. Time seemed to stretch as they clashed, the tension in the air palpable. After several tense runs, Rodrigo landed a blow on Lord Felipe, and he flew off his horse. The crowd erupted in jubilant cheers, chanting Lord Gutiérrez's name, the energy of their excitement filling the arena.

As the cheers faded, the audience surged with soaring spirits toward the pavilion outside, where food and mead awaited. The jousting match had come to a thrilling end, leaving the crowd buzzing with excitement and the knights basking in the glory of their performances.

CHAPTER 53

A Friend's Advice

As Lord Rodrigo and Lord Felipe strolled out of the arena, their camaraderie was evident as they playfully patted each other on the back. Once in the stables, Felipe, the more serious of the two, grew even more somber as he placed a hand on Rodrigo's shoulder. "I have some news for you, my friend," he said quietly. "I discreetly questioned your staff, and they spoke freely regarding rumors of Lady Magdalena." He lowered his voice. "I overheard whispers of her secret rendezvous with Juan, the stable hand."

Rodrigo narrowed his eyes and nodded slowly.

Felipe chewed his lip and took a deep breath. "But there's more. Yesterday, on my way to my chambers, I encountered Lady Magdalena. Leaning seductively against her door, she was stunning, flirtatious, and inviting. She pulled me into her room and offered an enticing proposition—to meet her in the attic loft." He looked down at the ground. "I am a weak man in the face of such beauty, and I regret to say I accepted her invitation. I am ashamed, Rodrigo, and if you wish, I will leave at once with Lady Elena."

Rodrigo stared at Felipe in disbelief, and the silence between them grew heavy with unspoken tension. Then, unexpectedly, he erupted into laughter. "Oh, Felipe! If only you could see your guilt-ridden expression. It's truly priceless!" His joy was infectious, and a glimmer of relief flickered in his eyes. "But worry not! Since I do not intend to marry Lady Magdalena, I do not care what you do with her. Your actions have sparked a brilliant idea. If I catch her in the act with another man, I'll have the perfect excuse to call off the wedding!" Rodrigo's laughter echoed in the stables, adding a touch of humor to the tense situation.

He clapped Felipe on the back and spun around, whistling a merry tune as he strode out of the stables.

Felipe shook his head, still taken aback, but a small grin crept onto his lips. "You're welcome, Rodrigo. Any time!" he called after him, feeling a mix of surprise and admiration for his friend's unyielding spirit.

CHAPTER 54

The Garden Confrontation

As the sun poured into my room the next morning, I felt a strong need for some alone time and quiet solitude. After getting dressed, I made my way to the bustling kitchen, where I exchanged a brief greeting with Clara before slipping out the back door, eager to find peace and solitude in the castle gardens. Taking a seldom-used path, I discovered an isolated bench surrounded by bushes, offering a perfect view of the fountain and the tranquil pond. Settling in, I breathed in the crisp morning air and felt the world's troubles melt away.

The sky was a deep azure, and the warmth of the sun enveloped me like a cocoon, making me feel relaxed and sleepy. I closed my eyes, allowing my mind to wander, unaware of the world's whispers around me—until I was jolted from my reverie by the sounds of a couple lost in passion nearby. Just as confusion began to settle in, a twig snapped to my right, and I turned to find Lord Rodrigo stealthily inching toward the source of the noises. He raised a finger to his lips, signaling for silence as he ducked behind a nearby bush.

Intrigued yet wary, I decided to retreat to my room. After the chaos of the ball, the last thing I wanted was to entangle myself in any more drama.

Since his conversation with Felipe, Rodrigo had taken it upon himself to keep an eye on Lady Magdalena's whereabouts. He took what he hoped looked like a casual stroll through the castle, and when he spotted her slipping out from her chambers, cloaked and hooded, looking left and right as if checking to see if anyone was watching her, a sense of purpose surged through him—he had to follow. Maintaining a careful distance, he trailed her through the grounds until she vanished behind a cluster of thick bushes. He was deciding whether to stay put or make his way through the dense foliage when Juan appeared, nervously meandering through the garden before disappearing behind the same bushes Lady Magdalena had just squeezed past.

Several minutes later, Rodrigo could hear the unmistakable sounds of passion reaching his ears. He smirked, silently thanking Felipe for unwittingly providing a catalyst for this cunning plan. It was time for action. Quietly, he approached their hideaway and cleared his throat. Lady Magdalena lay on her back in a compromising position with Juan draped over her body, her hair wild and messy, with a look of ecstasy on her face.

"My apologies, but I am searching for my betrothed, Lady Magdalena," he declared in a loud voice. "Oh, there you are!"

Juan's eyes widened in terror, and he bolted away as if the hounds of hell were at his heels. Lady Magdalena, however, remained unfazed, lounging with a defiant look, her skirts hiked up indecorously. "Darling, would you care to join me?" she teased, her voice dripping with insincerity.

Lord Rodrigo stood frozen, a storm of emotions swirling within him. "Ah, Lady Magdalena, I see that your true colors have finally revealed themselves," he said, his tone steady. "As a result of your indiscretion, the wedding is now canceled. Paulo will escort you to the midwife's cottage in the valley, where you will remain until after your child's birth. I have arranged for you to stay in a château in France. If you decide that you do not want to be a mother to this child, I will ensure it has a secure home at the castle."

Lady Magdalena remained nonchalant, her eyes glinting with a mixture of challenge and amusement as she took in his words.

Resolute in his decision, Lord Rodrigo called for his guard, Paulo, who was waiting nearby. "Paulo, please escort Lady Constanza to the midwife's cottage and ensure she does not escape," he instructed, handing over a note and a bag of coins for the midwife's assistance in the delivery.

"Yes, sir," Paulo responded, his demeanor formal. "My lady," he said, extending his hand to Lady Magdalena.

She took his hand, rising with a haughty flourish. "Oh, Paulo, I trust my new accommodations will be delightful. Farewell, Lord Gutiérrez," she threw over her shoulder, her tone dripping with sarcasm.

Rodrigo stared after her, a surge of joy washing over him, so relieved to have finally severed ties. He turned to go find Lady Maryann, eager to share the news, but the garden bench where he last saw her was empty. He shrugged it off, confident he'd have plenty of time to tell her the good news after the afternoon stag hunt.

Lady Magdalena rode away, furious, with bitter realization that she'd been caught red-handed. Claiming innocence would be futile. There would be no contest about who was telling the truth. All her carefully orchestrated plans in ruins, all because of a silly dalliance in the garden. She was furious with herself.

What have I done?

Why do I keep making such bad decisions?

Am I beyond hope and redemption?

CHAPTER 55

The Stag Hunt

Yellow ribbons danced in the gentle breeze, swaying from the branches of trees that framed the stag hunt venue. The sun filtered through the leaves, casting a golden glow over the clearing where Rodrigo, Felipe, Pedro, and a group of twenty men were gathered, each mounted on strong steeds armed with knives, bows, and lances. The air thrummed with anticipation. The first to kill a stag would be declared the victor.

The hunters erupted into action at the signal, galloping into the sprawling forest before them. Behind them, a group of elegantly dressed women adorned with delicate hats waited with subdued excitement. The attentive castle staff stood ready next to the prepared food and drinks for the hunters' return.

Rodrigo, Felipe, and Pedro rode together, their eyes scanning the thick foliage, honed senses alert for any movement. Rodrigo and Felipe were seasoned hunters who had long mastered the art of the chase, but even Pedro, having hunted side by side with his father for many years, knew what to do and held his own in their midst. After a while, Pedro tapped his father's shoulder, and he gestured toward a magnificent stag, its silhouette framed in a sunlit clearing just a few hundred feet away.

After the trio had dismounted, their movements deliberate and silent, Rodrigo turned to Felipe, his voice a low whisper. "Should we let Pedro take the first shot? He spotted it, after all."

Felipe nodded, pride glimmering as he gestured for his son to advance.

Pedro crept forward, bow poised, the tension palpable in the air. Carefully nocking an arrow, he took a steady breath, aimed with unwavering focus, and released. The arrow sliced through the air with deadly precision, finding its mark in the stag's chest and instantly bringing the animal down. Cheers erupted from Rodrigo and Felipe as Pedro beamed in the glow of his triumph.

Seizing the moment, Rodrigo sounded the bullhorn, a clarion call that echoed through the trees, signaling to the other hunters that a stag had fallen. They swiftly converged on Pedro, lifting him onto their shoulders in a triumphant display of camaraderie. Blankets unfurled across the ground while the castle staff provided a lavish feast to celebrate the day's victory.

Amid the revelry stood Lady Elena, a solitary figure radiating discontent. Her face twisted in a scowl, simmering with palpable frustration, a sharp contrast to the other revelers.

As the hunting party returned to the castle, Rodrigo tasked his butler with delivering a carefully penned notice to the guests' chambers, each letter unveiling a shocking announcement:

Dear Esteemed Guests,

Upon deep contemplation, I announce the cancellation of my wedding to Lady Magdalena Constanza due to private reasons. You are all invited to stay and enjoy the last sporting event tomorrow.

Sincerely,

Lord Rodrigo Gutiérrez

Rodrigo's relief sank in. He was free at last. There was one thing niggling him, though. He'd not yet found the moment to share this news with Lady Maryann, although he'd sent a notice to her room earlier. He'd hoped to tell her in person during dinner that evening. He wanted to see how she took the news. Would her joy match his own? Would those beautiful eyes of hers sparkle at the thought of nothing standing in the way of them being together?

There was only one way to find out.

CHAPTER 56

The Meadow Painting

Painting supplies were delivered to my room that morning. I was so excited that I decided to spend the day painting while most guests were at the stag hunt. I chose a simple lilac day dress, donned a feathered straw hat, and ventured out of the castle with a small wagon hitched to my horse, laden with my supplies: a cozy blanket and a lunch Clara had thoughtfully prepared.

About a mile from the castle, I came upon a breathtaking meadow. Wildflowers danced in a riot of colors under a clear blue sky with fluffy white clouds. My heart raced as I set up my easel, knowing I was about to be in my element once again. As my eyes swept across the vibrant landscape, a picturesque gothic-style church in the distance caught my eye—a perfect backdrop for my painting.

As I immersed myself in the moment, memories came rushing back of the last time I'd painted. How my life had changed since I'd stumbled onto those Celtic stones and been whisked away through time. I glanced around the surrounding area to ensure no partially buried ancient pillars were nearby. Though pangs of longing occasionally tugged at my heart for my past life, this world had become my home. I still held onto the hope that somehow a miracle would bring Rodrigo and me together.

With my thoughts quieting, I poised my paintbrush over the canvas, surrendering to the tranquility of the serene and lovely meadow. Hours slipped by in blissful solitude until my growling stomach became too much of a distraction.

Clara had thoughtfully packed me a lunch of succulent chicken, sweet, honeyed bread, and fragrant wine. What more could a woman ask for? After I had my fill, I reclined on my blanket, surrendering to the sun's embrace, and soon the world faded as I drifted into a peaceful slumber.

CHAPTER 57

The Mad Inquisitor

When I awoke, the sky had darkened considerably, casting long shadows across the meadow. A sudden chill ran up my spine as I sat up, and an unsettling sensation came over me—someone was watching. Slowly, I turned, my heart racing, and my chest tightened when I saw who it was.

Father Santiago.

He stood just a few feet away, his presence like a dark shadow that made me freeze. Before I could say or do anything, he lunged at me, muffling my screams by stuffing my mouth with a dirty gag. Bile rose inside of me, and my throat burned from the suppressed scream. The rope he used to bind my hands and feet cut into my skin, and as I struggled with everything I had, I caught sight of a hard, heavy object in his hand. It was heading straight for my skull at lightning speed.

And then everything went black.

The nausea hit me the minute I regained consciousness, and my vision blurred. I took in the dismal sight of a large basement or dungeon. When I looked down at myself, I realized I was naked and covered in a thin, dirty blanket, my limbs bound to the wooden table beneath me. Pain throbbed in the back of my skull where Father Santiago had struck me. I was thirsty, I was dizzy, and I felt like vomiting. I knew what this was, especially after sustaining that huge blow to my head. Concussion. I shivered violently.

My dream of Lady Magdalena in the dungeon came to mind as I

remembered that evil priest and his smug smirk before he hit me. This room resembled a dungeon, but its design was obviously for nefarious purposes. My eyes slowly roamed over the dozens of torture devices hanging on the wall, and I shuddered in fear. As my vision began fading, I tried everything in my power to stay awake. I pictured Rodrigo. His beautiful green eyes. His heart-stopping smile. His kindness.

I lost consciousness anyway.

CHAPTER 58

Lord Rodrigo's Angst

The great hall buzzed with even higher levels of excitement than usual as Lord Rodrigo and his guests gathered around the long formal dining table set for dinner. Prime cuts of stag meat roasted to perfection filled the air with an enticing aroma, yet the room held an undercurrent of unease. Whispers of the wedding cancellation spread among the guests, but no one dared to confront Lord Gutiérrez about the reasons behind his sudden decision to call off the wedding, for which he was grateful.

As laughter and clinking goblets broke the silence, Lord Rodrigo's eyes drifted around the hall, his thoughts consumed with worry for Lady Maryann. Where could she be? He should be celebrating, but her absence left a gaping hole, and it was all Rodrigo could think about.

About an hour into the meal, an urgent impulse surged within Rodrigo to find Lady Maryann. Excusing himself from the guests, he hastily ascended the grand staircase to her chamber. His heart raced as he knocked, but only silence greeted him. With growing dread, he opened the door, only to find her room untouched. The room, adorned with lovely colors and filled with the scent of her favorite flowers, was a stark contrast to the panic beginning to consume Rodrigo. Her unopened wedding cancellation notice only added to the confusion and dread.

He barreled down the hall, his heart racing as he met Maria. "Maria," he said, his voice a strained whisper, "have you seen Lady Maryann today?"

"No, Lord Gutiérrez. I haven't seen her since last evening," she replied, worry shining in her wide eyes and her voice trembling with fear. "I was on my way to check on her. What has happened?"

Rodrigo's fists tightened. "I don't know where she is. She never came to dinner, and now I can't find her anywhere. I must speak with Clara!" He nearly sprinted down the stairs toward the kitchen.

Bursting into the room, he caught Clara in the middle of baking, her hands dusted with flour. Breathless, he gripped her shoulders, his voice shaky but determined. "Clara, please tell me you know where Lady Maryann has gone. She missed dinner, and her room was untouched. I must find her!"

Clara recoiled, fear etched across her face. "Lord Gutiérrez, I last saw her around midmorning after I packed her lunch. She mentioned going outside to find a perfect painting spot and took one of the horses. If no one's seen her since . . . well, it's growing dark—I fear for her safety, sir!"

Rodrigo's stomach knotted.

The castle grounds were safe and well-defended, but there were still reports of small bands of thieves occasionally spotted on the castle's outskirts. Rodrigo's mind filled with a frantic fear. He commanded his trusted butler to fetch Felipe and four of his most trusted guards to meet him in the war room.

A sense of urgency fueled him as he paced the war room and gave his orders to the five men gathered around him. "Gentlemen," he declared in a grave tone, "Lady LeMaster is missing. Clara was the last to see her this morning as she headed out with her painting supplies. We must act swiftly. Gather your torches and prepare to ride. We'll search the castle grounds and venture several miles beyond its walls. Each of you will take a horn. Blow it if you discover her. We must bring her back!" With a rallying cry, the men dispersed in different directions, the weight of the evening heavy upon them as darkness began to creep in.

CHAPTER 59

The Dungeon

Terror gripped me the moment I awoke to the sound of ragged breathing filling the room. I forced my eyes open, and there he was again—Father Santiago.

Naked.

He was clearly aroused, his chest heaving and his body trembling. He was no more than twenty feet away, searching through an array of rusty torture tools, his lips moving as though in prayer—or madness.

My stomach rolled, and I fought the urge to retch. *Don't move. Don't make a sound.* My body trembled violently beneath the bindings, but I willed myself to stillness. I drew each breath quietly and deliberately, desperately praying he wouldn't hear or notice me trembling.

Oh God, please let Rodrigo find my painting with the church in the background—let him piece together where I am. Let him save me before this monster does the unthinkable.

Father Santiago's muttering grew louder, his eyes wild.

"God, grant me the strength to resist these vile urges! This heretic stirs the devil within me. I must make her repent, or I'll be damned for eternity!" His words broke into a frenzied, feverish pitch.

I clamped my teeth down hard on the gag, desperate not to whimper, terrified of what would come first—Father Santiago's lust or his thirst for violence.

I didn't know what scared me more.

CHAPTER 60

The Search

Rodrigo and his men regrouped a short distance from the castle, their horses kicking up dust as they formed a single line behind him. With a fierce glare, Rodrigo spurred his steed, heading toward the meadow of wildflowers. His eyes fixed on something in the distance, and hope pulsed through him. An easel and a lone pony grazing nearby. He raised his arm sharply, signaling his men to slow.

When they reached Maryann's abandoned easel, Rodrigo leaped from his horse. Sweeping the area frantically for clues, he noted an empty picnic blanket and moved closer, his stomach tightening. The nearly finished painting was a breathtaking scene of vibrantly colored wildflowers beneath a bright blue sky, with one ominous detail—the silhouette of Father Santiago's church looming darkly in the background.

The memory of Father Santiago's venomous rage toward Lady Maryann at that dinner not so long ago rushed back to Rodrigo. His pulse quickened with a dark realization.

"Men!" Rodrigo's voice rang out, sharp and commanding. "Father Santiago. He's taken her. To the church, now!"

They raced toward the church in a flurry of hooves, the staccato rhythm of the galloping horses pounding in his head like a war drum.

CHAPTER 61

The Mad Priest

Father Santiago had been standing stock-still when suddenly he jerked his head toward me, his eyes gleaming with madness as a ghoulish grimace stretched across his face, revealing yellow and rotting teeth.

"Witch," he hissed, venom dripping from his voice. "You think your beauty can save you? God has told me otherwise." His words slid under my skin like ice. "I will ruin your body and your face. Then I will begin the Lord's work."

The priest's laugh echoed throughout the room. He picked up a large knife, turning it over and testing its sharpness. My heart pounded so violently that I thought my chest would explode. Panic surged through me as my body thrashed against the ropes that dug further into my wrists the more I struggled. The gag muffled my desperate cries, and I knew my eyes were wide with terror as I pleaded for mercy.

But his face was devoid of empathy or mercy as he advanced, his knife gleaming under the dim light.

"Yes, be afraid, witch. When I finish with you, you will never again seduce another man!" Angling the knife toward my upper thighs, he made the first cut. Silent screams echoed in my head as I once again welcomed the darkness.

CHAPTER 62

Maryann

When Rodrigo and his men reached the church, Rodrigo leaped from his horse and pounded on the heavy wood with his fist. "Father Santiago!" he bellowed, demanding entrance, but the church was eerily silent. His men exchanged uneasy glances. With a nod, two of them hoisted Rodrigo up to the windowsill. After shattering the glass, he vaulted inside and rushed to the door to let his men in.

The men spread out through the dimly lit church, searching every corner for signs of life. But it was empty—too empty. Rodrigo clenched his teeth and began tearing at the rugs, searching for hidden passages. A picture of Maryann, alone and frightened, came into his mind, and desperation gnawed at him until a shout from one of his men shattered the silence.

"Here! A trap door!"

Rodrigo's pulse quickened. Signaling to his men to stay back, he descended the narrow stairs, every muscle taut with fear and determination. The dim light barely illuminated the horrific scene when he reached the basement. Lady Maryann lay strapped to a table, a thin blanket barely covering her nakedness, her hair trailing down to the cold stone floor. Father Santiago hovered over her, a gleaming knife poised above her abdomen. Blood dripped from the blade's tip, and Rodrigo's heart froze as icy fingers of fear gripped his heart.

"Stop!" Rodrigo's voice rang out, raw with rage. "Step away from her, Santiago!"

The priest turned, his eyes glazed with madness, his naked body trembling with a twisted mix of lust and mania. "She is a temptress! The devil works through her to corrupt me!" he raved, his voice cracking. "I must mutilate her—only then will I be free to do God's work!"

Rodrigo's blood boiled with fury as Santiago turned back to the table, poised to plunge the knife into Maryann. In desperation, Rodrigo charged, crossing the distance in a heartbeat and slamming the priest to the ground. Maddened by his delusions, Santiago fought with unnatural strength, rising quickly and lunging at Rodrigo with the blade.

"You are in league with the devil, Lord Gutiérrez!" the priest shrieked. "You must die!"

Rodrigo barely dodged the attack, rolling to the side as the blade slashed through the air mere inches from his chest. He was on his feet in an instant, sword drawn.

"Drop the knife, Father," Rodrigo warned, his voice steady despite his heart pounding. "Or I will end this."

Father Santiago's laugh was unhinged as it reverberated through the basement. "I am God's chosen one, and I will strike you down!" he screamed, rushing forward with the knife aimed at Rodrigo's chest.

In a swift, precise motion, Rodrigo plunged his sword into the priest's chest. Santiago's laughter died abruptly, replaced by a guttural gasp as the knife fell from his grip, clattering against the stone floor. His wide, crazed eyes flickered with disbelief as blood gushed from the wound. As he collapsed onto his knees, his eyes lingered on Lady Maryann one last time, a grotesque mixture of lust and hatred twisting his features before he slumped to the floor, lifeless.

Rodrigo wasted no time. He yanked his sword free, wiped the blood clean, and rushed to Lady Maryann's side. His hands trembled as he quickly removed the gag from her mouth and untied her restraints. Her skin was streaked with blood, but the cuts—thankfully—were shallow.

Relief hit him like a wave, and he leaned against the table, momentarily overcome. The thought that he had almost been too late twisted inside his gut. But Lady Maryann was alive. He carefully picked her up and held her, wrapping his cape around her. Her eyelids fluttered, and when her eyes met his, wide with terror, they softened in recognition and relief. Tears ran down her cheeks as her body began to shake. Rodrigo held her tightly.

"You're safe now, my love," he whispered, his voice thick with emotion. "It's over. He's gone."

With Lady Maryann cradled in his arms, Rodrigo slowly ascended the stairs, where his men stood waiting, their faces pale with worry.

"She's alive," Rodrigo said, his voice strained. "Cuts on her skin, but nothing too deep. She's in shock."

His men nodded solemnly, visibly relieved. Rodrigo's eyes swept over them. "Thank you," he said, his voice breaking. "Without your help, this could have ended much worse. I owe you all a debt."

CHAPTER 63

In Shock

When they reached the castle, Rodrigo dismounted carefully and carried Lady Maryann through the back entrance to avoid curious eyes. The kitchen staff gasped as he passed, but he kept moving, intent on getting her to safety. Clara, pale with fear, rushed forward.

"Lord Gutiérrez—will she be all right?" she asked, her voice trembling.

"Yes, she'll recover," he said, though his heart still ached. "But she's in shock and needs care. Bring bandages, healing ointment, and your herbal tea."

Clara nodded quickly. "I'll fetch them right away, sir!"

Rodrigo carried Maryann up the back stairs to his room, grateful that the halls were empty. He carefully laid her on his bed and began tending to her wounds, applying the healing ointment and wrapping the cuts with linen. Once she was cleaned and dressed in one of his shirts, he sat beside her and held her hand, brushing stray strands of hair from her forehead.

His chest tightened with an unfamiliar protectiveness, a fierceness he hadn't known he possessed. The thought of losing Lady Maryann—of arriving too late—was unbearable. And now that she was safe, the full realization of how much he loved her was crystal clear. "I love you," he whispered, though she was too deep in sleep to hear it.

CHAPTER 64

Recovery

I awoke slowly, my body heavy with exhaustion. Confusion clouded my mind. Rodrigo was there as my eyes fluttered open, his face etched with worry.

"Are you all right?" I rasped in a weak voice through dry, cracked lips.

He scoffed softly, shaking his head. "Am I all right? That madman of a priest almost mutilated you! I'm more concerned about you, my love. How do you feel? Are you in pain?"

I tried to sit up but winced as aches surged through my body. "My head feels like it's splitting, and everything hurts," I admitted, my voice barely above a whisper. Glancing down, I noticed multiple bandages covering my upper legs, and I was wearing one of Rodrigo's shirts. My stomach fluttered with gratitude and vulnerability.

"How bad are my injuries?" My voice trembled.

Rodrigo brushed a strand of hair from my face, his touch soft and full of tenderness. "Superficial cuts, all of them. You were fortunate."

Relief washed over me, though the memory of what had happened still lurked at the edges of my mind. "Thank you for saving me," I whispered, my throat dry. "I thought . . ." I trailed off, unable to finish the thought. "May I have something to drink?"

Without hesitation, Rodrigo fetched a glass of water and helped me sit up as I took slow, grateful sips. The cool water soothed my parched throat, making it easier to speak.

"What will the guests think if I'm discovered in your room?"

He chuckled with both amusement and disbelief. "A lot happened today, my dear. The wedding was called off."

The words sent my mind spinning. Was it over? Did this mean . . . ? "Wait, slow down," I said, my voice still shaky. "What happened?"

"Well," he began with a smirk, "right after I saw you in the garden, I discovered Lady Magdalena and Juan together. Let's just say they were making themselves quite comfortable behind a bush."

I blinked, shocked but oddly relieved. "Lady Magdalena wasn't ashamed when you caught them?"

Rodrigo's smile widened. "No. After Juan ran off, she had the nerve to ask if I wanted to join her."

I gasped and tried to suppress a laugh. "And did you?"

He shot me a playful look. "What do you think?"

"I think not," I replied with a grin, "because I know another woman has already captured your heart."

His face softened, and he leaned closer, his voice thick with emotion. "After what happened today, I realize how deeply I love you, Lady Maryann. I've never met anyone like you—strong, brave, stubborn, and so full of love. You're everything to me."

He paused, his eyes filled with intensity as they locked on mine. It made my breath catch. "Marry me, Lady Maryann. Be my wife."

Tears welled up in my eyes as his words sank in. My heart swelled with so much emotion that I could hardly speak. I threw my arms around him, pressed my face to his chest, and cried, letting the joy and relief wash over me. After a few moments, I finally found my voice.

"I can't think of anything that would make me happier," I whispered, looking up at him with tear-filled eyes. "Yes, of course I will marry you. I love you with all my heart." His lips found mine in a gentle, lingering kiss that held the promise of everything we had yet to share. When he pulled back, I could see the depth of his love shining in his eyes. My heart soared.

But a sudden thought interrupted the bliss. "What about your reputation?"

I said, pulling back slightly. "The guests—how did they react when you canceled the wedding?"

"I sent out wedding cancellation notices after the stag hunt, informing the guests that Lady Magdalena and I would not be marrying. I wasn't there to witness their reactions, but I'm sure they felt scandalized," he replied with a laugh.

The news piqued my curiosity. "And what happened with Lady Magdalena?"

"After I caught her and Juan in a compromising position, Paulo escorted her to the midwife's cottage in the village. She will be sent to France when she's recovered. If she refuses, I won't hesitate to lock her in the dungeon."

I shuddered at the thought. "You wouldn't truly imprison Lady Magdalena, would you?"

Rodrigo's face hardened slightly. "I would if it meant keeping you safe. I won't allow anyone to threaten you again, Lady Maryann. Not her, not anyone."

I bit my lip, unsure of how to feel. Rodrigo's protectiveness was comforting, but the idea of imprisoning someone still unsettled me. I changed the subject. "Who knows that I'm staying here with you tonight?"

"Only our closest friends. You'll stay in my bed to rest and heal," he said softly, pulling me closer. "No one will disturb you."

I couldn't resist teasing him. "And what if I don't want to rest? What if I want to make passionate love to you tonight?"

His eyes sparkled with a mix of amusement and restraint. "As much as I look forward to that, my love, we will wait for our wedding night," he said, his voice full of patience.

He coaxed me into finishing Clara's healing tea despite its bitter taste, and soon my eyelids grew heavy and closed. I suddenly recalled two of the words Rodrigo used to describe me—*brave* and *strong*. Thinking of my mom, I smiled and sent a thought out to her—*I wish you could see how happy I am, Mom. I love you.* I snuggled deeper into Rodrigo's arms, drifting off to sleep, feeling safe and loved.

CHAPTER 65

Brian Golding

As Brian's bus rolled to a stop in the quaint town of Zafra, he stepped off, immediately taken by the charm of the old-fashioned streets and cobblestone pathways. His footsteps echoed against the weathered buildings, and the scent of fresh produce and spices from a small market across the street filled the air. He walked through the near-empty store and approached the customer service booth.

"Excuse me, ma'am," he said, his voice friendly yet intense. "Could you please direct me to the local police station?"

The clerk's face brightened, and she gestured toward a dilapidated sign across the street that read "Zafra Police Station."

"Thank you!" Brian replied, a flicker of hope igniting within him. He crossed the street briskly and pushed through the station's door.

Inside, he approached the receptionist, a young woman with a kind face. "Hello, my name is Brian Golding. I need to speak with someone about a missing person."

"Of course, sir," she responded in a kind tone, smiling. "Please follow me. Detective Romero will be with you in a moment."

Moments later, Brian found himself in a cramped, dimly lit room. The air was thick and stale, and he felt like the walls were closing in as he sat at the solitary, scuffed table. He absently tapped his fingers against the table's surface, each sound ramping up his anxiety as he waited.

A sharp knock interrupted his thoughts, and a middle-aged man with a sturdy build entered. He settled into the chair across from Brian and nodded. "Good day, Mr. Golding. I'm Detective Romero. How can I assist you?"

"Detective," Brian began, his voice trembling, "I'm looking for my ex-fiancée, Maryann LeMaster. She came to Zafra a few months ago on vacation. After she missed her return flight and stopped answering her phone, I started to worry. I caught the first flight here."

Detective Romero's demeanor turned serious. "Mr. Golding, Miss LeMaster was reported missing a month ago. We have done everything possible to locate her, but she has seemingly vanished without a trace. At this point, there is no evidence to suggest that any crime has occurred. You need to understand that our resources are limited, and there's nothing more we can do at this time. Hopefully, Miss LeMaster will show up soon with a perfectly reasonable explanation for her absence."

The detective stood up as if to leave the room, then turned back toward Brian. "By the way, the last known contact she had was with Francisco Gutiérrez, who resides in the castle atop the mountain. He may be able to provide more information about Miss LeMaster's state of mind just before her disappearance. Good day, Mr. Golding, and I wish you the best of luck. I sincerely hope Miss LeMaster is found soon." The detective gave Brian a curt nod before exiting the room.

"Thank you, Detective Romero. I appreciate everything you have done." As the door shut behind the detective, Brian's heart sank, his mind full of terrifying thoughts of kidnapping and ransom notes. He needed to get to that castle. With a tight throat and a spinning mind, Brian made his way back over to the receptionist. Desperation crept into his voice as he asked, "Who can I call for a ride, ma'am?"

"I can arrange transportation for you," the receptionist replied with a hint of sympathy. "Just wait on the bench outside." After making a quick call, she said, "Your ride will arrive in approximately fifteen minutes."

"Thanks." Brian managed a grateful nod before stepping back outside. He sank onto the bench, his thoughts racing. Just as the receptionist had promised, a horse-drawn carriage appeared precisely fifteen minutes later.

The driver approached, tipping his hat. "Where to, sir?"

"Take me to the castle, please," Brian instructed, strengthening his voice.

The carriage clattered along the cobbled lanes, and he stared ahead, praying Maryann was safe and doing his best to stop his mind from imagining all the worst scenarios. Half an hour later, they stopped before an ancient yet sturdy castle.

CHAPTER 66

Francisco

Brian stepped down from the carriage, thanked the driver, and made his way up a winding cobblestone path. The impressive castle loomed above him, still imposing despite the signs of age. Just as Brian raised his hand to knock on the enormous wooden door, it swung open, revealing an aristocratic-looking man in his early thirties.

"Greetings, I am Francisco Gutiérrez. What can I do for you, sir?"

Brian Golding stood at the threshold, anxiety gnawing at his belly. "Hello, Mr. Gutiérrez. My name is Brian Golding. I'm searching for my ex-fiancée, Maryann LeMaster. She arrived in Zafra for a vacation several months ago. I have just learned from Detective Romero that you reported her missing and that you might be the last person who saw her before she disappeared," he exclaimed, feeling concern and fear for Maryann.

Francisco's expression turned solemn. "Please come in, Mr. Golding," he said, gesturing with a sad but welcoming expression. "I'll be glad to share what I know. Follow me into the drawing room, and I'll fetch some refreshments."

As Brian settled into the lavishly decorated drawing room, he noticed an adjacent wall adorned with period portraits. Curiosity tugged at him as he admired the faces of men captured in their prime. All bore the Gutiérrez surname, and their shared features told a lineage story. Fascinated, he couldn't seem to take his eyes off them.

Moments later, Francisco returned with a tray full of cheese, crackers, and a bottle of wine. He handed Brian a glass of wine and nodded toward the wall behind him. "That painting was created by Miss Maryann just before she disappeared."

Brian turned and gasped at the striking castle depicted in the artwork. "This captures her signature style," he observed. "But who are the three figures standing before the castle?"

Francisco's gaze fell to the floor, his fingers nervously fidgeting with his attire. After a heavy sigh, he met Brian's steady eyes. "The man is my seventeenth-century ancestor, Lord Rodrigo Gutiérrez. The woman he's embracing is shrouded in mystery. While digging through an old chest, Miss Maryann and I discovered a gold locket containing a woman's portrait—astonishingly similar to the woman in the painting. The locket had an engraving from RG to ML."

Brian nodded slowly, as if he knew how Maryann would have been excited by that discovery.

"Miss Maryann was fascinated," Francisco continued, "because of the coincidence of the ML initials. I had speculated that RG might be Lord Rodrigo and that the unknown woman could have been his mistress. However, her identity remains elusive, a mystery that has intrigued us for years."

"Is Lord Rodrigo Gutiérrez's portrait among your ancestral pieces?" Brian asked, intrigued despite his worry.

"Yes," replied Francisco, pointing to a striking portrait of a handsome young man with light brown hair and vivid green eyes. "This is Lord Rodrigo Gutiérrez."

Brian studied the painting intently. "Maryann truly captured his essence. But what of the pregnant woman lurking behind the couple?"

"That woman resembles Lady Magdalena Constanza, who was briefly engaged to Lord Rodrigo," Francisco explained. "Miss Maryann's choice to paint her is curious." He bit his lip. "I never showed her Lady Constanza's portrait. A family tale told over countless generations describes a tragic romance—Lady Constanza became pregnant with Lord Rodrigo's child. In a twist of fate, he offered his hand in marriage out of honor, only to discover her infidelity. Devastated, she lost the baby and descended into madness. She was then imprisoned in the dungeon, where she cursed Lord Rodrigo and all his future male descendants. While I don't lean into superstition, many of my ancestors did. Oddly, every male heir since her death only sired one son, and often their wives died shortly after childbirth."

Brian's eyes bulged. "That's fascinating," he said, absorbing every detail. "But how was all this connected to Maryann's disappearance?" Tension pulled at his muscles. He had to find her.

"Miss Maryann often painted alone and didn't always check in with me, so unfortunately, I can't pinpoint the exact day she vanished. And if you're wondering, there was no noticeable shift in her demeanor before her disappearance. Her belongings remain at her cottage untouched," Francisco added, sorrow filling his eyes. "If you find her, please let me know, Mr. Golding. I'm praying for her safety."

"Of course. I'll keep you posted, Mr. Gutiérrez. Do you know the address in Zafra where Maryann stayed?" Brian pressed.

"Regrettably, I do not," Francisco admitted. "But I can call your driver back. He may know."

"Thank you, Mr. Gutiérrez. That would be wonderful. I appreciate your hospitality and your insight. I'll be in touch," Brian said, shaking Francisco's hand firmly.

Half an hour later, the same driver, a middle-aged man with a friendly face, arrived at the castle. "Where to next, sir?" he inquired.

"Are you familiar with the cottage where Miss Maryann LeMaster stayed before her disappearance?" Brian asked, bracing himself and praying the answer was yes.

"Yes, sir." The driver nodded. "It's just a twenty-minute drive from here."

Anxious, Brian sat forward in his carriage seat, juggling a mix of hope and dread, as the carriage traveled down the mountain road.

CHAPTER 67

Maryann's Cottage

The carriage arrived at a quaint white cottage, which appeared secluded. Taking a deep breath, Brian stepped out on unsteady legs and handed the driver the fare.

As he approached the front door, a knot tightened in his stomach. The noxious stench of spoiled food immediately assailed him as the door creaked open. With a handkerchief pressed against his nose, he ventured deeper into the dimly lit interior, pushing aside the nausea. All that mattered was finding Maryann.

Aside from the rotting remnants of spoiled food, everything appeared unsettlingly in place: Maryann's clothes lay neatly folded, her pocketbook rested innocently on the table, and her passport sat open. But where was her phone? A fresh wave of fear crashed over him.

With no clear leads, Brian stepped outside and wandered the perimeter of the cottage, his need for answers burning in his mind. While gulping down some long breaths of fresh air, he spotted a narrow dirt road barely visible amid the foliage. Intrigued, he followed it, each step fueled by his desire to discover the truth.

After about ten minutes of walking, he stopped to catch his breath beside a fallen log. Two ancient stone pillars, partially concealed by earth and moss, captured his attention. He drew closer and noticed strange symbols intricately etched into the stones. A shiver ran down his spine—these markings seemed to belong to a forgotten Celtic era.

Crouching down, he brushed away the dirt, eager to decipher the cryptic designs. But as he leaned over, he lost his balance and instinctively grasped the cool, weathered stone beside him. A jolt ran through his hand, a powerful vibration that resonated deep within him. Startled, he pulled back, and the vibrations ceased, as if silenced by his retreat.

His eyes widened, and he braced himself before placing both hands firmly on the stones again. The ground beneath him trembled violently, and the world spiraled into chaos. Brian's heart raced as a strange, haunting melody surrounded him, echoing in his mind just before losing consciousness.

CHAPTER 68

Brian's Adventure

Brian found himself sprawled on the grass beside a dirt road when he awoke, confusion swirling in his mind like a fog. The partially buried stone pillars were gone, leaving only a well-worn path winding up the mountain. Compelled by curiosity and a faint sense of purpose, he followed the trail.

After half an hour of climbing, he reached the mountaintop to a breathtaking sight—a grand castle that towered majestically against the sky. This beautiful castle was not Francisco's. It was unmistakably newer. The sound of children's laughter floated through the air, drawing his eyes to a cluster of Romani caravans nestled nearby. Was he still asleep? He shook his head in bemusement and continued toward the castle's entrance, unable to ignore the enigmatic aura surrounding the place.

He knocked on the heavy wooden door, which creaked open moments later to reveal a young woman wielding a feather duster. Her eyes sparkled with kindness as she spoke in halting English. "What can I do for you, sir?"

"I am looking for a friend—Miss Maryann LeMaster. Is she here by chance?" Brian asked, trying to keep his voice steady.

"Yes, sir, please come in and have a seat," she replied, curtsying gracefully. "I will let Lord Rodrigo Gutiérrez know that you are here."

Brian's mind buzzed with confusion as Francisco's brief history lesson popped into his mind. Didn't Francisco have an ancestor by the name of Lord Rodrigo Gutiérrez? Shaking his head, he thought it couldn't be. He was impressed by the scale of luxury in the castle. The furnishings, while antiquated in design, appeared almost new. He sank into a beautifully carved French chair, his mind a whirlwind of unanswered questions. Was this a historic Airbnb? Even if it were, he could not imagine Maryann abandoning the cottage and her belongings without a word to anyone. An uneasy feeling settled in his stomach.

As Brian waited for Lord Gutiérrez, his eyes wandered around the room before landing on a wall adorned with portraits. His breath caught in his throat. Many of the faces were eerily familiar. As he inspected the room again, his unease deepened—this drawing room mirrored one of the rooms in Francisco's castle almost perfectly. The difference? These antiques looked newer. Were they reproductions?

Just then, the sound of approaching footsteps broke Brian's concentration. When he looked toward the sound, his heart thudded so loudly he thought it would jump out of his chest. There was Lord Rodrigo Gutiérrez in the flesh, confidently striding toward him and looking exactly as he had in his portrait—a regal figure with striking features and green eyes.

Brian tried to grasp the whirlwind of thoughts racing through his mind. In his peripheral vision, he noticed several couples in period clothing milling around, and he estimated the style to be several centuries old, at least.

Lightheaded and disoriented, he instinctively gripped the back of the chair for support as dizziness threatened to overcome him. He inhaled deeply to steady himself.

Lord Rodrigo approached Brian confidently, stopping just a few feet away. "Welcome, sir. I am Lord Rodrigo Gutiérrez. How may I assist you?"

Summoning all his composure, he replied, "I am Lord Brian Golding, sir. It is an honor to meet you. I'm a family acquaintance of Lady Maryann LeMaster. After her mother's recent passing, my parents grew concerned for her well-being. They asked me to find her to ensure that she is all right."

Rodrigo's eyes narrowed, suspicion brewing beneath his polite demeanor.

"Sir, what precisely is your relationship with Lady LeMaster, and how did you know she would be here in Zafra at my castle?"

Caught off guard by the directness of the inquiry, Brian was momentarily stunned into silence. A familiar-looking auburn-haired beauty entered the room at that moment, radiating grace and charm. He couldn't help it as a gasp escaped him.

CHAPTER 69

Lord Golding

When I stepped into the room, everything inside me tightened with shock, and a surge of anxiety coursed through me.

Brian Golding? I wondered if I was dreaming again. *He couldn't be here. Could he?*

If he is, this is it for my new life. It's over. If people here knew my secret . . . I bit my lip in an attempt to stop myself from spiraling.

He looked pretty real. And if he was, what was he doing here? Riding the wave of anxiety, I managed to mask my nervousness.

"Lord Golding, what a delightful surprise!" I managed to say in a calm and welcoming voice. "I see you've met my fiancé, Lord Rodrigo Gutiérrez. What brings you to Zafra?"

Brian lowered his head and took my hand, his lips brushing against my skin with hesitation. I noticed the tension in his features.

I blinked twice, a silent plea for him to follow my lead, but he spoke up first. His concern was palpable, and I struggled to maintain my composure.

"Lady Maryann, my family grew worried when you failed to arrive in Madrid. They sent me to search the port townships. I'm relieved to find you—and see that their concerns were unfounded."

"How very considerate of your family," I replied, forcing my mind to stay quiet and calm, just long enough to keep the worst of the turmoil at bay. "But as you can see, I'm quite well. How is your family in Germany?"

"They're doing well, thank you. Considering their close ties to your late parents, they want to ensure you are safe."

Rodrigo cleared his throat to interject. "Lord Golding, you can rest assured that Lady Maryann is well. I am looking after her well-being," he declared with confidence. "By the way, I'm hosting a sporting event tomorrow. You're welcome to stay and join us. My butler can retrieve your trunks, sir."

"Thank you, Lord Gutiérrez. Unfortunately, I left in such haste, I'm afraid I only have the clothes on my back," Brian replied, laughing nervously.

Rodrigo's brows furrowed in confusion. "No matter. You and I are of similar stature. I'll have my man fetch a suitable garment for you to wear for dinner." He then turned, signaling for his butler, who instantly appeared as if conjured. "Dinner will be in the formal dining room in one hour. Until then, Lord Golding!"

As he followed the butler, Brian couldn't shake the bewildering thoughts swirling in his mind. Once they reached his room, he settled on the bed, grappling with the idea of time travel and its implications. The concept seemed unfathomable, and Brian struggled to comprehend it. More than anything, he longed to understand how Maryann, who appeared undeniably happy, had arrived here and soon after had become engaged to Lord Rodrigo Gutiérrez, a man from a different era.

As he splashed cold water on his face, a knock at the door jolted him from his thoughts. "Come in," he called, drying his hands as the butler entered bearing several elegant-looking outfits. Brian thanked him, and the butler nodded before retreating, leaving Brian to contemplate the unfamiliar outfits laid out before him.

Brian chose one of the finely tailored outfits and got dressed. Casting a glance in the ornate mirror, satisfied with how the clothes fit, he exited the room. Pausing to take several deep breaths to calm his frayed nerves, he went in search of the dining room, praying he would blend in with the other guests.

CHAPTER 70

A Formal Dinner Affair

Brian followed a group of guests into a sprawling formal dining room. The sheer elegance of the space captivated him—the classic sculptures and exquisite paintings lining the walls were a feast for his eyes. Moments later, a server rang a bell, commanding attention.

"Lord Rodrigo Gutiérrez and his fiancée, Lady Maryann LeMaster," the server announced, and Brian's heart raced again, a tumult of conflicting emotions swirling within him.

A momentary hush enveloped the room as the handsome couple strolled in, their smiles and nods doing little to dispel the palpable tension. The faces of the guests around the long table reflected the same shock and disbelief Brian felt, which added to the charged atmosphere. Lord Rodrigo and Lady Maryann took their seats at one end of the table, their confidence contrasting with the turmoil among the guests.

Lord Rodrigo cleared his throat while the staff gracefully served the meal, his voice cutting through the murmurs. "Ladies and gentlemen," he began, commanding the room's attention with an air of authority, "I would like to address the cancellation of my engagement to Lady Magdalena Constanza."

Confused gasps rippled through the room as he continued. "While we were informally engaged, I had intended to offer a settlement instead of pursuing marriage. Then, wedding invitations were sent out unbeknownst to me. As responses arrived, I felt obligated to follow through with the wedding." He paused, scanning the room. "However, after much discussion, Lady Constanza and I agreed that it was in our best interests to part ways."

Turning toward his betrothed, a radiant smile illuminated Rodrigo's face as he proudly helped her to her feet. "It is with immense joy that I introduce the woman I adore and plan to marry—my fiancée, Lady Maryann LeMaster." His words hung in the air, and shock registered on the guests' faces.

"Rest assured, you will all be invited to our wedding. Thank you all for being so understanding. I hope you will stay for our final sporting event tomorrow. Now enjoy the meal!"

Disbelief pulled at Brian's mind as he recalled Francisco's family tale of scandal—of Lord Rodrigo Gutiérrez and Lady Magdalena Constanza's intended union. Could fate have orchestrated such a tangled web and then sent Maryann across time to become engaged to Lord Rodrigo? If so, why? The more Brian pondered this, the more questions arose.

The vibrant conversations swirled around him as he savored the delicious meal, grounding himself in the moment to cope with the overwhelming uncertainty and the looming possibility of being stranded in this century.

His questions for Maryann would have to wait.

From my seat beside Rodrigo, my heart sang with gratitude for how things had turned out. My eyes flitted to Brian, who sat at the far end of the table. Despite the chaos swirling around him, he appeared calm, effortlessly engaging with the guest beside him as if he'd resided in the seventeenth century all along. Thank goodness he'd had the presence of mind to play along. What an extraordinary night this was turning out to be!

My mind drifted back to when I'd first met Brian, a pleasant memory wrapped in the warmth of a sunlit gallery. I'd been absorbed in an eighteenth-century neoclassical painting, its colors stirring something profound within me, when a rich and engaging voice broke through my reverie. "There's something extraordinary about neoclassical art, wouldn't you agree, Miss?"

I'd turned to find a handsome young man standing behind me, his tousled blond hair and bright blue eyes striking against the museum's elegant backdrop. He was wearing a navy three-piece suit that seemed tailored to perfection. His tall, muscular frame leaned effortlessly against a pillar, and his hands were casually tucked in his pockets.

Taking a few steps closer, he extended his hand with a charming smile. "I'm Brian Golding."

With piqued interest and curiosity, I shook his hand. "I'm Maryann LeMaster. It's a pleasure, Mr. Golding. Are you a lover of neoclassical paintings?"

"Not quite a lover, but I appreciate a classic piece," he replied, his smile broadening. "How about you, Miss LeMaster?"

I confessed with a hint of shyness, "I'm an amateur painter. I draw a lot of my inspiration from the masters. When I examine a painting like this, I try to envision what the artist's thoughts were as they were creating the masterpiece."

"Fascinating," he said, his eyes lighting up. "Would you care to join me for a cup of coffee at the diner down the street?"

"Sure, Mr. Golding. Lead the way," I replied, excitement igniting within me.

Our coffee then led to dating, which soon morphed into a carefree romance, but as soon as we became engaged, the tides began to shift. Brian's once-charming old-fashioned ideals started to feel suffocating. Every decision felt like a negotiation. Although he cherished the notion of treating a woman like a queen, my spirit craved freedom, and something had to give.

Snapping back to the present, I turned to Rodrigo, squeezing his hand with affection. The desire in his eyes sparked joy in my heart, and as he leaned in to kiss my cheek, I realized how fortunate I was to have found my soulmate. Living in an era when women had few rights, I'd been embraced by Rodrigo as an equal partner. He treated me with the respect and love I'd always desired. I was grateful for the stones not just because they'd led me to him but because they'd also led me to continue pursuing my passions and dreams. I felt very fortunate indeed.

CHAPTER 71

The Pheasant-Shooting Event

The morning light filtered through the castle windows and brightened the room as I eased myself out of bed. The ache in my thighs still throbbed faintly, a haunting reminder of the ordeal at the church, yet it couldn't dampen my spirits. Since our engagement had been announced, the joy swirling within me overshadowed any lingering pain.

Maria and Amalia fluttered about my room, their hands buried in fabrics as they debated my attire for today's pheasant-shooting contest. I reached for the simpler beige gown that felt right for the occasion, but Maria snatched it from my grasp before I could slip it on.

"Oh no, my dear, this won't do," Maria scolded, her eyes glinting with mischief. "The yellow dress is much more fitting for Lord Gutiérrez's betrothed. You must look the part."

"Maria, don't you think the yellow gown is too fancy for shooting birds?" I asked, hesitating as she held up the sunny yellow dress, its soft sheen catching the morning light.

Maria tapped her foot impatiently. "Nonsense. You're no longer just Lady Maryann. You're *his* Lady Maryann now," she said, beaming. "You must reflect that."

Amalia chimed in, her face flushed with excitement. "Miss Maryann, it's so romantic. You and Lord Gutiérrez are the talk of the castle." With an audible sigh, she continued. "Love truly does conquer all!"

I couldn't help but grin at her romantic words. Their excitement washed over me, settling deep into my bones. Still, I tried to steady my breath as I glanced at my reflection and admired the bright fabric that practically radiated under the sun's touch.

"Miss Maryann," Amalia began again, her voice dropping conspiratorially. "I forgot to tell you—Mr. Bruno Pilato, the nephew of the local Romani trader Stefan Pilato, is officially courting my mother!"

My breath caught. "What was the man's name again?" I asked, a tremor in my voice. I hoped they hadn't noticed.

"Bruno Pilato," Amalia replied, smiling. "His father passed away when Mr. Bruno was just a boy, and he and his mother survived thanks to a kind couple. His red and green carriage sign, 'Pilato's Fine Gypsy Wares,' is in Romani and English, a tribute to both worlds."

A cold wave washed over me, though the room had not chilled. I knew that name, and not from here—Bruno Pilato, my driver and friend from the twenty-first century. I couldn't forget his brightly painted sign. The shock of this revelation was like a physical blow, leaving me in disbelief. How could it be? How could he and Brian *both* be here? Those stones really had been busy . . .

Before I could dwell on the strangeness, a knock rapped sharply at the door, pulling me back to the present. I opened it to find Rodrigo looking dashing in a brown leather vest, breeches, and tall boots that casually hugged his form.

"My lady," he greeted, bowing with a smile that made my heart race. "You look breathtaking. Are you ready?"

"Yes, of course," I replied. My mind was still spinning from Amalia's revelation as I slipped my arm through his. Together we descended the stone steps of the castle, and I focused on the cool air, which was filled with the lively sounds of the day's preparations.

Amid the chattering gamekeeper and the male guests, a large cage of restless pheasants stood in the courtyard. The women, wrapped up in their conversations, seemed uninterested in the event, while my mind was fixed firmly on the competition ahead.

As I glanced at the line of men preparing to shoot, memories stirred of long hours practicing archery, perfecting my aim. I didn't want to be here just to watch.

I leaned closer to Rodrigo and whispered, "Are women allowed to compete in this event, Lord Rodrigo? I would like to participate if it is allowed."

Lifting his brow in surprise, Lord Rodrigo's eyes sparkled in admiration. "If you can handle a bow, my love, I would be honored to see you compete." Without hesitation, he clapped his hands, calling for attention.

"Ladies and gentlemen, it seems we have a rare treat," his voice boomed over the crowd. "There are rumors that some of the women here today possess archery skills. I want to invite any capable lady to join the contest." A cacophony of surprised voices erupted after Rodrigo's proclamation, but no other women stepped forward.

The air thickened with anticipation as Lord Rodrigo stepped up for his turn. With a confident grip on his bow, he nocked an arrow and raised it high, nodding at the gamekeeper to signal his readiness. The gamekeeper opened the cage with a flourish, releasing a bird that soared gracefully above the castle. Rodrigo's eyes locked on the bird, and with a precise aim adjustment, he let the arrow fly. It whistled through the air, striking true and sending the bird spiraling down. The crowd erupted in triumphant applause.

As my turn approached, the confidence that had surged in me moments before seemed to waver. Sensing my hesitation, Rodrigo stepped in, offering a reassuring smile and a slightly smaller bow. His unexpected encouragement strengthened my resolve. With shaky hands, I accepted the bow and nocked my arrow as I steadied my breathing. I pointed it skyward, just as Rodrigo had, and nodded to the gamekeeper.

"Release it," I whispered to myself, my heart racing. As the bird took to the sky, I raised my bow, my focus unwavering. I adjusted my aim with a deep breath and let the arrow fly on the soft exhale. It soared, cutting through the air with purpose. When it struck its mark, Lord Rodrigo's eyes widened, and his astonishment transformed into an infectious grin. He laughed as he swept me up in a joyous spin. The cheerful roars of the men drowned out the surprised gasps of the women who watched, taken aback by our exuberance. In that whirlwind of celebration, I could only see Rodrigo's radiant face, full of pride and joy.

CHAPTER 72

Mistress Esmeralda

I approached Esmeralda as she poured herself a cup of mead from the barrel underneath the pavilion tent, where colorful banners fluttered in the breeze.

"Lady Maryann, that was an incredible shot! Where did you learn to shoot with such skill?" she exclaimed, her eyes sparkling with admiration and excitement.

"Good afternoon, Mistress Esmeralda! Thank you for the kind words. My father hired a master archer when I was Amalia's age, and I practiced tirelessly. By the way, where is your daughter? I hear she's been busy helping her aunt."

"She has indeed been helping out," Esmeralda replied, pride shining. "I saw her earlier with that nice young man, Pedro, but I can't help but feel anxious for them. Their future worries me—she's Romani, and he's the son of a lord."

I squeezed her hand reassuringly. "You needn't worry. Lord Gutiérrez has assured me they have Lord Velasco's blessing if they choose to wed. And speaking of blessings, I want to congratulate you and Mr. Bruno."

"Thank you, Lady Maryann," she replied, happiness shining through her eyes. "Mr. Bruno was concerned for your well-being when he first arrived. I assured him you were well and staying at the castle. I believe you'll both have the chance to speak soon. And congratulations on your engagement to Lord Gutiérrez—I'm overjoyed for both of you!"

"Thank you, Mistress Esmeralda," I said, embracing her. As I pulled away, my gaze landed on Brian standing alone a short distance away. I excused myself as the joyful murmurs and laughter continued to swirl around us.

CHAPTER 73

Lord Golding

"Lord Golding," I exclaimed, feigning astonishment. "What a delightful surprise to see you!"

"Lady LeMaster," Brian replied and bowed dramatically, his voice laced with playful sarcasm. "I must commend you on your archery prowess. The guests' expressions were priceless when you landed that perfect shot! More than that, seeing you looking so happy and well is a relief." His tone softened as he continued, "But tell me—how did you end up here?"

I glanced around us in every direction to ensure no one was listening. I told Brian my story of how I came to be here, as well as the haunting melody I'd heard just before I lost consciousness.

Brian didn't look fazed in the slightest. "That sounds similar to my own experience," he said, his eyes lighting up with excitement. "I flew to Zafra to search for you when you missed your flight home. I also stumbled upon a pair of half-buried ancient stone pillars, and the rest is history. You've been here for some time, Maryann. Do you have any theory as to why the stones brought us to this particular time? And here's the million-dollar question—have you discovered a way back?" There was a hint of hope in his voice.

I swallowed hard. This was going to be hard for him to hear. "No," I confessed, my heart steady in its conviction. "I don't know if there's a way back, nor do I wish to leave. I believe I was drawn here to find my soulmate." I chuckled at his bemused expression. "Come on, Brian, wipe that silly grin off your face,"

I said, suppressing a chuckle as I raised an eyebrow at him.

"All right, I'm sorry," he replied, a crooked grin creeping onto his lips. "I promise to keep an open mind. Please, continue."

I recounted the whirlwind of events since my arrival, touching on the drama with Lady Magdalena and my harrowing encounter with the priest.

Brian paled and managed to blurt out some supportive words, his voice low and earnest. His expression darkened in sympathy as he took in my hardships. "I'm so relieved Lord Rodrigo came to your rescue in time. I understand he was supposed to marry Lady Magdalena this week. Why was their wedding canceled, and how did your engagement come to be, if you don't mind me asking?"

"When Lord Rodrigo discovered that Lady Magdalena had forged the wedding invitations, he was furious. He didn't see any way out of the wedding without a valid excuse, so he began watching Lady Magdalena closely, hoping to catch her in a compromising position. A few days ago, he followed her to the gardens and caught her and Juan, the stableman, in a very compromising act. That was all he needed to call off the wedding. He knew she would not challenge him, in fear that rumors of her tryst with Juan would become public knowledge."

"Wow," Brian exclaimed, shaking his head. "And where is the illustrious Lady Magdalena now?"

"She's confined to the midwife's cottage until after the birth of her child," I explained. "Unfortunately, she is likely to be banished to France after she recovers, and the child will probably be raised at the castle."

"That's so sad," Brian sighed. "It's clear she must have endured a difficult life. I hope things improve for her."

"It's ironic you say that," I mused. "You and I are probably the only ones here who empathize with her and genuinely wish her a better life. It's a pity there are no therapists now—as she would certainly benefit from seeing one."

"I agree, from the sound of things." He shook his head.

"Oh, another time traveler has recently arrived." My voice brightened. "His name is Bruno Pilato—my carriage driver in Zafra. I just learned that he's courting a lovely Romani woman named Esmeralda. Perhaps we were all chosen to travel through time to meet our soulmates. I'm curious to see if you might also find yours, Brian." I flashed him a mischievous grin and winked.

"Count me in!" he declared, grinning widely. "Let the quest begin!"

CHAPTER 74

Maryann

Spotting Rodrigo nearby, I waved at him and headed in his direction.

"How are you feeling, my love?" he asked, his voice gentle but edged with concern. "After everything you've been through recently, I would think you'd be tired. Would you care to rest before dinner? After all, it hasn't been that long since your ordeal."

A sigh escaped me. I hated admitting the truth, but my body felt heavy, each step a reminder of my exhaustion. "I admit it. I am worn out, and the soreness lingers. A hot bath and a nap sound like heaven."

Rodrigo chuckled softly, a glint of admiration flashing in his eyes. "You hid it well earlier with your impressive display of archery. You were remarkable." Curiosity shone in his eyes. "How did you become so skilled, my dear?"

A small smile tugged at my lips. "My father hired a master archer to teach me when I was young. I practiced for years, and I suppose it stuck."

Rodrigo laughed heartily, the admiration deepening in his eyes. "A woman of many talents. You were magnificent today, truly." His hand brushed against mine as we neared the castle entrance. "Come, my love. Soon you'll be able to rest."

Inside my room, the air was warm and fragrant from the freshly heated water poured into the tub. The maids worked quickly, and when they left, we were finally alone. Rodrigo's presence filled the space, making it feel smaller and more intimate as he reverently pulled me into his arms. His lips brushed against mine as he held me securely.

A surge of boldness rose in me—we were now engaged, after all. I wrapped my arms around Rodrigo's neck, pulling him closer and deepening the kiss. The moment our lips touched again, something inside me ignited. My heart pounded against my ribs, every part of me wanting more, needing more.

Rodrigo groaned softly, barely able to restrain his desire. He pulled back, his hands lingering on my shoulders. "If we keep this up, I'll end up in that bath with you," he whispered, his eyes dark with longing, his breath ragged. His words were both a promise and a warning. But instead of yielding, he kissed my forehead almost chastely and stepped back with a sigh. "Rest, my love. And by the way, don't you think we should be on a first-name basis at this point in our relationship, at least in privacy, my love?"

Giggling, I replied, "I do think so, Rodrigo."

Rodrigo's face lit with joy as he laughed and embraced me again. "See you soon, Maryann." With a sexy smirk and a wink, he retreated from the room, leaving me flushed and wanting.

CHAPTER 75

The Nightmare

I sank into the hot water and sighed as the heat seeped into my tired, aching limbs. The water seemed to cradle me, soothing the soreness and melting away the tension from the day. My eyes fluttered shut, the gentle steam curling around me like a blanket as I drifted off to sleep.

But sleep did not bring peace.

The dream came on fast and vivid.

Back in that wretched dungeon, the stone walls were cold and damp around me. The crazed priest's mutterings echoed in the chamber, his voice a low, evil hum that grated against my bones. I tried to move, to escape, but my arms and legs were bound, the leather straps digging into my skin. Panic welled up inside me, and my chest tightened as I struggled in vain.

Then he turned. The priest looked at me with an eerie grimace stretching across his face. His eyes gleamed with a dark madness. He revealed yellowed and rotted teeth as he grinned—a ghastly, twisted grin that sent shivers through me. I pulled harder against the restraints, desperation clawing at me. He stepped closer, and in his hand was a knife, long and glinting in the dim light.

"No," I whispered, my voice trembling, barely audible. But the priest heard. He loomed over me now, his breath foul and heavy. His mouth widened grotesquely as he raised the knife high above my chest.

"No!" I screamed.

The knife plunged downward, straight for my heart. The pain—oh God, the pain. I felt it as the blade pierced me, slicing through flesh and bone. Blood pooled, and darkness followed.

I woke up thrashing in the water, gasping for air. The scream that tore from my throat echoed through the room, a sound of sheer terror. My body trembled uncontrollably, causing water to slosh over the sides of the tub.

The door flew open, and Rodrigo rushed in with his sword drawn, his eyes wild with alarm. The moment he saw me alone in the tub, his sword clattered to the floor. Crossing the room in two strides, he wrapped his arms around me and pulled me from the water, quickly wrapped his cape around my shoulders, and held me close. Still shaking from the terror of the nightmare, I clung to him in desperation.

"My love," he murmured, holding me tightly. "I'm here. You're safe now. I'm here."

But the nightmare clung to me and refused to let go. I buried my face in his chest, sobbing uncontrollably, shaking like a leaf in a storm. "Rodrigo, it was the dungeon. It was so real. The priest stabbed me in the heart. I felt it!"

Rodrigo stroked my hair, his voice a low, comforting murmur. "It's over now, my love. It was just a nightmare, a cruel echo of what you went through. Sometimes after a trauma like that, the mind plays tricks on you. But you're safe here with me."

"I'm afraid to fall asleep again," I whispered, clinging to him. "Rodrigo, will you . . . will you stay with me tonight? I don't want to be alone."

Tightening his arms around me protectively and reverently kissing my forehead, he softly replied, "Yes, my love, but only to keep the nightmares away. If you keep tempting me like this, I may not be able to resist your charms." He flashed a sexy grin.

Laughing through my tears, I cuddled deeper into his embrace. "I love you, Rodrigo."

"And I love you, Maryann," he whispered back.

CHAPTER 76

Motherhood

Lady Magdalena paced restlessly within the small confines of the midwife's cottage, her frustration mounting with each passing hour, feeling trapped as if she were locked up in a dungeon. Two of Lord Rodrigo's guards stood outside to ensure she remained where she was. She knew of Lord Rodrigo's plans to send her away, far from Zafra, to France, where she'd live in some distant château. On the one hand, the thought of starting anew in a land of promise was tempting—a fresh beginning where the weight of her past might not follow.

But Zafra was her home.

She'd known its warm sun, dusty streets, and shadows her whole life. How could she leave? As if in response to her turmoil, a sharp pain lanced through her abdomen, forcing a gasp from her lips. Doubled over in agony, she frantically clutched her stomach as a second wave of pain surged, fiercer this time. She barely had time to register the sudden warmth spreading down her legs before the realization hit her: her water had broken.

"Julia!" she cried out, panic rising with the pain.

The midwife rushed over, her hands steady and practiced as she gently guided Lady Magdalena to the bed. After she examined her quickly but thoroughly, she looked up with an excited expression. "The baby is coming, my lady. It won't be long now."

Lady Magdalena's body felt foreign, as if it were no longer her own. Each contraction tore through her, reducing her to gasps and groans as her muscles clenched in relentless rhythm. The pain was unimaginable—worse than anything she'd known. Whenever she thought she couldn't endure another wave, it crashed over her with even greater force. Sweat trickled down her temples, and her breaths came in ragged bursts.

"Focus, Lady Magdalena," the midwife urged, her voice a beacon of calm amid the chaos. "You're almost there. Keep going."

Hours passed by like a blur, marked only by the intensifying agony, and time seemed to stretch as though she'd been trapped in this moment forever. Magdalena's strength was ebbing, her mind teetering on the edge of despair. She wanted to stop, lie back, and let the darkness take her. But the midwife's voice kept pulling her back, insisting she continue to push and urging her not to give up.

"You can do this," Julia whispered, leaning close. "I see the baby's head. One more push, Lady Magdalena. Just one more, and your child will be here."

Through the fog of pain, Magdalena summoned every last bit of strength. With a final, primal scream, she pushed, her body giving everything it had left. Then suddenly the pressure was gone.

The seconds stretched unbearably. Lady Magdalena's breath caught in her throat as she waited for something, anything. Then a sharp, piercing cry filled the room, breaking the silence like a promise of life itself.

Her baby was alive.

Julia swaddled the newborn with practiced ease before placing the tiny, fragile bundle in Magdalena's arms. She looked down at the baby for a brief, heart-stopping moment.

A daughter.

So small and fragile.

So beautiful.

She could feel the baby's warm body through the blankets and hear the soft, helpless sounds as the baby squirmed.

Suddenly, the joy disappeared, and a cold wave of dread washed over her. This child—this innocent life—had come from her, yet she couldn't bear the weight of it. Fear twisted like a knife in her chest. How could she ever be a good mother? How could someone like her, who had lived in darkness for so long, nurture something so pure and beautiful?

"Take her to Lord Gutiérrez," she cried, her voice breaking. The baby's soft cries clawed at her heart, but she couldn't look at her anymore. "Please, take her away."

Julia hesitated, her eyes filled with sympathy, but she did as she was asked. Lifting the child from Lady Magdalena's trembling arms, she delicately placed her in a wicker basket, tucking a small blanket around her.

When Julia opened the door, Paulo stood ready as though he were expecting the baby, his face somber. He exchanged a few words with the midwife, then took the basket, cradling the precious bundle as if the world's weight rested in his arms.

When the door closed and the baby was gone, a silence heavier than before filled the room.

Magdalena collapsed back onto the bed, her chest heaving as sobs overtook her. She hadn't thought it would hurt this much. She'd convinced herself that she would feel nothing—that the child was just a consequence of a life she hadn't chosen. But when Julia had taken her daughter away, it felt as if something had been ripped from her soul.

Her sobs turned into deep, wrenching cries. She'd given up her child, a symbol of love, hope, and pure goodness. Now, only emptiness and dread remained. She would never again experience the touch of that tiny hand or the sensation of her baby's breath against her skin. Alone and drained, she curled into herself, the exhaustion pulling her under like a tide. The tears blurred her vision, and the ache in her heart was far worse than the pain of childbirth.

CHAPTER 77

A Child

The castle had settled into a quiet routine since the wedding guests had departed. The absence of their laughter and celebration left the halls feeling cavernous as the sense of normalcy slowly returned. As we sat for supper, the soft clinking of silverware filled the room until the large oak doors suddenly creaked open. Paulo appeared holding something in his arms, and the air in the room shifted.

Lord Rodrigo raised an eyebrow, half curious, half concerned. "Paulo, what have you brought with you?" he asked, eyeing the basket cradled in Paulo's hands.

Everyone at the table turned their attention to the large wicker basket as Paulo wordlessly handed it to a nearby maid, who carefully placed it on the dining table in front of Lord Rodrigo.

A hush fell over the room as Lord Rodrigo leaned forward and carefully peeled back the edge of the blanket. His breath caught audibly. Nestled inside, sound asleep, was a tiny baby, her dark black hair softly framing her serene face, swaddled snugly with meticulous care.

For a moment, time froze. I felt my heart leap, then stall, as if my body couldn't fully comprehend the sight before me as I watched the exchange between Rodrigo and the baby.

Lord Rodrigo's eyes softened. In a reverent tone, he whispered, "Paulo, is this . . . is this Lady Magdalena's child?"

Standing with the weight of his responsibility heavy on his shoulders, Paulo nodded. "Yes, my lord," he said quietly. "This is her newborn daughter. The midwife says she was much further along in her pregnancy than anticipated. Lady Magdalena, though devastated, believes the child will have a better life here in the safety of the castle."

Rodrigo's face was a complex landscape of emotions—admiration, awe, and perhaps a thread of sorrow for Lady Magdalena's plight. He reached out slowly and touched the baby's soft, delicate cheek with the back of his finger, his voice thick with emotion. "She's beautiful."

Maria shot to her feet, her movements brisk and decisive. "Lord Gutiérrez," she began with a spark of determination in her voice. "There's a widow in the valley with an infant about three or four months old. She's still nursing. Shall I ask if she will act as a wet nurse for this baby?"

Lord Rodrigo's shoulders seemed to relax slightly, as if Maria's practical suggestion had solved the overwhelming situation. "Yes, Maria, I would appreciate that. Please offer her the position and promise that she and her child will be well cared for. Paulo, would you mind taking Maria to the widow's home?"

"No, sir. I do not mind at all."

Maria and Paulo's swift departure left the room in a pensive quiet. As we waited, our attention returned to the baby, who slumbered peacefully, unaware of the uncertainty of her future. It wasn't long before the sound of carriage wheels crunching on the gravel announced their return. Maria was the first to enter the castle with a woman walking hesitantly behind her, a child balanced on her hip. Sara was in her late twenties, with a weathered but kind face that spoke of a life of hard work and resilience. She had a nervous but resolute look about her. Though neatly mended, her clothing bore the marks of hardship, the patches in her dress evidence of a life lived with little. Despite her modest appearance, her eyes gleamed with quiet dignity.

"Lord Gutiérrez," Maria said, "this is Sara and her daughter, Alicia."

Lord Rodrigo rose, his presence commanding yet cordial. "It's an honor, Sara," he said, his tone soothing as he extended a hand to her. "Thank you for coming on such short notice. If you agree to act as this baby's wet nurse and nanny, you and your daughter will be well provided for. You will have a comfortable chamber, and anything you require will be available. The castle will be your home."

Sara's eyes widened at the generosity of the offer, and she nodded, clearly moved. "I would be honored to care for the baby, my lord," she said softly, a touch of gratitude in her voice.

Rodrigo nodded in a friendly manner, the tension in his shoulders easing further. "Wonderful. Please come meet your new charge."

Sara stepped forward, and her expression softened as her eyes fell upon the sleeping infant. Her maternal instincts seemed to take over as she softly touched the baby's cheek, and her face lit up. "She's lovely, my lord," she whispered. After a pause, she asked, "What is the child's name?"

Rodrigo turned to us, a playful glint in his eyes. "Ladies, we have a most important decision—what shall we name her?"

Suggestions fluttered around the table like petals in the breeze. Names were spoken—each considered, some quickly discarded. But when I suggested Sophia, Rodrigo's eyes sparkled.

"Sophia," he repeated, testing the sound on his tongue. "Sophia Constanza." He looked around the room with satisfaction. "Yes, that will be her name."

With a sense of completion, Rodrigo turned back to Sara. "Please, Sara, sit and join us for dinner. We are informal here, and you are now part of this household."

"Thank you, Lord Gutiérrez," Sara replied shyly, as she took a seat beside Maria with her daughter, Alicia, snuggled in her arms.

CHAPTER 78

The Library

Restless and uncomfortable, I tossed and turned in bed, the fear of reliving my nightmare keeping me awake. I slipped into my robe and quietly walked down the dim hallway toward the library, seeking the comfort of solitude.

Moments later, I was curled up in my favorite chair near the crackling fireplace, the heat of the flames easing my nerves. My fingers traced the familiar pages of my favorite book of poetry, each verse a temporary escape from the haunting images that lingered in my mind.

An hour passed in peaceful quiet when a soft knock on the door pulled me from my reverie. Rodrigo's face peeked in, his eyes twinkling in merriment.

"I thought I might find you here, Maryann," he said, his voice carrying affection. "Do you mind if I join you? The last time we met in the library, things . . . well, they didn't exactly end calmly," he added with a playful smirk.

I couldn't help but grin back, feeling the tension melt away. "Please join me, Rodrigo." With a teasing glint in my eye, I added, "I wouldn't mind reliving that epic kiss you gave me—if you're offering."

His expression softened as he approached, and the passion between us seemed to ignite like the fire in the hearth. "Careful now, my love," he murmured, his voice deep and sultry. "You're making it very hard to keep my hands to myself. Would you consider shortening our courtship?" His tone was laced with longing and sincerity. "A month seems impossibly long when

I only want to make you my wife."

I stood slowly, my deep and sincere love for him filling my chest. "Rodrigo," I whispered, meeting his eyes. "I would marry you tomorrow if it were possible. I don't need grand festivities or lavish celebrations. All I need is you—us, surrounded by the people we love."

His eyes darkened with emotion as he stepped closer, his arms enveloping me in a secure, protective embrace. "Three days, then," he said with a grin that held joy and mischief. "I'll make it happen. Maria would never forgive me if she didn't have time to create a wedding gown for you."

My belly flipped at the thought of our wedding in just three short days. I sighed happily, resting my head against his chest and feeling his heartbeat beneath my cheek. "Three days sounds perfect," I whispered, letting the weight of anticipation settle over me. "I can't wait to be your wife."

Rodrigo tilted my chin, his touch gentle but filled with the intensity of his love. His lips met mine in a kiss that made my heart race, filled with promise and passion that felt impossible to contain.

His green eyes blazed with desire when we parted, tempered only by the tenderness he always showed me. "If only we were married now," he confessed, his voice rough with restraint. "Every moment with you feels like torture, not being able to love you fully."

I held him tightly, my own emotions a mirror of his longing. "Soon, Rodrigo. I feel it, too, but soon," I reassured him, feeling the certainty of our future together in every beat of his heart.

CHAPTER 79

Reunion

As the days slipped by in a flurry of joyful anticipation, the castle staff immersed themselves in preparations for our wedding.

Seeking solace from my swirling thoughts and the anxiety gnawing at my heart, I wandered into the garden. I breathed in the fragrant blooms with each step, trying to find clarity. I shouldn't be starting married life with a secret between us. I needed to tell Rodrigo the truth of how I'd arrived here, yet fear gripped me. What if he reacted negatively? The mere thought made my heart race.

I heard my name called. Turning around, I was delighted to see Bruno Pilato approaching, a wide grin lighting up his face.

"Miss Maryann! How delightful to find you flourishing in this century!" he exclaimed, his joy infectious. "When you vanished, I was apprehensive. Francisco was the first to alert the police about your disappearance, but soon the case grew cold. Did you arrive here through the Celtic stones?" He wiggled his eyebrows playfully, his signature smile brightening the garden.

"Bruno! You have no idea how happy I am to see you!" I exclaimed, returning his grin. "Yes, I arrived through the stones. And shortly after, so did my former fiancé, Brian Golding—Lord Brian Golding, now a guest at the castle. Remember the dreams I shared? They were all warnings about this very adventure!"

Bruno laughed heartily, his eyes sparkling with mischief. "Ah, if my memory serves me right, I did mention that the meaning of those dreams would reveal itself when the time was right. Looks like I was spot-on!" he said, showcasing his signature grin.

"Yes, you were!" I chuckled, feeling lighter in his presence. "But how did you end up here?"

"Well," he began, after first looking around to make sure no one was in hearing range, "I was heading to my sister's house when the road became impassable from the heavy rains. I took an unfamiliar alternate route, and as soon as my carriage rolled over two partially buried stone pillars, everything—my carriage, horses, and I—was somehow whisked back in time! But I am so happy to be here, as I met my ancestor and my lovely fiancée, Mistress Esmeralda. I hear that congratulations are in order for you as well, Lady Maryann." His eyes twinkled with mischief as he bowed to me.

"Oh, Bruno, I've missed your humor!" I laughed, my heart lifting. "And I'm thrilled for you and Esmeralda! She's such a wonderful woman. I have a theory about why we all traveled through the stones. Would you like to hear it?"

"Absolutely! Please, enlighten me," he implored.

Taking a deep breath, I said, "We were meant to find our soulmates in this era. Brian Golding, my former fiancé, also traveled here. I suspect that he will also meet his soulmate soon. Isn't it curious that all three of us ended up here? What do you think about that, Bruno?"

"Remember, I'm Romani, and I believe in magic," he replied with a hearty laugh. "But seriously, I agree. We were destined to walk this path to find our soulmates here. There are no coincidences. The three of us are like a time-traveling family, perhaps meant to support each other in this journey. Didn't you feel that immediate connection when we first met? Like we were long-lost friends?"

"Absolutely! I trusted you implicitly from the start," I said, my heart swelling with gratitude. "And I could use your support and advice right now, Bruno." I took a steadying breath. "Before marrying Rodrigo, I need to tell him my secrets about time travel and my former engagement to Brian. But I'm terrified."

Bruno's expression shifted to one of understanding. "I can relate. I feel the same way about my secrets with Esmeralda. I plan to tell her when the time is right, but I won't reveal my origins to Uncle Stefan!" His voice trembled, underscoring the gravity of his words. "Romani people are superstitious, and I don't want to add fuel to that fire, especially with Uncle Stefan's unpredictable temper. I would appreciate it if you would please keep my name out of the conversation, at least until I speak with my Esmeralda."

"Of course, Bruno," I assured him. "There's no reason to mention your name. I do have to reveal my true origins to Rodrigo, but I don't think it's a good idea to reveal my past relationship with Brian just yet."

"If you don't mind me asking, when and why did your engagement to Brian end?" asked Bruno.

"Well," I began, gathering my thoughts, "Brian and I dated for years, and we had a great relationship, filled with fun and laughter. But once we got engaged, everything changed, and I ended our relationship. He's old-fashioned, likes making the decisions, and relishes the role of protector. Those traits are perfect for here and now, but they didn't work with me, probably because I'm such a strong and independent woman. We are much better suited as friends," I explained, laughing lightly. "But seriously, Bruno, I'm terrified of how Rodrigo will react to the notion that I'm a time traveler. It's a fear that's gnawing at me." I trembled slightly.

"I'm sure Rodrigo will come to understand time travel eventually," he said, his advice carrying the weight of his wisdom. "But as far as how he'll react to Brian being your ex-fiancé, I can't say. I'd suggest talking to Brian before you speak to Rodrigo. I wish you luck, Maryann."

CHAPTER 80

Confession

My nerves twisted like a coiled spring. The need to confide in Brian gnawed at me as the day passed. Yet in this era, I couldn't just approach him without crossing the boundaries of propriety. With a heavy heart, I feigned a headache and retreated to my chamber. It wasn't long before a gentle knock at my door broke the silence.

"Come in," I called softly.

Maria entered, her usual exuberance dampened by concern as she hurried to my side.

"Maria, please, no more fussing," I declared in a serious tone. "I have something to tell you, and you might think I've lost my mind."

"Lady Maryann, you're scaring me!" Her blue eyes widened with worry. "What is it?"

Taking a deep breath, I steeled myself for the truth. "Maria, I'm from the twenty-first century," I confessed, watching her expression shift from concern to bewilderment.

Her face paled, and she fell silent, clearly grappling with my revelation.

I rushed the rest of the words out. "During a trip to Zafra, I encountered two Celtic stone pillars partially buried in the ground. When I touched them, everything began to spin. I heard a haunting melody, and then nothing. I woke to find myself in this century, where I met Lord Gutiérrez." The weight of my revelation hung heavy in the air, a confession that could change everything.

Maria stared at me, her shock palpable. It took several long moments before she managed to respond. "I am speechless," she finally said, her voice trembling. "The tales of time travel through the singing Celtic stones have been whispered among my Romani ancestors for ages. I always dismissed them as mere folklore." Her disbelief was almost tangible.

"Well, it seems the legends are true," I replied. "But there's more. Lord Golding is also from the twenty-first century. We were once engaged, and now, just days before my marriage to Lord Rodrigo, I feel compelled to reveal my past to him, or rather, the future. It's all rather confusing. But I fear how he might react."

Maria nodded slowly, and after what felt like several minutes, her eyes filled with sympathy. "I must be honest, Lady Maryann. I doubt Lord Gutiérrez will believe your story, at least at first. And when he learns of your previous engagement, it may shatter him."

"Oh, Maria," I lamented, guilt consuming me. "I can't marry Lord Rodrigo while I still have secrets. I owe him the truth, but I need to speak with Lord Golding first."

With a comforting hug, she promised, "First, I will arrange for you to speak with Lord Golding. After that, we'll devise a plan for you to disclose everything to Lord Gutiérrez. Don't worry. You have friends who care for you dearly, and your current fiancé adores you."

CHAPTER 81

The Bench Meeting

I sat on a bench in a quiet corner of the castle garden, anxiety and nerves getting the better of me as I waited for Brian. I felt an instant relief when I caught sight of him approaching.

"Are you all right, Maryann?" he asked, his brow furrowed with concern. "I understand you need to speak with me."

"Please sit, Brian," I urged, my voice unsteady. "Stress is wearing me thin, and I desperately need your guidance. I want to tell Rodrigo about my true origins and our past engagement, but I don't know how to break the news to him without devastating him. I want to reveal my time travel origins first, and once he's accepted that, I'll tell him about our former relationship. What do you think, and are you okay with me revealing that information?"

"Maryann, if you're brave enough to confront Rodrigo with the truth, then I must be equally brave for whatever consequences follow," he replied, resolve lacing his tone. "He may be troubled by our history, but I will assure him of your love and devotion to him. I now realize that we are only meant to be good friends. You are so fortunate to have found true love with Rodrigo. Surely, my soulmate must be out there as well, right?" He smiled wistfully.

"Brian, you're a true friend," I replied, my heart full of gratitude. "And yes, I'm sure your soulmate is here somewhere. Are you sure you're all right with this?"

"Of course," he affirmed without hesitation. "I understand why you need to unburden your secrets before you marry Lord Rodrigo. And if he asks, I'll share my experience about time travel and reassure him of your commitment to him."

"Thank you," I replied, squeezing his hand tightly. "I need to get back to the castle now. You are a dear friend, Brian." I smiled with gratitude.

As I walked toward the castle, my emotions were all over the place—a mixture of anxiety and relief. The gravity of revealing my past and the truth of my time travel to Rodrigo loomed over me—yet I knew I had to take this daunting step to achieve the life I longed for with the man I loved.

CHAPTER 82

Gentlemen's Drawing Room

Rodrigo and Brian settled into their seats in the drawing room, and Rodrigo poured a healthy dram of brandy into them. Composing himself, Rodrigo addressed the lingering questions weighing on his mind.

"Brian," he began thoughtfully, "I need you to be completely honest about your past relationship with Lady Maryann. There is an undeniable familiarity between the two of you that somehow feels more than just friends. Furthermore, when you both arrived, I inspected the Zafra port records and learned that no ships had docked on the day you arrived. If you are my friend, then please tell me the truth."

Brian let out a heavy sigh as if realizing the importance of his forthcoming words. "Rodrigo, I understand that what I'm about to say may be difficult to believe, but you deserve to know the truth. I'm betraying Lady Maryann's confidence, because she planned to tell you before the wedding. All I ask is for you to keep an open mind."

Brian paused to gather his thoughts when he noticed the tense and impatient expression on Rodrigo's face, so he took a deep breath and forced himself to continue. "Lady Maryann and I are both from the twenty-first century. We were engaged to be married, but she ended it several months before coming to Zafra. Women of the future are remarkably independent. They have the same rights as men and are considered equal. If they choose, women can obtain an education and work in any field they desire, including politics. In the future, people travel on flying transport machines called airplanes that soar through the skies at incredible speeds. There are also gas- and electric-powered horseless cars. There are so many wonders to behold in the future. In America, Lady Maryann taught Spanish to children, and as you can probably guess, her favorite pastimes were painting and music. Taking a break from her job, she'd traveled alone from America to Zafra to stay for an extended holiday. While painting the castle, she fell near two partially buried stone pillars with Celtic symbols. When she touched the stones, she was transported here."

Rodrigo's green eyes were locked onto Brian in stunned silence. The air in the room felt heavy and dense as Brian's nonsensical words whirled around in his mind. After what seemed like hours, he finally roused himself. Shaking his head in disbelief and irritation, he declared, "Brian, the whole idea of time travel is absurd. While I was a boy, I heard many wild tales about time travel through magical Celtic stones, but they are simply folklore. Please enlighten me on how you truly arrived here in Zafra, and please tell me the truth as to why you came here looking for Lady Maryann!"

"I assure you, Rodrigo, I am telling you the absolute truth," Brian asserted earnestly. "When Lady Maryann failed to return to America, I was concerned for her safety, so I flew to Zafra to look for her. After arriving, I learned from the local authorities that she'd vanished without a trace, leaving behind all her personal belongings."

Lord Rodrigo's voice took on a colder tone as he probed further. "Tell me, Brian, if you and Lady Maryann are no longer engaged, why would you come to this castle searching for her?"

"As I mentioned earlier, she had not returned from her trip abroad. Although our engagement had ended, I still cared enough for her well-being to search for her and ensure she had not met with foul play or injury. While I was out searching for her in Zafra, I stumbled upon two partially buried ancient-looking stone pillars that appeared to be of Celtic origin. When I touched them, I heard a haunting melody and lost consciousness. After I came to, I walked to your castle and was shocked to find a much newer version of your descendant's castle. I recognized the portraits on your wall because I had seen them on your descendant's wall. When you walked out to greet me, I recognized you from your portrait, and it was at that moment I realized that I'd somehow traveled back in time. I was both shocked and relieved to find Lady Maryann here."

Rodrigo pursed his lips. "I will most certainly talk to Lady Maryann about this, but I have to tell you that I just don't believe this time travel story."

"I understand that this must be difficult to grasp," Brian said, rising from his seat in frustration. "But please believe me when I say Lady Maryann's love for you is genuine. None of this was orchestrated or planned in any way. I've shared the truth about our arrival, past engagement, and the incredible circumstances that brought us here. I apologize if it's hard for you to accept, but it is the reality we find ourselves in."

After Brian excused himself, Rodrigo remained seated as he contemplated the wild tale. His mind spun with paranoid conspiracies and conflicting emotions. Could there be a hidden agenda behind Maryann's actions? He wondered—could she have conceived a scheme to marry him and orchestrate his accidental death to secure her position as the lady of the castle? She would then be free to marry whomever she wished. Would she choose Brian? As outlandish as it seemed, Rodrigo was overwhelmed with questions and suspicions. Yet despite these crazy, unsettling thoughts, his genuine love and connection with Maryann remained. He had to confront her and seek the truth, no matter how disturbing it might be.

CHAPTER 83

Secrets Unburdened

Tonight was the night to reveal everything about my past to Rodrigo, and my stomach churned with every emotion possible. With my determination set, I walked down the hallway toward the library. As I stood in front of the library door, I took several fortifying breaths to gather my courage before knocking on the door. I thought I heard Rodrigo's voice, so I gingerly opened the door and entered, finding Rodrigo sitting in one of the two chairs in front of the fireplace. He was deep in thought, holding a glass of brandy. "Rodrigo, may I come in?" I asked, my voice steady despite my nerves.

"Of course," he said. "Please come in and sit down. Would you care for a cup of brandy or some wine?" He downed the brandy in one gulp. As he waited for my answer, he refilled his cup.

"Oh, no, thank you. I've something important to tell you, and I prefer to do so with a clear head."

"Well, sit down then. I hope you don't mind if I have a few glasses of brandy while you tell me whatever is on your mind," he said in a slurred voice.

I narrowed my eyes at him as he took another gulp of brandy. "Well, perhaps I should wait until tomorrow when we are both clearheaded," I replied, preparing to turn around and leave.

"My dear, I am not so gone that I can't understand whatever you say. Go ahead. I am listening."

Alarm bells went off in my mind. I had to talk to Rodrigo tonight, but it didn't feel like a good time to have a serious conversation. Yet, I was out of time, and I had no choice but to see this through. "All right, Rodrigo." I took a deep breath and dove into my story. "I am not from France. I left my home in the Americas in 2026 and traveled to Zafra for an extended vacation." I held my breath as I looked at Rodrigo, waiting for his reaction, but I was met with silence. Feeling confused and frustrated, I asked, "Rodrigo, why don't you seem surprised?"

"I am not surprised because I recently spoke with Lord Golding," he replied slowly as if in a daze. "He mentioned that you planned to speak with me. However, I convinced him to tell me his side of the story first. As I told him, I do not believe in time travel. I checked the port records and confirmed that no ship landed in Zafra when you arrived, and again later on the day Lord Golding arrived. Are you going to also tell me that you arrived through the Celtic stones, Maryann?" His sarcasm was quite apparent from the tone of his voice.

This conversation was not going as I had envisioned, but I could hardly stop now. "Rodrigo, you do not believe in time travel, but that is exactly how I arrived here. Somehow, I will find a way to prove this to you. There is something else you should know. Lord Golding and I were once engaged, but I broke it off several months before traveling to Zafra. I consider him a dear friend, but that is all. Looking back, I now realize that my feelings for him were not love, just fondness. We were good friends before we had a relationship, but when we became engaged, our relationship deteriorated because we were never meant to be anything but good friends. I did not know what love was until I met you. Nothing in this world compares to the deep, passionate, all-encompassing love that I have for you, Rodrigo, nothing! What do I need to do to convince you of that?"

Suddenly, Rodrigo abruptly stood up with an urgency that startled me, pulling me closer to him. "Maryann, I love you more than life, and I want to believe you, but these revelations have me feeling conflicted. Convince me beyond any doubt that your love for me is true," he pleaded.

I knew that mere words wouldn't be enough to assuage his doubts. I had to demonstrate my love through action. Without hesitation, I reached up with both hands to cradle his face. Drawing his head down close to mine, I captured his lips in a wildly passionate, searing kiss. Our emotions and passion intensified as I wrapped my arms around his neck, pressing my body against his, as I poured all the love and passion I felt for him into that fervent kiss. It was a kiss that surpassed anything I'd ever experienced. Lost in the passionate kiss, we teetered on the edge of surrender, our desires threatening to consume us. Rodrigo eventually broke away, leaning his forehead on mine as our breaths mingled. As our hearts continued to pound in unison, he pulled back slightly to look at me, his beautiful green eyes now filled with desire, love, and certainty.

"Maryann," he said, his ragged voice laden with love and conviction. "I believe you. I believe in the love you've shown me. Do not worry, my love. We will find a way to work through everything. Your past engagement with Lord Brian is of no concern to me, as I know it is over between you two."

"And what about time travel, Rodrigo?" I asked hesitantly, bracing myself and hoping for an open-minded response.

"We can set aside that discussion for another day, my love," he replied, his voice brimming with reassurance. "Right now, let us focus on our wedding. Our love is unwavering, and I am confident that in time we will address any lingering doubts together."

CHAPTER 84

The Big Day

The big day was here, and Rodrigo and I were finally getting married. The castle's great hall had been transformed with an abundance of fragrant flowers, their vibrant colors softly illuminated by the golden glow of countless candles. At the head of the room stood a beautifully crafted arched arbor entwined with jasmine vines, their delicate blossoms releasing subtle perfume. Beneath the arch stood Father Díaz, a gentle priest and a good man. He stood with his Bible open, ready to guide us through this sacred union.

My dearest friends—Clara, Maria, her sister Esmeralda, and Bruno—were seated in the first rows, each face alight with happiness. Just behind them, Pedro and his Aunt Angelina whispered excitedly with Amalia, while Brian, Sara, and her young daughter sat across the aisle. Rodrigo's elite guards were also there, as was a somber Lady Magdalena. Baby Sophia was asleep upstairs, while a trusted maid vigilantly watched over her.

Rodrigo stood tall at the altar, looking as handsome and confident as ever, wearing elegant white silk breeches and a flowing white shirt that emphasized his incredibly muscular form. His hair was loose, framing vibrant green eyes that sparkled with love. I stood in the doorway, and our eyes met; the room faded, and the love in his eyes grounded me in the moment we'd both been waiting for.

I stepped into the hall, my heart swelling with joy. My gown, Grecian in style, flowed around me in soft white satin embroidered with tiny flowers. A garland of fresh flowers crowned my hair, and as I took my first steps, I felt the love radiating from our friends sitting in the pews, eager to witness our vows.

Father Díaz's gentle voice echoed through the hall. "Lord Rodrigo Gutiérrez, do you take this woman, Lady Maryann LeMaster, as your wife and promise to cherish her always in sickness and in health, in poverty and in wealth, and to be true to her in all things until death alone shall part you?"

Rodrigo clasped my hands, his gaze steady. His voice resonated with certainty as he replied, "I do."

Turning to me, the priest asked, "Lady Maryann LeMaster, do you take this man, Lord Rodrigo Gutiérrez, as your husband and promise to cherish him always in sickness and in health, in poverty and in wealth, and to be true to him in all things until death alone shall part you?"

A wave of emotion overwhelmed me, and tears glistened in my eyes. "I do," I whispered, my voice catching as I steadily held Rodrigo's gaze, feeling the weight of the moment.

Lord Velasco stepped forward with the wedding rings at a signal from Father Díaz. Rodrigo took the first ring and faced me. With a steady voice, he said, "With this ring, I, Lord Rodrigo Gutiérrez, take you, Lady Maryann LeMaster, as my lawfully wedded wife." Sliding the beautiful and delicate gold band onto my finger, his words rang with emotion as he said, "Loving what I know of you and trusting what I do not yet know, I will respect and have faith in your abiding love for me through all our years and all that life may bring us."

My hands trembled as I carefully picked up the remaining ring, my heart racing as I looked into his eyes. "With this ring, I, Lady Maryann LeMaster, take you, Lord Rodrigo Gutiérrez, as my lawfully wedded husband," I vowed, slipping the ring onto his finger. "I promise to love, trust, and remain true to you. I will always respect and have faith in your love for me through all our years and all that life may bring us." My voice cracked, and my eyes stung with happy tears.

The priest closed the Bible, smiling, his voice ringing joyfully. "By the power vested in me by God and the Catholic Church of Spain, I now pronounce you husband and wife!"

A triumphant cheer filled the hall, along with clapping, whistles, and joyful shouts from our guests and friends. Rodrigo wrapped me in his arms, his lips meeting mine in a tender, electrifying kiss—a promise sealed in love. The kiss lingered until the priest's gentle cough brought us back to the moment.

"Congratulations to Lord Gutiérrez and Lady Gutiérrez!" the priest announced. "May your lives together be filled with joy!"

CHAPTER 85

Wedding Reception

The reception was alive with laughter and the clinking of glasses as we made our way around the room, accepting heartfelt congratulations and toasts from each of our friends.

Lord Velasco stepped forward, his face beaming with affection. "My friend," he said, turning to Rodrigo, "I never thought I'd see the day you found true love. And to find a woman as perfect as Lady Maryann, well, it's nothing short of a miracle."

He turned to me, his eyes full of humor. "My dear, you must be a saint to have navigated through all the madness in the last several weeks. Rodrigo had better keep a tight hold on you, or I might leave Elena and steal you away!" His hearty laugh rippled through the room, bringing happy smiles to everyone around us. "Congratulations to you both, and may you find joy in every moment."

As the celebration continued, Brian's eyes fell upon a beautiful woman with long, wavy black hair standing alone across the room, her gaze distant and nostalgic. A sad and melancholy grace softened her striking features. Feeling an impulsive tug, he navigated around the guests toward her.

When he reached her side, he bowed respectfully and took her hand.

"My lady, it's an honor to meet you. I am Lord Brian Golding, a friend of Lady Maryann's."

The woman offered a tentative smile. "A pleasure, Lord Golding. I am Lady Magdalena."

Brian subtly flinched with recognition. *This* was Lady Magdalena? But he offered a welcoming smile, undeterred by whispers of her past, preferring to make up his own mind about her. "Lady Magdalena, I'm grateful you could attend today. I am so glad to make your acquaintance."

A shadow crossed her face, and she looked away. "There is no need to feign kindness, Lord Golding. I am well aware of the rumors surrounding me. I've made mistakes I cannot undo, and forgiveness feels beyond reach."

"Lady Magdalena," Brian replied in earnest. "I care little for rumors. Let us look toward the future, not the past. What is important is what you choose to do from this moment forward."

Her eyes softened, though doubt lingered. "That is a rare perspective, Lord Golding. Your kindness is appreciated, but my path is one of repentance. Good day, my lord." With a grace that felt like a queen dismissing her subject, she stepped away, her figure soon flanked by two guards who escorted her from the hall.

As Brian watched her leave, an unfamiliar feeling stirred within him—a connection, an emotion he didn't quite understand. Her sadness left a trail in her wake, and all he wanted to do was hold her and tell her everything was going to be all right. Seriously, what was going on with him today?

CHAPTER 86

The Happy Couple

Rodrigo and I reveled in the camaraderie and love of our friends surrounding us when he suddenly leaned in close and whispered in my ear. His playful grin lit up his face as he took my hand and led me out of the room. Before our friends had a chance to notice our absence, we were already climbing the grand staircase, our laughter echoing through the quiet corridors. He paused at our chamber door and, with a triumphant grin, scooped me up and carried me across the threshold.

Inside, the room was aglow with the soft light of flickering candles. A large tub of steaming water awaited me, delicate ripples shimmering on its surface. With a knowing look, the maid added a fragrant oil to the water before quietly exiting.

Rodrigo kissed my forehead, his eyes filled with excitement. "Take your time and enjoy your bath, my love. I'll join you soon." His words wrapped around me like an intimate embrace as I made my way to the inviting bath, the steam rising like tendrils of magic.

Twenty minutes later, I emerged from the tub and slipped into a silk nightgown. As I brushed my damp hair, a sense of anticipation coursed through me. I climbed into bed and waited nervously for Rodrigo. Moments later, he entered, the smoldering desire in his eyes making my heart race.

"Lady Gutiérrez, are you ready to consummate our marriage?" he teased, his soft murmur laced with both mischief and tenderness.

"Yes," I replied with a nervous laugh as his dark eyes held mine. The intensity in his gaze sent a flush to my cheeks, and my breath hitched as he leaned in, his lips brushing mine with a gentleness that belied the hunger simmering beneath.

Our lips met tenderly at first, a hesitant exploration. However, as the moments passed, the kiss deepened. The nervous flutter in my chest dissolved, replaced by an intense passion and desire that made my core clench. Rodrigo's hand slid to the small of my back, pulling me closer, while his other hand cradled my face, his thumb softly stroking my cheek.

The world around us dissolved, leaving only the quiet hum of the crackling fire and the steady cadence of our breathing. We moved together in perfect harmony as if we'd danced this intimate waltz a thousand times before. Every touch, every sigh, every whispered murmur wove an unbreakable bond, solidifying our love in ways words could never capture. Time seemed to stretch and blur, the boundaries between us fading as we explored the contours of each other's hearts and bodies. The night embraced us in its quiet intimacy, a witness to the promises we made without speaking. The world fell away, leaving only us wrapped in a haven of love, peace, and a shared future that began in this perfect, tender moment.

As dawn broke, Rodrigo held me close, gazing at me with a love that made my heart swell. We shared a gentle embrace, the memory of our union still fresh between us. When I noticed a small splotch of red on the sheets, I flushed with embarrassment.

"Maryann, please don't be embarrassed. I cannot express how honored I am to be your first," he said softly, his voice filled with reverence and love. "I hope I didn't hurt you too much."

"There was only a moment of pain, but it quickly faded into pure pleasure," I reassured him, a mischievous grin curling my lips. "Dear husband, I look forward to exploring the art of lovemaking further if you have the patience to teach me."

He chuckled, a glint of mischief in his eyes. "You vixen. I'll have to check my busy schedule to see if I can arrange some time for that, my dear," he replied with a crooked, sexy smile.

I playfully smacked his arm and snuggled closer, feeling grateful for my decision to remain a virgin until marriage. We were blissfully content, our hearts full and our souls intertwined.

CHAPTER 87

Lady Magdalena

One crisp morning, several weeks after our wedding, an unexpected visitor arrived at the castle—Paulo. He approached Lord Rodrigo, his face etched with concern. "Sir, may we speak in private? It's about Lady Magdalena."

Rodrigo hesitated but then nodded. "It's all right, Paulo. You may speak freely in front of Lady Maryann."

Paulo took a deep breath. "I fear for Lady Magdalena's health—both physically and mentally. She hardly eats, and I'm deeply concerned that she is losing her will to live." His voice quivered with genuine concern.

I reached for Rodrigo's hand. "Perhaps she would fare better here in the castle near her child," I suggested softly. "Now that we're married, she poses no threat to us, and with Sophia nearby, she might find peace. We have to show her compassion in her suffering."

Rodrigo studied me for a moment, the weight of the decision evident in his eyes. "If you're certain, my love, I will allow her to stay under one condition: Paulo must keep an eye on her to ensure she doesn't harm herself or others."

"I am certain of it. Thank you, Rodrigo," I replied, my heart swelling with gratitude.

The following day, we met a much-changed Lady Magdalena. She appeared thin and tired, a shadow of her former self, her eyes heavy with an unspoken sadness. Her once radiant complexion was now pale, her once lively eyes dull, yet she was still beautiful. She greeted us silently before following a maid to her new chamber, and her fragile demeanor tugged at my heart.

Later that evening, Lady Magdalena appeared refreshed and rested when she entered the dining room. She exuded a newfound tranquility, and her face appeared softer and more at peace. Before taking her seat, she turned to me, her voice gentle yet firm.

"Lady Maryann, I owe you an apology. I used to be envious of your bond with Lord Gutiérrez, and my actions were inexcusable. I am partly responsible for Father Santiago's treatment of you and am deeply sorry. Seeing you both together now, I realize how perfect you are for each other."

Tears welled in my eyes as I acknowledged her words, grateful for this moment of honesty.

Lady Magdalena then turned to Rodrigo, her vulnerability palpable. "Lord Gutiérrez, I am so regretful of my past actions. I once believed that I loved you. I longed to be the lady of this castle. But I now understand that those feelings stemmed from my insecurities. I thought achieving that role would fill the void within me—but I was mistaken." She paused, her head bowed. "Please forgive me."

Rodrigo responded kindly yet firmly. "Lady Magdalena, I accept your apology. You are welcome to stay here indefinitely. If you choose to bond more with Sophia and transition to full-time motherhood, know that we will support you—but ultimately, the choice is yours."

"Thank you," she said, her voice trembling. "I'm unsure if I can be a good mother, but I want to try. I hope that one day, Sophia can learn to love me."

"Please take a seat, Lady Constanza," I said, my voice shaky. The gravity of the moment weighed heavily on me. "I'd like you to meet a dear friend of mine, Lord Brian Golding of Germany." Turning to Brian, I said, "Lord Golding, may I present Lady Magdalena Constanza?"

Brian stood and bowed gracefully, kissing Lady Magdalena's hand, and gave her one of his charming smiles. "It's a pleasure to see you again, Lady Constanza."

Brian then turned to me and grinned sheepishly. "Lady Constanza and I became acquainted at your wedding."

As the meal progressed, I caught subtle glances between them, each look brimming with unspoken fascination. Brian seemed utterly entranced by her beauty and newfound grace. Beneath the layers of her past misdeeds and mischief, I sensed a transformation happening within Lady Magdalena. She'd shown strength and courage by apologizing to me and Rodrigo. Perhaps redemption was not just possible for Lady Magdalena—maybe it had already begun.

CHAPTER 88

Confessions and New Beginnings

Days later, Brian came upon a radiant Lady Magdalena laughing in the garden with Sophia, the morning light casting a bright halo of sunshine over them. Brian's heart fluttered as he watched the pure joy on Lady Magdalena's face as she interacted with her daughter. Summoning his courage, he approached her.

"Lady Constanza, you look lovely today. It's so heartwarming to see you and your daughter together enjoying yourselves," he said, smiling affectionately at mother and daughter.

Lady Magdalena's eyes brightened as she looked up, her face a mixture of surprise and delight. "Thank you, Lord Golding. It's nice to see you as well." Her grin widened. "Would you like to join us? I'd love to hear more about your life in Germany."

With a shy grin, Brian took a seat nearby. "There's not much to tell," he replied modestly. "My family originated from Germany generations ago, and I've recently inherited a modest estate along the Rhine. My real passion is writing—especially about events that shape our world." He paused, glancing at her. "But I'd much rather hear about you, Lady Magdalena."

Lady Magdalena's eyes softened as a shadow crossed her face. "My past has been difficult. Do you really want to hear about it?" she asked.

"Only if you want to talk about it. It might help release pent-up emotions you may still be carrying around," he replied, smiling encouragingly.

"All right, but you might be sorry you encouraged me, Lord Golding," she said in a serious tone. Taking a deep breath, she began. "When I was eleven years old, my mother and I moved into a room above the tavern where she worked. When she was working, I was left unattended. One day, I was playing in the alley behind the tavern when two men approached me."

She paused to dab her eyes, her voice shaking. "They attacked and beat me, leaving me unconscious. My mother discovered me a few hours later and took me to a Catholic convent to recover, but she never returned. Living there was a nightmare; I endured grueling chores and long hours of prayer, during which I was punished if I fell asleep. After two years, I ran away.

"I'm sorry, Lord Golding. This is hard for me," she said, dabbing her moist eyes.

"Take your time, Lady Magdalena. You're doing well," he encouraged, squeezing her hand.

"I was lucky to meet a kind woman who took me in, but she passed away several years later. Homeless and desperate, I turned to prostitution. One day, I met Lord Rodrigo at a restaurant. Believing he was interested in me, I drugged his mead and stole his coins to pay for a room."

Fidgeting, Magdalena continued, "The next morning, he assumed we had been intimate, but we hadn't. I was already pregnant. I lied and told him the child was his. He did the honorable thing, and we became engaged. I am now ashamed of my actions."

She lifted her gaze with determination and continued. "After Sophia's birth, I felt hope for the first time and wanted to change. Afraid and unsure where to start, I gave her over to Lord Rodrigo, knowing she would have a better life, though it nearly broke me," she added, hands shaking.

"Lady Maryann showed me kindness when she arrived at the castle, but I was jealous and tried to make her life difficult. Amazingly, she kept forgiving me. I'm learning to forgive myself by Lady Maryann's example. But it was Sophia who gave me the reason to live."

Brian gazed at the lovely woman pouring her heart out and admired her strength. "Lady Magdalena, you shouldn't be ashamed of your past. What matters is what you do from here on. Seek Lady Maryann's friendship—it could lead to something good."

"Thank you for listening, Lord Golding. I've never shared my story. I feel lighter and freer," she said with a radiant smile.

CHAPTER 89

Pelota Ball

In recent weeks, Brian had spent much of his time with Lady Magdalena. He appreciated her intelligence and wit. Although he intended to propose, he didn't want to put any pressure on her because she was still in the process of discovering herself.

Today marked the first official pelota game to be played on the newly constructed pelota court, built by Rodrigo's workers. Magdalena and Brian were to face off against Rodrigo and Maryann. Although the game of pelota is ancient, it is very similar to the more modern American handball game.

The ball was three-quarters the size of a baseball, made from virgin rubber, and covered in linen thread and goatskin. The objective of the game was for each player to hit the ball with the palm of their hand hard enough for it to connect with the wall and bounce back to the opposing team. The first team that failed to hit the wall with their ball would lose the round. The team that won the most out of ten rounds would be the champion.

They positioned themselves within the pelota court and prepared to face off against each other. Brian served the first ball, and Rodrigo easily volleyed it back. They continued hitting the ball back and forth until Maryann got a hit in. After she hit the ball, it bounced back to Magdalena, and then the women volleyed back and forth until Magdalena missed the wall, making their team lose the round. For never having played before, she quickly grasped the rules of the game. By the middle of the game, their team was slightly ahead of Rodrigo and Maryann, but in the end, Rodrigo and Maryann won by one point.

After switching sides, the competition grew fiercer. In game ten, the men picked up the pace. They began volleying the ball back and forth so hard that the women stepped out of the court to let them finish the game one-on-one.

After leaving the court, Magdalena and I sat down on a nearby bench under a large, shaded willow tree, in clear view of the men as they continued their fierce, competitive game.

Turning toward her, I asked, "Have you ever played pelota before, Lady Magdalena?" My curiosity was evident in my voice.

"No, this is my first time, Lady Maryann. Have you ever played?" she asked, smiling.

"Yes, I have, although it wasn't called pelota," I replied. I thought back to the handball game I had played just days before my fateful flight. The wind suddenly picked up, and a few leaves from the tree scattered around the bench where we sat.

"I'm so happy to see you doing so well, Lady Magdalena," I exclaimed, smiling. "And it delights me that you and Lord Golding appear to be getting along so well!"

"I'm working hard to better myself, Lady Maryann," she responded, smiling and nodding. "But when I think back on my past bad behavior, it makes me shrink. I now realize that I craved attention because of my insecurities. It was like I was caught in a vicious cycle of self-destructive behavior, but I couldn't seem to stop myself. I know that you tried to get through to me, but at the time, I only saw you as an adversary." A shadow of sadness passed over her features.

"We can only move forward in our lives by learning from our past mistakes," I said, smiling encouragingly. "You shouldn't feel ashamed, Lady Magdalena. Look how far you have come, my friend!" I squeezed her hand in support.

"I'm happy we've become friends, Lady Maryann. You know, I always admired you in secret, although I certainly didn't show it, did I?" she said with a laugh. "As for my relationship with Lord Golding, it's going very well, but he seems to be taking forever to ask for my hand. I've dropped numerous hints, but they don't seem to be getting through to him." She smiled, almost rolling her eyes.

I burst out laughing. "Oh, Lady Magdalena, I believe you may be the perfect match for Lord Golding. It's obvious to everyone how you both feel about one another. He's probably just giving you more time to discover yourself. I'm so proud of you, my friend. It's incredible how you've turned your life around in such a short time. I always knew you could do it!" I said, smiling proudly.

"Thank you, Lady Maryann," she replied, giggling. "I'm enjoying life so much now that I am making a real effort to be a better person and a good mother to Sophia. I'm so in love with my wonderful daughter, and I cannot imagine life without her. And without your friendship and kindness over the last few weeks, I don't think I could have come this far."

"I'm glad we're finally friends, Lady Magdalena," I said. "It has made me incredibly happy to watch your amazing transformation!"

Suddenly, the men cheered in triumph, jumping around the court with their arms raised, yelling, "It's a tie, it's a tie!"

Lady Magdalena and I just looked at each other and laughed as the men entertained us with their silly antics.

CHAPTER 90

Bruno and Esmeralda's Nuptials

After a joyful yet brief courtship, the wedding day of Bruno and Esmeralda had arrived. Several large pavilions had been set up on the castle grounds for the special day. The castle staff had prepared a succulent smoked pig on a spit, along with several delicious vegetable side dishes and an array of colorful fruits and mouth-watering desserts, and the aroma of freshly baked bread filled the air.

Romani caravans had begun arriving the night before, bringing dozens of guests dressed in brightly colored attire. It was heartwarming to see all the additional faces that had also arrived from the Spanish communities to show their support for the happy couple. The castle courtyard bustled with activity as the lines between the Romani and Spanish communities seemed to blur, their differences melting away in shared joy.

A lone guitarist began to play a lovely Romani song as Mistress Esmeralda slowly emerged from the crowd. She walked gracefully toward Bruno, dressed in a stunning, colorful, and elaborate traditional Romani gown, with a matching headscarf. Beautiful golden earrings adorned her ears, and her long hair was worn loosely, nearly touching the ground.

At the head of the room, Stefan Pilato stood proudly next to his nephew, Bruno. "You look a bit nervous, nephew," he said jokingly in a low voice. "If you can't manage your bride, I'd happily take on the task. It will stay in the family, eh?" He chuckled as he winked. "But first, let's get you married." Then he cleared his voice and began.

"Bruno Pilato, do you promise to be true and love Mistress Esmeralda Portola for better or worse during your marriage?" Stefan asked.

Bruno clasped Esmeralda's hand, his voice low and respectful as he vowed his love. "With all that I am, I swear to love this woman and honor her above all else."

"Mistress Esmeralda, do you promise to be true and love Bruno for better or worse during your marriage?" Stefan asked.

The crowd watched, enraptured, as Esmeralda stepped forward and softly spoke with equal sincerity. "Yes, I will love Bruno for all my days," she declared, her voice firm. "And with luck, I will give him many Pilato sons!" She smiled radiantly.

A wave of applause rose from the crowd as Stefan proclaimed them wed. Without hesitation, Bruno swept Esmeralda into his arms, their kiss igniting cheers from the guests as the celebration began in earnest.

Everyone was in high spirits as the festivities began. Couples began dancing to the lively music played by a solo guitarist. I noticed Grandmama Portola dancing slowly off to the side with one of the older Romani gentlemen, and it brought a smile to my face. Even Rodrigo jumped into the fray of people and tried his best to emulate the Romani dancing style. As the women giggled, they rallied behind him. Watching Rodrigo dance filled me with joy.

From the corner of my eye, I observed Brian and Lady Magdalena sneaking away, hand in hand. Love was definitely in the air.

CHAPTER 91

The Proposal

The Romani wedding festivities were beginning to wind down when Brian took Lady Magdalena's hand and guided her to a secluded bench within the castle gardens under a twilit sky painted with hues of pink and lavender. She looked up at him, curiosity bright in her eyes.

"Lady Magdalena," he began, his voice thick with emotion. "I won't mince words. I've fallen in love with you and wish to make you my wife." He paused, inhaling deeply. "But before you answer, there is something you must know."

Her eyes softened. "Please, continue," she whispered encouragingly, her eyes steady, yet something in her expression told him she understood this was no ordinary confession.

Brian lowered his voice, his heart thundering. "What I'm about to share must remain between us," he said, glancing around. "Lady Maryann and I . . . we're from the twenty-first century." Lady Magdalena's eyes widened, yet she sat perfectly still, only a slight tremor in her fingers betraying her surprise.

Brian continued, confiding in her his greatest secret. "Lady Maryann and I were once engaged, but she ended our relationship months before traveling to Zafra. We remained friends, and when she vanished, I went to Zafra to search for her. Upon my arrival, I discovered a pair of partially buried ancient Celtic stone pillars. When I touched them, I heard a haunting melody just before losing consciousness. When I awoke, I found myself in this century."

Lady Magdalena gasped but quickly recovered, her steady eyes on Brian as she leaned in closer. Brian dropped to one knee, reverently taking her hand in his. "Lady Magdalena, would you do me the honor of becoming my wife and returning with me to the twenty-first century? I wish to legally adopt Sophia as well, with your permission, of course."

Dead silence followed for what seemed like an eternity, and Brian's heart sank into his stomach. What had he been thinking, expecting her to believe all this, let alone agreeing to leave her whole life behind for him?

The drawn-out silence continued between them until Lady Magdalena finally drew a breath. "Lord Golding," she began, her voice soft yet determined, "I would follow you across centuries as long as you will accept me along with my past indiscretions."

Brian lifted her hands to his lips, his gaze unwavering. "Lady Magdalena, you are the bravest soul I know," he murmured. "The past is a chapter we've both left behind. If anything, I admire you more and am more certain than ever that I want to share my life with you."

Lady Magdalena's bottom lip quivered slightly before a soft smile broke out across her lovely face. She leaned toward Brian, her lips a breath away. "Lord Golding," she whispered with a sly sparkle in her eye, "I may know where you can find a pair of Celtic stones here in Zafra!"

With awe, wonder, and love in his eyes, Brian rose in one smooth motion and gathered her into his arms, sealing their love with a passionate kiss.

CHAPTER 92

The Announcements

The joy was palpable as friends and loved ones gathered around the formal dining room. Brian stood up at one end of the table and cleared his throat. "Friends, I want to announce some wonderful news. Lady Magdalena has accepted my wedding proposal! We plan to get married as soon as possible and embark on a trip to Germany the day after our wedding. I have inherited a sizable estate on the Rhine River in Germany, and we plan to make it our permanent home." Glasses clinked, toasts were raised, and laughter echoed across the room.

Still standing, Brian's eyes fixed lovingly on Lady Magdalena. "I am endlessly grateful for Lady Magdalena, my soon-to-be wife," he said, his voice full of pride. "And to Lord Rodrigo and Lady Maryann for welcoming us with such open hearts."

Rodrigo rose next, his eyes softening as he regarded the couple. "Let us raise our cups and toast Lady Magdalena and Lord Brian! And we are all so proud of Lady Magdalena and the wonderful mother she has become to Sophia." Rodrigo cleared his throat as he continued. "Lord Brian, I know you'll be a steadfast husband and a good father," he stated, as he smiled at his friend. Claps and cheers filled the room.

When it had quieted down again, I stood up and raised my cup. "To Lord Brian and Lady Magdalena," I declared. "I wish you all the joy and love that life offers."

"And," I turned to Rodrigo and smiled shyly as I clasped his hand, "I also have an announcement . . . Lord Rodrigo and I are expecting a child!"

Rodrigo shot to his feet with a joyful grin and laughed out loud as he lifted me into his arms. Cheers erupted around the table, and in that perfect moment, surrounded by laughter and love, I looked into Rodrigo's eyes and knew my happiness was complete—save for one truth he still struggled to believe.

CHAPTER 93

Eve of Brian and Magdalena's Wedding

The castle was abuzz with activity as the final wedding preparations were underway. While Lady Magdalena was trying on the gown that Maria had made her, Brian found his way to Rodrigo's study, determined to convey the truth of his and Lady Magdalena's impending journey—a truth Rodrigo had so far been reluctant to accept. They planned to depart the day following their wedding ceremony, with everyone believing they'd be sailing for Germany. Only a select few, including Maria and Bruno, were aware of their intended passage through time.

Pouring brandy into two glasses, Rodrigo welcomed Brian with an affectionate pat on the back. "Congratulations on your upcoming nuptials tomorrow, Brian."

"Thank you, Rodrigo," Brian said, accepting the brandy respectfully.

"I'm so happy for you and Lady Magdalena. I know you will both be wonderful parents to Sophia. And I must say that I'm amazed at Lady Magdalena's positive transformation in such a short time. It's truly remarkable!" Rodrigo raised his glass. "I hope we'll stay close despite the distance. You will always be welcome here."

Brian sighed with disappointment tinged with sadness. "Rodrigo, we've discussed this. Lady Magdalena, Sophia, and I are bound for the year 2026." He paused, hoping his sincerity would bridge the gap between belief and disbelief. "Perhaps if you came with us to the Celtic stones, you could witness it firsthand."

Rodrigo chuckled skeptically in response to Brian's proposal. "Your loyalty to this tale is admirable. But no, I won't join in what I believe is folly. I have instead a different gift for you and Lady Magdalena."

Rodrigo retrieved a small velvet pouch from his desk and handed it to Brian. Inside, Brian found a collection of twenty gold Spanish coins, each one gleaming with immense value.

"Rodrigo, this is too much. In my time, these coins could fetch a fortune," Brian said, overwhelmed.

Rodrigo chuckled, impressed by the idea. "Then consider it a head start on a life of comfort. I may not share your belief, but I do value your friendship. Take it as a token of our bond."

Brian's gratitude softened his voice. "Thank you. You have my deepest respect and admiration. I am grateful you and Lady Maryann have found such joy together." They exchanged farewells, yet Brian felt the familiar ache of Rodrigo's disbelief as he left. He resolved to speak with Maryann one last time before their departure.

It was the day of Brian and Lady Magdalena's wedding, and most of the castle staff were busily preparing the celebratory feast. I was still abed, my head nestled in Rodrigo's lap while enduring another wave of morning sickness.

"Brian and I spoke again last night," Rodrigo murmured, stroking my hair. "He still insists he's taking Lady Magdalena and Sophia to another century. Maryann, I've been trying to push this notion of time travel aside, but it lingers. Nonetheless, the only truth that matters is that we are here together with a child on the way."

I took his hand, my gaze steady. "It pains me that you don't believe me, Rodrigo. If you accompanied us to the stones, you could witness their departure. But if you don't see it, I can hardly expect you to understand."

Rodrigo frowned, letting out a deep sigh. "The answer is no, Maryann. They're departing by ship tomorrow. I've seen the manifest myself." He hugged me close. "Please, let's not argue, my love. I don't wish to upset you."

Though frustration simmered within me, I managed a calm expression, squeezing his hand as I considered my options. A reckless idea surfaced: What if I could somehow bring Rodrigo to the Celtic stones and force him to witness Brian's journey through time with his own eyes? But how? The wedding left precious little time. I needed help.

Several hours later, Amalia arrived with an elegant gown Maria had fashioned for me to wear to the wedding. I embraced her warmly. "Please thank your aunt. Her work is stunning," I said, admiring the fine craftsmanship. "I'll see you and Maria at the ceremony soon!"

As Amalia departed, I glanced out the window, determination settling over me. Tomorrow would be a test for Rodrigo and me. I was determined that one way or another, he would be going to the Celtic stones to witness the departure of Brian and Lady Magdalena.

CHAPTER 94

Brian and Magdalena's Nuptials

Rodrigo and I descended the grand staircase and encountered Brian and Pedro in quiet conversation. We joined them and headed toward the chapel, where Bruno and Esmeralda waited patiently. Maria and Amalia stayed behind to assist Lady Magdalena with her final preparations. Excitement was palpable in the air.

The small white chapel was beautifully adorned with vibrant flowers arranged throughout the church. I noticed a gleaming new harpsichord set to one side, a lovely addition. I leaned into Rodrigo with a playful grin, gesturing to the instrument. "Husband, do you know if anyone will play today?" I asked, smiling as I nodded toward the harpsichord.

Rodrigo's eyes lit up, and a glimmer of admiration softened his expression. "Would you like to play the harpsichord for the service, my dear?" he asked. "With all your other talents, I wouldn't be surprised if you were also a gifted musician."

"Well, I know a few tunes." I laughed softly. "There's a piece from my homeland, a simple wedding song. It's called 'Here Comes the Bride.'"

Rodrigo's expression shifted, his fondness evident. "Then it will be beautiful, just as you are," he said, brushing a light kiss on my cheek.

A gentle hush fell ove[illegible]hapel as I began to play the song's first notes. Brian nodded at me gr[illegible]e recognized the music and mouthed, "Thank you."

Standing before Father Díaz, Brian straightened, his face a mixture of nerves and joy as Lady Magdalena appeared at the chapel doors. Her white gown was elegant yet unpretentious, framing her in soft lines that caught the golden light. Loose curls fell down her back, adorned by a simple crown of flowers, and her eyes sparkled, her smile shy yet unwavering. Brian's eyes filled with love and admiration, clearly unable to look away from his bride.

Glancing over, I could understand his awe. Lady Magdalena moved with such grace that it seemed time had paused in her honor. When their hands joined, I had to blink away my tears. Leaning into Rodrigo, I felt his arm tighten around me, a steadying comfort as happiness filled me to the brim.

After the brief, heartfelt ceremony, we gathered outside the chapel to embrace the newlyweds, sharing laughter and congratulations. The tables under the pavilion were laden with food and drink, prepared with loving care by Clara and her kitchen staff. For once, I was not nauseous, so I gratefully ate and enjoyed the abundant bounty of food and the delicious flavors of the dishes before me.

CHAPTER 95

Brian

As soon as the lovely wedding was over, Rodrigo was called away, leaving me with a precious moment to approach Brian while he was momentarily unoccupied. I took a steadying breath and moved toward him. "Brian, congratulations! Please forgive me for intruding so soon after your wedding, but I need to talk to you. It's important."

He nodded, his expression softening with understanding. "It's all right. Tell me what's on your mind."

I bit my lip, gathering my thoughts. "As you know, Rodrigo refuses to believe in time travel. He still insists you and Lady Magdalena are bound for Germany simply because your names are on the ship's manifest. I begged him to accompany me to the stones tomorrow to witness your departure, but he refuses. I know it's a great deal to ask, but would you help me find a way to ensure his presence when you leave?"

Brian sighed deeply, glancing toward the horizon as though gathering courage. "I knew this moment would come," he said, his voice laced with sadness. "After my conversation with Rodrigo last night, I realized he is still deeply skeptical—almost painfully so. He cares for you more than anything, but his need for tangible proof outweighs his trust. I don't want his disbelief to chip away at the love you share. If this plan is what's needed, I'm willing to help."

Relief washed over me, and I placed a hand over my heart. "Thank you, Brian. If I can gain Bruno's cooperation, we might be able to make this work.

Rodrigo must be near the carriage. If he's close enough, perhaps the two of you could secure him inside. I know it's asking the impossible—"

He placed a reassuring hand on my shoulder. "Say no more. I will help. Speak to Bruno. I'll do whatever I can to see this through, even if it risks Rodrigo's wrath."

CHAPTER 96

Bruno

I spotted Bruno by the pavilion, sipping a mug of mead. It was now or never. I had to speak with him. Willing myself to remain calm, I took a deep breath and braced myself for his reaction to what I was about to ask.

"Bruno, when you arrive tomorrow to pick up Brian, Lady Magdalena, and Sophia for their journey to the stones, I need your help gagging and restraining Rodrigo before placing him in the carriage."

Bruno's eyes bulged, and he laughed loudly before seeing my serious expression. He quickly steeled himself. "Forgive me, Maryann. I could have sworn you just asked me to gag, restrain, and kidnap your husband," he replied. "Boy, it's been a long day!"

I could have wept. Forcing the man I loved to go anywhere against his will was the last thing I wanted. But it was for the greater good. "No, you heard me correctly," I said with a hint of desperation. "Rodrigo must witness Brian and his family's departure through the stones to see the truth with his own eyes. He's convinced that I've deceived him about my arrival here, and if he continues down this path, it may destroy the love and trust we share."

Bruno studied me for a long moment before sighing. "Very well. It's an extreme measure, but one I understand. I've come to care deeply for you and Rodrigo both."

A wave of gratitude filled me, and I clasped his hand, my relief spilling over. "Thank you, Bruno. I can't express how much this means. You'll not only be helping Rodrigo witness the miracle of time travel, you'll also be helping to secure our future together."

The weight of our plan hung heavily in the air, yet as I looked toward Rodrigo in the distance, I knew this was our best, if not only, chance.

CHAPTER 97

A Moment of Peace

Rodrigo stood near the church, waving goodbye to the priest as he rode away in his carriage. When I reached him, I met his affectionate gaze as he turned to me and folded his arms around me. I let out a soft sigh as he tucked my head beneath his chin, the familiar strength of his embrace making me feel safe and cherished.

"Wasn't it a beautiful wedding?" I murmured, the joy of the day still lingering.

Rodrigo's smile softened as he looked down at me, his voice a warm rumble. "It was magnificent. To see Lady Magdalena transform so fully and find such happiness is a wonder. She and Sophia reunited at last, and now with Brian, she has found love and a new life. Three weddings in such a short time . . ." He leaned toward me, a playful glint in his eye. "Perhaps there is something in the air," he teased, brushing a light kiss across my forehead. We shared a quiet laugh before Brian appeared nearby, clearing his throat with a grin.

"Lady Golding and I are returning to the castle, as we need to rest and prepare for our journey tomorrow," he announced, but his sparkling eyes gave away his true intent. Laughter rippled through our group, each of us fully aware of the newlyweds' eager anticipation to spend their first night together as husband and wife.

The joy was infectious, and as I looked around, I felt deeply grateful to be surrounded by such love and companionship.

CHAPTER 98

Last-Minute Planning

Before retiring for the evening, I felt compelled to speak with Maria. She'd been good to me, and she deserved to know the truth of what I was planning. When I reached her chambers, I gave a gentle knock. The door opened almost immediately, and Maria greeted me with a bright smile.

"Lady Maryann! What a lovely surprise," Maria exclaimed, gesturing for me to enter. "Please, sit down. You look a bit worn out. Can I get you some water or a glass of wine?"

I settled into a chair. "No, thank you, Maria. I'm all right, just under a lot of strain," I replied, noticing the slight tremor in my hands. "And I might need your help tomorrow with something . . . difficult."

"Of course, whatever you need," she assured me, reaching out her hand to cover mine in a steadying touch. Her eyes were filled with concern. "You're worrying me. What's troubling you?"

I took a deep breath, my words faltering as I looked into her compassionate eyes. "Lord Brian and Bruno have agreed to subdue Lord Rodrigo tomorrow," I began. "The plan is for them to bind Lord Rodrigo, gag him if necessary, force him into the carriage at their departure, and make him witness Lord Brian and his family's disappearance through the stones." My voice dropped to a whisper. "I may need you to distract the guards as we approach the carriage."

Maria's eyes grew wide, but her expression quickly shifted to determination. "Lady Maryann," she said softly, "I'll help you. But please try to calm yourself. I agree this may be the only way to make Lord Rodrigo understand. I'll be ready. Tomorrow I'll keep an eye out from the kitchen window. Once Lord Brian and Lady Magdalena are in the carriage and I see you and Lord Rodrigo approaching, I'll handle the guards if necessary, depending on where they are. Don't worry—you can rely on me."

Grateful beyond words, I accepted the glass of wine she offered as she affectionately held my hand. "Thank you, Maria. I have to believe this will work."

"It will," she replied with quiet certainty. "Everything will fall into place, you'll see. Now, go get some rest. You can't let Lord Rodrigo sense your nerves, or he may grow suspicious." She gave my hand a final squeeze, then pulled me into a comforting hug.

"Good night, Lady Maryann. Tomorrow we'll see this through together."

CHAPTER 99

Departure Day

The castle was alive with activity on the morning of Brian, Lady Magdalena, and Sophia's departure. Servants darted about, gathering belongings and helping with the final packing. Lady Magdalena appeared radiant in a sky-blue dress that matched Sophia's adorable little outfit. Brian had chosen to wear his modern clothes, drawing a few curious glances but no comments.

Seated on a love seat, I patted the spot beside me, and Lady Magdalena took a seat while Brian held Sophia nearby. I could feel her nervous energy as she clasped her hands tightly in her lap, her eyes filled with excitement and apprehension. I reached over and held one of her hands. "Are you nervous?" I asked softly.

She nodded, letting out a small sigh that carried the weight of her worries. "Yes. I worry about adjusting to Brian's time. What if I embarrass him—or fail him as a wife? Sophia will adapt without even realizing it, but I worry. I don't want to disappoint him," she whispered.

I gave her a reassuring nod. "I once felt that same fear. When I realized I'd traveled back in time to this century, I was terrified—completely alone, keeping my secret, afraid to draw attention and risk exposure to the Inquisition. Ironically, my worry only brought more attention my way. And I even first thought of you as my enemy." I chuckled.

Lady Magdalena's cheeks flushed with regret. "Oh, Lady Maryann, I am so sorry. I was deeply jealous of you. At first, I thought to make you uncomfortable, but I never intended to do true harm to you. When I convinced Father Santiago you were a heretic, it spiraled out of control. I have lived with that guilt ever since," she said, sighing.

I gently patted her arm. "I forgave you long ago. Now it's time for you to forgive yourself. Trust me, Lady Magdalena, you will thrive in the twenty-first century. You already know about this journey. You have Brian by your side and a beautiful daughter to cherish. I promise you will learn to love the wonders of the future. And remember, in the future you'll need to drop the Lord and Lady titles when addressing others."

Her eyes filled with gratitude, and she embraced me tightly. "I will, and I appreciate the kindness and friendship you have shown me, Lady Maryann."

The clatter of wheels on cobblestone pulled me from our conversation—Bruno's carriage had arrived. My heart raced. Rodrigo hadn't come down yet. I leaned close to Brian. "Please don't leave without us. I'll go find Rodrigo."

Brian nodded as he and his family hurried toward the waiting carriage. Turning to Maria, I whispered, "I need your help. Rodrigo is somewhere in the castle!"

She placed a calming hand on my arm. "I'll search here. You check upstairs—and try not to worry. Everything will be fine."

I hurried up the stairs, starting in our chambers and then moving to the library. He wasn't in either. Suddenly, I remembered the war room on the top floor—a place I'd never ventured to. I climbed the last set of stairs, peeking into rooms along the corridor until I finally reached a larger door at the end of the hallway. Holding my breath, I knocked softly, and when no answer came, I turned the knob and slipped into the vast room.

Rodrigo was seated at the far end of a long wooden table facing a window, lost in thought. I cleared my throat to get his attention, and he turned, a welcoming, bright smile lighting his face.

"What brings you here, my love? Is everything all right?"

"Yes. Lord Brian, Lady Magdalena, and Sophia are waiting in the carriage. Will you come with me to see them off?" I asked, my voice a little breathless. "I may need to lean on you as we go down the stairs."

“Of course,” he replied, offering his arm. I rose on my tiptoes to kiss his cheek, then I looped my arm through his. As we walked down together, sweat trickled down my back, and my hands grew clammy. This plan was not for the faint of heart.

When we reached the main floor, Maria, watching from a nearby window, gave me a slight nod. “We’ll be back shortly, Maria.” I winked. “Just bidding our friends farewell.”

CHAPTER 100

A Kidnapping for the Greater Good

Bruno's carriage was parked a short distance from the castle, cleverly positioned out of view. My eyes darted from left to right. Not a guard was in sight. Bruno tipped his hat in greeting. Inside, Lady Magdalena was seated, her face calm yet hopeful, knowing her role in the plan. Brian stood waiting beside the carriage.

"I wish you and Lady Magdalena a safe journey," Rodrigo stated, sincerity shining in his eyes. "I enjoyed our time together. May fortune favor you and your family."

Brian clasped Rodrigo's shoulder. *This is going to be hard.* Brian then employed a sudden and unexpected kung fu maneuver that brought Rodrigo to the ground, his face slackened with surprise, and his eyes clouded with confusion. Checking to make sure he was not seriously harmed, Brian then loosely bound and gagged him. "I'm sorry, my friend. I didn't want to have to do this," he said regretfully.

"We must leave quickly," I urged, and Brian and Bruno helped place Rodrigo inside. I took the seat beside him and carefully removed his gag. Rodrigo's eyes met mine, a mix of shock and disappointment in his eyes. Brian and Lady Magdalena sat across from us as Bruno climbed to the driver's seat and started down the mountain road.

Looking into Rodrigo's confused face, I spoke, my tone heavy with regret. "I'm sorry, Rodrigo. None of this would have been necessary if you'd agreed to join us willingly. But I need you to see the truth of the stones for yourself."

Rodrigo's expression was unreadable as he leaned back, not saying a word. As the carriage reached the valley, Lady Magdalena signaled to Bruno, who slowed to a halt and guided the carriage off the road. We disembarked, and Brian removed Rodrigo's restraints.

We all walked along a narrow path toward the secluded clearing where the two Celtic stones were partially buried. Rodrigo, now intrigued and finally showing interest, moved closer to inspect the ancient carvings on the stone pillars.

I hugged Lady Magdalena tightly. "I wish you the best of luck. I know you'll adapt beautifully. Be happy, my friend."

Turning to Brian, I clasped his hand. "Thank you for being such a steadfast friend. I wish you and your family a wonderful life together."

Unexpectedly, Rodrigo stepped forward and placed his hands on Brian's shoulders. "Brian, I forgive you. I know your intentions were pure. But until I see you disappear, I cannot believe it. Still, I wish you both happiness."

As we stepped back, Bruno said his farewells, and Brian gathered Sophia close as Lady Magdalena took his arm. He squatted, pressing his hands to the stones. Suddenly, the ground trembled, and Lady Magdalena lost her footing and tumbled to the side.

I rushed to her without thinking, steadying her as the ground began to vibrate beneath me. I held onto her shoulders, guiding her back into Brian's arms—but before I could release her, a dizzying wave hit me. Everything blurred, and I heard Rodrigo loudly shouting my name, until his voice faded as darkness closed around me.

CHAPTER 101

Tragedy Strikes

Rodrigo's heart seized with fear as Maryann lunged forward to help Lady Magdalena. He called to her to be careful, but then the unthinkable happened, and he blinked as time seemed to stand still. They all vanished before his eyes. Rodrigo's stomach lurched, and he cried out in disbelief. Collapsing onto his knees, he sobbed and continued to call out to Maryann in anguish. Why hadn't he believed her? And more importantly, how was he ever going to get her back?

Turning to Bruno, his face paled with desperation. "Bruno, tell me how to return her! How do the stones work?" His voice was raw.

Bruno's expression was ashen, his voice faltering. "Place a hand on each stone and concentrate on Lady Maryann."

Rodrigo did as instructed, pressing his hands against the stones, but nothing happened. After several minutes, he dropped his hands, a guttural cry ripping from his chest as he fell to his knees. Tears streamed down his face. His heart ached with the thought that he had lost Maryann forever.

Bruno stepped closer, placing a gentle hand on Rodrigo's shoulder. "I'm sorry, Lord Rodrigo. The stones allow passage for some but not others, and there may be limits on how often one can travel through them. But if Lady Maryann can return, I know she will."

Rodrigo rose, his face etched with despair yet hardened with determination. "Then I will wait here until she does," he vowed, his voice resonating with his unwavering love for Maryann.

Bruno nodded solemnly. "As you wish, Lord Rodrigo. If I could bring her back myself, I would. But the mysteries of time travel are beyond my understanding."

CHAPTER 102

Back in the Twenty-First Century

Sprawled on the ground in the twenty-first century, Brian lay flat on his back, the baby safely snuggled against his chest. Magdalena was beside him, gripping his hand as they tried to orient themselves to their surroundings. I sat nearby, overcome with grief as tears spilled down my face.

"Maryann, what happened?" Magdalena asked, her voice trembling. "I thought you'd let go of me!"

Through my tears, I looked at them, the weight of my sudden separation from Rodrigo settling painfully. "I didn't mean to come with you," I said miserably. "And now I . . . I can't get back."

Brian frowned. "What do you mean? Why can't you return?"

I pointed at the Celtic stones. "I just tried going back before you both woke up," I whispered with grief. "Nothing happened."

"Don't worry, Maryann," Brian said softly, his voice calm. "We'll work it out. We're staying for at least a week. We can return to the stones tomorrow, and you can try again. Is there room for all of us at your cottage?"

"Yes, of course. There is plenty of space," I replied, though my voice was shaky. "I can sleep on the couch in the living room. Come on, let's go. I could use a hot shower and some comfortable clothes."

The walk to the cottage was short, but the stale smell of spoiled food hit us when I opened the door. I flung open the windows, propped the door wide to air it out, gathered the offending waste, and tossed it quickly into the bin outside.

"I'll head up the road to see if I can flag down a carriage," Brian said. "We need groceries. And when I get back, Maryann, could I use your computer to contact a friend to get proper documentation for Magdalena and the baby?"

"Of course," I replied, my voice thick with sadness. "I can't stop thinking about Rodrigo. He's probably waiting for me, expecting me to reappear." I covered my face as fresh tears started to fall.

"Brian, I'll stay with Maryann. You go to the market."

"All right, my love." Brian gave her hand a reassuring squeeze. "I'll be back soon. Why don't you two go back inside? The cottage should be aired out by now."

Magdalena and I stepped inside, closing the door against the chill. She held a sleeping Sophia in her arms as she looked around the room, her face filled with wonder. The room's cozy atmosphere enveloped us, and I could see the flicker of the fire in the fireplace reflecting in Magdalena's eyes.

"I'd like to look around after I put Sophia down for a nap. Is there somewhere I can lay her down?" Magdalena asked.

"Yes, of course," I replied. "You can lay her on the bed if you like."

Magdalena took a quilt from the love seat and carefully laid Sophia on the bed, covering her with the soft fabric. After planting a tender kiss on her daughter's forehead, she joined me in the kitchen.

I flicked on the overhead light, and Magdalena's eyes grew wide as she looked around in awe at the light and the modern appliances. Her eyes flitted from the refrigerator to the oven and finally the microwave. "Could you show me how everything works?" she whispered reverently, as if she were in the presence of the miraculous. For her, perhaps she was.

By the time Brian returned with the groceries, Magdalena was practically glowing from learning about the "magic" of modern technology. Brian set the bags on the counter. They were filled with chicken, fresh vegetables, and, to Magdalena's surprise, baby supplies: disposable diapers, formula, and bottles.

Magdalena reached for a disposable diaper, studying it curiously. "Brian, what are these?"

"Those are disposable diapers for the baby. You don't have to wash them. You just throw them away when soiled." He held up the formula. "This is a milk substitute for babies. Add a scoop to the bottle, mix in water, and heat it over the stove."

Magdalena's eyes lit up as she took it all in. "That's incredible!" she exclaimed, laughing. "Could you show me how to use it the first few times?"

"With pleasure," he replied with a grin. As he began putting away the groceries, Magdalena eagerly helped, soaking up each new detail.

I slipped away to the bathroom. Stepping into the hot shower, I sighed in pleasure, closing my eyes as the steaming water washed over me. As much as I missed Rodrigo, it felt heavenly to rinse off. Twenty minutes later, I dressed in comfortable yoga pants and a tank top, braided my hair loosely, and applied a hint of light pink lipstick to brighten my face.

Brian and Magdalena sat on the love seat in the living room, hands clasped. Magdalena's eyes widened when she saw my outfit.

"Before you say anything," I laughed, "let me show you what women's fashion looks like in the twenty-first century." I took her hand, led her into the bedroom, and opened my closet to reveal an array of dresses, blouses, skirts, and pants. Magdalena's mouth fell agape as I laid out fitted yoga pants, cargo shorts, and sundresses.

"Do women go about with their legs uncovered?" she asked, fingering the fabric with care.

"Absolutely! Here, try on anything you like. But first, you *must* try the shower." I grinned, guiding her into the bathroom. I explained the use of each fixture—the toilet, sink, and shower. "Here are some towels and a robe for afterward. I'll be in the other room if you need any help."

Magdalena gave a tentative nod, clearly overwhelmed but eager to try. I left her to explore, joining Brian in the living room. He gave me an encouraging smile.

"We'll go to the stones tomorrow," he said. "Just stay positive, all right? I'm certain you'll be back with Rodrigo soon."

"All right." To distract myself, I moved over to the old piano in the corner, closing my eyes as my fingers glided over the keys, filling the room with a calming melody.

A few minutes later, Magdalena appeared at the bedroom door wrapped in a robe, her hair loose and fresh from the shower. "Maryann, could you help me choose something suitable to wear?"

I winked at Brian, then followed her back to the bedroom. Twenty minutes later, Magdalena stepped out looking stunning. She wore a sky-blue sundress and wedge sandals, her hair falling in soft curls around her shoulders.

Brian's eyes widened in appreciation. "Magdalena," he said, his voice filled with admiration, "you look beautiful!"

Magdalena smiled shyly, the soft fabric of her dress rustling as she moved. She looked at me with a soft laugh and winked. "Now I understand why women wear these clothes—they're so flattering and comfortable!"

"Exactly!" I said, laughing with her.

Brian whistled, still visibly impressed. "Magdalena, you look incredible."

She flushed with pride, settling beside him on the love seat. Just then, I thought of something. "Magdalena, do you play chess? Brian is almost impossible to beat."

"Oh, I do play," she replied with a mischievous grin. "And I'd love to challenge Brian in a game."

Excited, I set up the chessboard and watched them engage in a strategy battle for the next hour. Finally, Magdalena moved her piece with a triumphant grin. "Checkmate!"

Brian's expression of surprise was priceless, and I clapped with laughter. "Well done, Magdalena! I've never seen Brian lose a game."

Outnumbered, Brian laughed in good humor and helped us set the table for dinner. Magdalena observed what I was doing as I cooked dinner. Forty minutes later, we sat down to eat, toasting with a glass of chardonnay that Brian had picked up.

After dinner, Magdalena began washing the dishes by hand. "Wait," I said, smiling, "you don't have to do that." I loaded the dishes into the dishwasher, explaining each step.

Magdalena's eyes sparkled. "The conveniences of this time are remarkable," she said.

Later, we gathered in the living room, and when Sophia stirred, Brian showed Magdalena how to prepare a formula bottle and use a disposable diaper. After feeding, Sophia quickly fell back asleep. Brian fashioned a makeshift crib from a laundry basket, lining it with soft blankets, and carefully placed Sophia inside, tucking her in.

"Good night, Maryann," said Brian, closing the door softly.

"Good night," I whispered, curling up on the love seat. As I drifted off, I held close the comforting thought that maybe tomorrow I would find my way back to Rodrigo.

CHAPTER 103

A Return Trip

The following day I woke up early, excited about returning to Rodrigo and the seventeenth century. I set the kettle on to boil, and as it began to whistle, Brian and Magdalena joined me. I prepared a light breakfast of scrambled eggs, toast, and fresh strawberries. While Brian took a shower, I tidied up the kitchen, and Magdalena fed baby Sophia.

We left the cottage thirty minutes later, taking off for the short hike to the Celtic stones. My stomach churned, my nerves winding tighter with each step. I took deep breaths, trying to keep calm as we walked the familiar path. Brian, who knew the way best, led the way. After following a narrow trail and turning off the main path, the clearing finally opened to reveal the ancient stones.

My heart pounded as I approached the stones, and I clutched the bag with the seventeenth-century clothes I'd brought. After I said goodbye to Brian and Magdalena, I wasted no time. I knelt between the stones, placing a hand on each. Closing my eyes, I focused on Rodrigo's face in my mind's eye. I waited, every second stretching painfully. Minutes passed, and still the stones remained silent. After fifteen minutes, I slowly stood, feeling the weight of defeat, and met Brian and Magdalena's sympathetic faces.

Unable to speak, I turned and began the walk back to the cottage in silence, every step taking me closer to my breaking point. Brian and Magdalena, as if sensing my need for solitude, stayed quiet. Back at the cottage, I took a detour to the stream beside it, needing time alone to process the reality that I would never see Rodrigo again—or that the child I carried would never meet his father.

It was more than I could bear.

CHAPTER 104

A New Start

Entering the cottage sometime later, I joined Brian and Magdalena, who were seated at the kitchen table with cups of tea, and they each took one of my hands. Brian spoke first, his voice calm and steady.

"Magdalena and I talked, and we'd like you to come live with us in Germany. The estate is enormous, and you'd have a suite of rooms all to yourself—and for the baby, of course."

"It's funny," I replied, managing a sad smile. "I was just thinking that I can't return to San Diego. I didn't realize it before, but a fresh start is just what I need."

The offer of a new life in Germany, albeit one without the love of my life, brought me some comfort amid my emotional turmoil.

Magdalena squeezed my hand with affection. "Maryann, you mean so much to us both. Please say you'll come. I am worried about the future and Sophia's adjustment, but I know we'll adapt with you. Our children can grow up together, and we'll be a family. You're the sister I always dreamed of. Please come with us."

Tears filled my eyes, and I dabbed them away, nodding. "Yes, I'd be honored. You have no idea how much this means to me. Thank you both."

Later that afternoon, I found my computer among my things and set it up for Brian on the kitchen table, plugging it in to charge. "Here you go, Brian," I said, handing him a sticky note with my username and password.

Brian logged in and opened his email to contact his friend Edgar, a tech-savvy friend from San Diego who specialized in creating fake identifications, passports, and birth certificates as a side job. In his message, Brian requested an expedited birth certificate, passport, and California identification card under the name Magdalena Constanza and a birth certificate for Sophia Golding. He then took several headshots of Magdalena with his phone, uploaded them, and attached them to the email before hitting send. Edgar replied ten minutes later, confirming he'd have the documents delivered to the post office in a few days.

As Brian continued working on the computer, I turned to him, thinking of my unfinished business. "Brian, since I'm here to stay, I must let the local authorities know I'm not missing. I'd also like to stop at the castle to let Francisco know I'm okay. Would you mind if I ride with you both to town?"

"Of course not," Brian replied. "Would you like company when you visit Francisco?"

"No, thank you. I'll be quick," I said, smiling. "I want to collect my painting and let Francisco and his father know I'm all right. But I need a story to explain my absence. Any suggestions?"

Brian's eyes lit up with a grin. "I have an idea. You could say your friend, Magdalena, who lives in France, was out shopping when her house burned down. She called you in a panic, so you rushed over and forgot your purse, but luckily you had enough cash for the ferry. You didn't bother packing because you thought it'd be a quick trip, and then you stayed to help her with the insurance claim before returning to Zafra."

"Wow, Brian." I laughed, impressed. "You're good at making up stories—no wonder you're such a great journalist!"

He chuckled. "I've spun a story or two in my day."

CHAPTER 105

Missing No Longer

After arriving in town, Brian thanked the carriage driver as we climbed down and gave him a generous tip. He and Magdalena headed to the post office, and I walked across the street to the police station. Entering the small building, I hesitantly approached the young receptionist and waited until she'd finished her phone call. As she hung up, she nodded to me in a welcoming, professional manner.

"Good morning, ma'am. Can I help you?"

"Yes, I hope you can," I replied, trying to ignore the nervous butterflies in my stomach. "My name is Maryann LeMaster, and I understand someone filed a missing person report on me. I'm here to clear that up. I've just returned from visiting a friend." I added a nervous laugh, wondering how long I'd been gone. It felt like months, but I'd yet to learn if time flowed the same here as in the past.

The receptionist scanned her files. "Yes, ma'am, the report was filed several months ago. I'm glad to see you're all right. Detective Romero is out today, but I can take your statement. He may still reach out to you with follow-up questions."

"That would be fine," I said. "I'm staying at the cottage outside town if the detective needs to reach me."

The receptionist introduced herself as Lucía and requested to see my identification before inviting me to sit with her. "Miss LeMaster, could you tell me why you left so suddenly and what happened while you were away?"

I nodded. "Of course. My friend Magdalena lives in France. She called me in a panic because her home burned down while she was out shopping. She was distraught and needed my help. I was so rushed to get there that I left without my wallet. Luckily, I had enough cash on me for the ferry. I thought it would be a short visit, but she asked me to stay until the claim was settled." I bit my lip, hoping I was pulling it off. "The process took longer than expected."

Lucía jotted down notes and looked up. "Thank you, Miss LeMaster. What's your friend's last name? And could I have a phone number where we can reach you?"

"Her name is Magdalena Constanza," I replied, giving her Brian's number since I hadn't yet found my cell phone.

"Thank you. That's all I need for now," Lucía said. "Detective Romero may reach out if he has additional questions. Would you like help arranging transportation?"

"Yes, thank you, Lucía," I replied, relieved. Outside, I sat on the bench and waited.

Several minutes later, the carriage pulled up. "Where to, ma'am?" the driver asked.

"The castle, please."

CHAPTER 106

Francisco

Twenty minutes later, I arrived at the castle. I asked the driver if he could wait ten minutes at the most, and he agreed. Stepping down from the carriage, I walked toward the castle, feeling a comforting wave of familiarity.

When Francisco opened the door, his expression shifted from shock to joy. "Miss Maryann, you're back!" His eyes shone with genuine care and happiness. "Please come in!"

"Thank you, Francisco," I said, feeling welcomed and trying to keep my emotions in check. I followed him to the parlor, where we sat across from one another while Francisco waited for me to begin the conversation.

"I'm so sorry for leaving Zafra so abruptly," I began. "A close friend of mine in France had an emergency—her home burned down, so I left to help her. In my rush, I forgot my purse. Once her insurance claim was settled, I returned to Zafra."

Francisco sighed, his face lighting up with visible relief. "I'm just glad to see you safe. We were quite worried. Your friend Brian came by too, hoping to find you. Did he succeed?"

"Yes, we met up soon after I returned," I assured him. As I spoke, my eyes drifted to the wall behind him, where my painting hung prominently. Emotions tightened in my throat. I couldn't ask for the painting. I feared Francisco would ask too many questions that I wasn't ready to answer. I held back.

Taking a deep breath, I stood. "I'm sorry to cut this visit short, Francisco, but I really must be going. I'm returning to the States in a few days, and there's so much to do before I leave. I just wanted to let you know that I'm all right. Thank you for everything, and please give my regards to your father and aunt."

Francisco nodded, his eyes reflecting with understanding. "Of course, Miss Maryann. Have a safe journey, and if you're ever back in the area, please visit us."

I impulsively hugged him, moved by feelings of gratitude and fondness. "Thank you for being such a wonderful friend, Francisco," I said, smiling as I headed back toward the waiting carriage.

CHAPTER 107

The Cottage

When I returned to the cottage, Brian and Magdalena were seated in the living room, chatting quietly. "Hey, how did everything go in town?" I asked.

"Very well," Brian replied. "We stopped by the post office and informed them I was expecting a package in the next few days. How was your interview at the police station?"

"It went smoothly," I replied. "Detective Romero wasn't in, so I gave my statement to Lucía, the receptionist. They'll close the file unless the detective has additional questions."

"And how did it go at the castle?" Brian asked.

"It went well," I said wistfully. "I told Francisco the same story. I wanted to ask for my painting back, but when I saw it on the wall, I just couldn't. I was afraid he would start asking questions about it."

Magdalena broke into a proud grin. "Maryann, I made dinner with Brian's help. Of course, he did most of the cooking, but it was a start." She laughed, sending Brian an appreciative look.

"That sounds wonderful!" I replied, feeling my stomach growl. We all sat at the table as Magdalena served us a delicious-looking stew filled with tender beef, potatoes, carrots, green beans, and onions. After my first spoonful, I sighed in appreciation.

"Oh, Magdalena, this is delicious! Thank you so much."

Blushing, she replied, "I'm glad you like it, Maryann. Cooking is so much easier here, I must say."

"Has Brian told you about cars and planes yet?"

"Yes," she replied, "but I haven't seen any here in Zafra."

"True, Zafra is charmingly traditional," I said. "But when we leave for the airport, we'll travel in a gas-powered bus—a vehicle that carries many people at once. Then, once we arrive at the airport, you'll experience flying for the first time!"

Magdalena's eyes widened. "I'm intrigued, though a bit nervous about the bus and the airplane. It's all so new to me."

"Don't worry," Brian assured her, reaching for her hand. "You'll get used to it soon enough. And remember, we'll both be there with you."

CHAPTER 108

The Trip to Town

The next few days drifted by in a rhythm of simple pleasures. We hiked through the countryside, played card games, and spent evenings filled with music and laughter. I entertained Magdalena with funny stories about Brian, and we all waited for the arrival of his package from Edgar. Finally, the call came from the post office—Brian's documents had arrived.

When we arrived in town, Brian and Magdalena headed straight for the post office. I spotted a small boutique across the street and decided to check it out. I found a lovely, delicate lilac chiffon dress and a pair of white low-heeled pumps for Magdalena.

Brian and Magdalena were waiting for me across the street as I exited the boutique with my gift-wrapped items. When I reached them, Brian grinned and said, "Ladies, how about lunch at the café on the corner?"

Magdalena and I answered yes in unison, giggling as we linked arms and walked over to an old-fashioned diner next door to the post office.

Seated in a booth by the window, the waitress turned to Magdalena first. "What would you like to drink, ma'am?"

Magdalena looked to me for help, so I ordered for us both. "We will both have iced tea, please. Brian, what are you drinking?"

"Iced tea sounds perfect. Thank you," Brian replied.

I skimmed the menu and was surprised to see American food included. "Well, I know what I'm getting!" I announced with a grin. "I've been craving a good cheeseburger. Magdalena, do you feel like trying something new?"

She nodded eagerly, taking a moment to tuck the baby blanket snugly around Sophia, who was sound asleep in the baby carrier. When the waitress returned, Brian ordered three cheeseburgers with fries. While we waited, he opened Edgar's envelope, skimming through the documents.

"Looks like everything's in order," he said, satisfied. "I've got our bus and plane tickets booked for the day after tomorrow."

Turning to Magdalena with a twinkle in his eye, he asked, "So, how about we get married again tomorrow? Just a quick civil ceremony at the courthouse—Maryann can be our witness. That way, our marriage will also be official in this century."

"Well, I don't know, Mr. Golding. It's all so sudden," she teased, pretending to consider. "But yes." She laughed, taking his hand. "I'd love to marry you tomorrow."

Brian's expression softened as he squeezed her hand. The waitress brought out our food, and Magdalena's eyes went wide at the sight of the cheeseburger and fries. Her face lit up with delight after first biting into the cheeseburger. "Oh my! This food is delicious!"

I couldn't help but agree between mouthfuls. "Oh, I've missed this so much."

Brian nodded in silent agreement, too busy enjoying his burger to answer.

Once home, I gave the gift-wrapped items to Magdalena and hugged her. "This is a little gift from me for your wedding tomorrow."

"You didn't have to buy me anything, but I am very grateful." She reverently took the package and pulled me into a tight hug.

CHAPTER 109

A Beautiful Daydream

I spread a blanket over a grassy patch under the shade of a willow tree by the stream. Lying back, I closed my eyes, and my thoughts immediately turned to Rodrigo. I soon drifted to sleep in the sun's warmth, a vivid dream washing over me.

Rodrigo held my hand as we strolled through the castle gardens. Suddenly, a small boy with light brown hair and bright green eyes peeked out from behind a bush, grinning mischievously.

"Boo, Mother and Father!" he squealed before giggling and hiding behind another shrub.

It was a beautiful day. Sunlight poured through the trees, and birdsong filled the air. Rodrigo stopped and pulled me into his arms. His eyes glowed with an intense love that made my breath catch. His gaze dropped to my lips as he leaned in, pressing a soft, tender kiss.

Then a small war cry broke the moment as our son charged forward. "Arm yourselves, lord and lady! Enemies are at the gates," he yelled with a fierce determination that made Rodrigo laugh.

With a sparkle in his eyes, Rodrigo scooped up our son, spinning him in circles as his laughter filled the air. My heart swelled with joy as I watched them, savoring the love and life we had created.

As my eyes fluttered open, I blinked back tears and gazed at the willow tree's sweeping branches. I knew something for sure in that moment, and it made my heart swell. We were going to have a son, and I'd have a piece of Rodrigo to carry forward with me.

CHAPTER 110

Lord Rodrigo's Loss

Rodrigo hadn't moved from the spot where his beloved Maryann had vanished. Leaving would mean accepting that she was gone, and he couldn't do that. The long hours dragged as if they were years, and exhaustion and resignation crept in as the sun set for the second time. The bleak possibility that she might never return, or perhaps had chosen not to, filled him with a hollow despair. He turned and began the solitary walk back to the castle, the familiar path now seeming cold and foreign.

How could he go on without her?

The weight of his actions sank heavily onto his shoulders. He'd refused to trust Maryann, forcing her to bear his doubts alone. Now his skepticism had cost him everything—the woman he loved and the unborn child he would never meet. His only heir was now destined to grow up in a world centuries away from his reach. By the time Rodrigo returned to the castle, darkness had settled over the grounds.

Paulo, his ever-loyal guard, approached him with concern. "Sir, is everything all right?" His voice was quiet, hesitant.

"No. Nothing is right," Rodrigo replied, his tone weary and broken. "My wife has vanished, and I fear I may never see her again."

The color drained from Paulo's face. "But what do you mean, sir? Is there anything I can do to help?"

"There is nothing to be done," Rodrigo said, his voice rough and strained.

"Forces beyond our control are at play, Paulo. Whether Lady Maryann will return is beyond any of us. Only time will tell." He left Paulo as he continued silently up the steps and into the castle.

In the dimly lit kitchen, Clara looked up, her eyes swollen and red from crying. "Is she gone, Lord Rodrigo?" she asked, trembling.

He stopped, his heart heavy. "Yes, Clara, she's gone. And worse, I can do nothing about it." He passed by her, feeling the weight of loss settle over him like a shroud.

For days, Rodrigo confined himself to his chambers, his once vibrant and noble countenance now a mask of despair. Clara delivered meals to his door, though the plates remained untouched. By the third day, however, he forced himself to bathe, to eat a small bite, and finally to step outside, hoping the fresh air might soothe his troubled mind.

CHAPTER 111

Guardian of the Stones

While out strolling through the castle gardens, Rodrigo noticed an older woman seated on the stone bench, her figure swathed in a heavy woolen shawl.

"Can I help you, madam?" he asked, puzzled by her presence. "Are you in need of assistance?"

The woman looked up, her dark eyes glinting with a strange familiarity. "Lord Rodrigo Gutiérrez," she said in an inviting and steady voice. "I am Juanita Gutiérrez, a descendant from the twenty-first century. I am also an appointed guardian of the Celtic stones in Zafra."

Rodrigo stared, his mind struggling to grasp her words. Then a surge of hope pulsed through him. Finally, someone who might understand what had happened. His heart skipped a beat. "If you are a descendant from the future, Lady Gutiérrez, then you must know of my wife, Lady Maryann."

Smiling patiently, she said, "Yes, I'm here because Lady Maryann desperately wishes to return to you. Though I have refrained from interfering with those who travel through the stones, this matter is different—it concerns our family. I can glimpse the future and the past, especially of those souls drawn to the Celtic stones. Your wife and future heir are stranded in the wrong century, and if they remain there, the Gutiérrez lineage will face great misfortune. Lady Maryann's return to your time period is the key to our family's legacy."

Rodrigo's patience thinned, his tone sharpened by frustration. "Madam, why add to my torment if you cannot help?"

Juanita chuckled softly. "Ah, your impatience—one of the traits passed down through the ages." Her eyes twinkled with amusement. "If you follow my instructions, there may be a way to bring back your Maryann. I must warn you, however, that time is slipping away. She has resolved to leave for Germany with Brian and Magdalena. They depart this very afternoon. Once she is on the plane to Germany, I cannot intervene, as my abilities are limited by geography rather than time. You must find her before she leaves."

Rodrigo leaped to his feet, his jaw clenched with determination. "Then tell me what I must do! I will do anything to bring her back."

Juanita reached down, lifting a burlap sack from the bench beside her. "You will need to wear these clothes, young man. You must blend into the twenty-first century to retrieve your wife."

Rodrigo snatched the sack eagerly and stepped behind a nearby bush to change, muttering as he struggled with the strange garments. Hearing his muffled complaints, Juanita laughed. "If you need help, young man, just ask."

Emerging from behind the bush, Rodrigo wore a frustrated expression, his clothing somewhat disheveled. The buttons on his jeans gaped open, and he tugged uncomfortably at the hem of the snug shirt.

Juanita stifled a laugh, whistling in admiration. "Oh my, Lord Rodrigo, you'll turn heads in the future with those good looks! Allow me to assist." She patiently explained to him how to button the jeans and helped to tie his shoelaces. "Much better. Now follow me."

They wove through thick, overgrown foliage past the castle grounds until they reached a hidden clearing. Two massive, half-buried stones rested at its center, their surface weathered by centuries. Juanita paused, gesturing toward the stones.

"There are several Celtic stones scattered across Zafra. For reasons I don't fully understand, the stones do not necessarily remain in the same spot after traveling through them. Now, here's what you must do." She knelt between the stones, motioning for him to sit behind her. "You will hold tightly to my shoulders and not let go, no matter what happens."

"Believe me, I won't let go," Rodrigo vowed, his desperation driving him.

With a serious expression, Juanita added, "Good. A weak grip could leave you stranded in an unknown timeline. And remember, this journey is not for the faint of heart." She gave him a wry smile before placing her hands on the stones.

The ground trembled beneath them, and Rodrigo's vision blurred as the world spun out of control. The air filled with a strange, haunting melody that echoed around them, growing louder until it became almost deafening. Rodrigo's hold tightened, his eyes closed against the dizziness, and his mind reeled. And then—darkness claimed him.

CHAPTER 112

Modern Times

Rodrigo found himself lying on his back in a clearing. Blinking, he looked around and noticed the stones were gone, though the clearing remained familiar.

"We've arrived, Lord Rodrigo," Juanita announced calmly. "You're still on the castle grounds, but this is the twenty-first century. You have twenty-four hours to find Maryann and bring her back here, or she and your son will be stranded in this time forever." Her voice was steady, but her eyes held a glimmer of concern.

Rodrigo's mind raced. Panic and determination warred within him. "Where should I look first, Lady Gutiérrez?" he asked. "Do you have any idea where she might be?"

Juanita nodded, a trace of sympathy in her eyes. "She was staying at a cottage that lies exactly where Esmeralda's does in your time. She's likely in town preparing to leave if she's not there. Remember, time is not on your side."

Rodrigo gave her a quick nod and turned to leave when Juanita cleared her throat. "Young man, a hand to help me up wouldn't go amiss," she said, amusement dancing in her voice.

Flushing, he quickly extended his hand to Juanita. "Forgive me," he muttered, embarrassed by his haste.

Once she was on her feet, Rodrigo took off down the path, his determination mounting with every step. The modern clothes felt surprisingly comfortable, and he marveled at how the strange shoes made running almost effortless. As he ran, he pulled the tie from his hair and jogged toward the valley.

Soon, the familiar sight of a small cottage emerged, nestled in the same spot where he remembered Esmeralda's cottage standing in his own time. He knocked on the door, but there was no answer. He peered through the window and saw trunks lined up on the floor—a sign that Maryann was preparing to leave.

Realizing she'd likely gone to town, he set off, alternately jogging and walking briskly. A passing carriage slowed, and the driver asked if he needed a ride. Rodrigo declined, not having any modern coins. By the time he reached Zafra's bustling main street, he was breathless yet determined, scanning the crowds with urgency for any sign of Maryann.

Zafra was both familiar and foreign to him at this time. Horses and carriages were the primary form of transport here as well, it seemed. Stripped-down trees connected by ropes coated in black material lined the streets, their purpose a mystery. The air felt thicker here, laden with unfamiliar smells, and his heart ached for the clean scent of the open fields in his own time.

Then, just as he was about to move on, a flash of auburn hair caught his eye—a woman in a short dress that fell just below her knees, revealing her legs. Rodrigo's heart skipped.

Maryann.

Good God, he thought, barely suppressing a gasp. *Could women of this time indeed expose so much of themselves in public?*

He moved to call her name, but his voice caught in his throat as he watched her enter a carriage. His heart dropped as he recognized Brian and Lady Magdalena seated beside her. Desperation gripped him as he called out, waving frantically, but the carriage began to pull away. Rodrigo cursed under his breath, knowing their next stop would be the cottage to collect their trunks. He ran, fighting his fatigue as he retraced his steps.

CHAPTER 113

Trip to the Airport

I must be losing my mind. I could have sworn I'd heard my name called as the carriage started down the road. Looking back in the direction of town, I saw a small figure waving his arms wildly in the distance. I could barely distinguish the figure of a man in jeans and a black T-shirt, his long hair loose and blowing in the breeze. The sight was strange, almost familiar, but we rounded a corner before I could give it another thought.

We soon arrived at the cottage, and Brian asked the driver to wait as we gathered our trunks. After loading them into the carriage, we set off again, this time for the bus stop in town that would take us to the airport in Mérida. My stomach churned with warring emotions, and I did my best to focus on the positive ones. I was about to start a new chapter and forge a whole new life for me and the baby. But the pain of Rodrigo's absence was difficult to ignore.

Halfway to town, Brian pointed out a lone figure jogging along the roadside, his head down, long hair obscuring his face. "Strange," he muttered. Minutes later, we reached the bus stop just as the charter bus pulled in.

Magdalena clutched Brian's hand nervously, her anxiety evident as they boarded the bus. Brian held her hand, squeezing it reassuringly as they handed the driver their tickets and settled into their seats. As the bus began to move, Magdalena covered her mouth and nose, and my heart went out to her. The sharp smell of fuel must be so unfamiliar and overwhelming for her.

Brian put a comforting arm around her, pulling her close. The gentle swaying of the bus soon lulled Magdalena to sleep as she rested her head against his chest.

Half an hour later, the bus pulled up at the airport. The moment we stepped outside, Magdalena's eyes widened as she took in the chaotic scene. The air was thick with fumes, and car horns blared as vehicles jockeyed for position. She looked at Brian in horror, covering her mouth and nose with her scarf.

"Brian, this is madness. You call this progress?" she asked incredulously.

Brian chuckled, squeezing her hand. "Progress has its price—pollution, traffic, and all the rest. Come, let's get inside where the air is clearer." He led us into the terminal with one hand holding the baby carrier and the other guiding Magdalena.

As we entered, I took a steadying breath, glancing around the crowded space. Part of me felt excited at the prospect of a new beginning, yet another part tugged me back to Zafra, to Rodrigo. I wrestled with the conflicting emotions as we settled on a bench while Brian went to check on our flight.

I turned to Magdalena, who looked anxious, taking her hand to offer comfort. "Try not to worry. I've traveled this way often, and I promise you'll be safe. Brian and I will be right beside you on the plane."

Magdalena gave me a shaky but grateful grin. "I can't imagine doing this without you. Brian has been wonderful, but your presence keeps my nerves at bay." Her voice was barely above a whisper.

Brian returned a few minutes later, his shoulders slumped. "I'm afraid all flights to Germany are delayed several days due to weather," he said, his tone heavy.

Magdalena and I exchanged relieved looks, and I couldn't help but laugh softly. "Honestly, I could use a few more days in Zafra. The cottage rent is paid until the end of the week, anyway."

Brian sighed, relenting with a chuckle. "It seems the two of you have made up your minds. I'll get us tickets for the return bus to Zafra."

As he walked away, I glanced at the bustling airport, an unexpected sense of relief settling over me. Time, it seemed, was giving us one last reprieve.

CHAPTER 114

Last Chance

Rodrigo had reached the cottage and was breathless with anticipation and exhaustion. His heart pounded as he ran up the path, knocking fervently on the door. Silence answered him. Refusing to believe he'd come so close only to be too late, he circled the side, pressing his face to the window. Inside, the cottage was quiet, the traveling trunks gone.

Despite the despair that washed over him, Rodrigo's resolve grew stronger. He remembered Brian's words about airplanes and the possibility they offered. Their next step was clear—they had to reach an airport to depart for Germany.

Revitalized, Rodrigo stood, dusted off his jeans, and entered the cottage, searching for anything that might prepare him for the journey. A curious metal box with a handle caught his eye in the kitchen. Opening it, he immediately felt a rush of cool air and a surprising discovery of food and drink. He took a long sip of cold water, then grabbed an apple and a banana, stuffing them into his pockets before setting off down the hill.

Returning to town, Rodrigo spotted a small brick building with a sign that read "Travel Agency." He pushed the door open, setting off a tiny bell above his head. An older man sat behind a counter, peering over his reading glasses as Rodrigo approached.

"Hello, young man." He eyed Rodrigo curiously. "Need help with something?"

Rodrigo hesitated, then asked, "Yes, thank you, sir. What's the best way to reach Germany from Zafra?"

The man raised an eyebrow as he looked Rodrigo up and down, presumably taking in his old-fashioned demeanor and slightly disheveled appearance. "The best way? The only way to get there is to take a bus to the airport in Mérida, and from there you'll fly to Germany. Looking to buy a ticket?"

"Not just yet," Rodrigo replied quickly. "Tell me, has a bus left recently for Mérida?"

"Left about thirty minutes ago," the man replied sympathetically, clearly not missing the disappointment that crossed Rodrigo's face. "And I'm afraid there's only one direct flight to Germany today. Leaves in about ten minutes."

Rodrigo's heart sank. "Thank you, sir," he managed, nodding stiffly before leaving the shop. With his head down and spirits crushed, he wandered, his mind reeling.

He had failed. But as he wandered back through Zafra's narrow streets, something pulled his gaze upward. Before long, he stood before the castle grounds, the gardens stretching ahead as if inviting him in.

CHAPTER 115

A Time of Reflections

As we stepped off the charter bus, I let out a sigh of relief, happy to be back in Zafra. Magdalena and I shared a look, grateful at the familiar sight of home. As Brian dialed for the carriage, I gulped down a long breath. The air felt clearer and calmer.

Moments later, the carriage arrived, and the driver greeted us. "Back to the cottage, folks?" Before Brian could respond, I spoke up. "Sir, could you please drop me off at the castle grounds?"

"Not a problem, ma'am," he replied with a tip of his hat.

Brian gave me an understanding nod. "Good idea, Maryann. A walk will do you good."

As the carriage ascended the mountain path, I felt my emotions swirling, a strange sense of anticipation growing within me. At the top of the hill, I climbed down, waving goodbye to Brian and Magdalena as they headed toward the cottage.

I strolled through the gardens, memories flooding back with each step. Rodrigo's face lingered in my mind. The feeling of his presence was so strong here that I half expected to see him appear among the rosebushes or beneath the sprawling oak tree. Reaching the stone bench where we'd often sat together, I closed my eyes, my heart aching. I could almost feel him beside me, his touch brushing away the tears that had begun to slip down my cheeks.

CHAPTER 116

Am I Dreaming?

A large hand tenderly touched my face, wiping away my tears. I felt a gentle kiss on my lips. My eyes flew open, and I gasped before falling very still.

Rodrigo? Surely this wasn't real. My heartbreak was probably messing with my mind.

He knelt before me, dressed in modern clothes that fit him so perfectly it was as if he'd always belonged to this time. He looked at me so tenderly that my heart felt ready to burst. I blinked. Maybe I was dreaming. But could it be . . . ?

Then he pulled me into his arms, his familiar scent and touch filling my senses, and I knew he was real. He was here. "Rodrigo," I whispered. Then the world tilted, my vision darkened, and I fainted.

CHAPTER 117

Francisco's Castle

As Maryann fainted, Rodrigo rushed to catch her, his chest tightening. He placed a gentle hand over her abdomen, praying that his wife and child would be well, then gathered her into his arms and carried her to the castle. He anxiously knocked on the front door, and moments later the door swung open to reveal a young man with dark, curly hair and brandy-colored eyes.

"Oh my, is Miss Maryann unwell? What's happened? Where are my manners? Please, come into the parlor and lay her down on the love seat while I fetch some refreshments."

My eyelids fluttered open, and I gasped, my eyes darting around the room. Rodrigo, Francisco, and his aunt Juanita stood nearby, their faces full of concern. Rodrigo was instantly at my side, his hand comforting and steady.

"My dear, I'm so glad you're awake," he said, a note of pride and concern in his voice. "I was just explaining to Francisco that you fainted because you're carrying our child. I also mentioned that we're to marry soon—you'll become Mrs. Roberto Díaz."

Now fully alert, I took in his words, realizing with a start that he wanted me to play along with his ruse. My questions would have to wait. I should be used to all of this strangeness by now. Grasping Francisco's hand, I turned to him, offering an apologetic smile. "I'm sorry for causing you any worry. I've had a few fainting spells since learning I'm expecting, but the doctor has assured me it's nothing serious."

At that moment, Juanita approached Rodrigo, a mischievous look in her eyes. "Hello, Roberto, I'm Juanita Gutiérrez, Francisco's aunt. It's a pleasure to meet you."

Then she turned to me and surprised me with a hug. "It's good to see you again, my dear." She winked.

I clasped her hand affectionately and said, "It's a pleasure to see you again, Lady Gutiérrez."

Juanita laughed, waving away the formality. "Oh, nonsense, I am no lady. Call me Juanita, please." Turning to Francisco, she said, "Francisco, would you be a dear and fetch us a bottle of wine?"

As Francisco stepped out of the room, Juanita leaned in, her grip surprisingly firm as she helped me to my feet. "Come, both of you," she urged in a low voice. "If you're serious about going home, we must leave before my nephew returns."

My eyes widened with sudden hope. "Juanita, do you mean . . . we can go back?"

"Yes, my dear," she said, "but we must leave now. Come quickly." Moving with surprising agility, she led us from the room. As we made our way outside of the castle, Juanita said something that shocked us. "I probably shouldn't be telling you this since you're returning to the seventeenth century, but I'll tell you anyway. From my mother's side, there is a long lineage of women with gifts, such as psychic abilities and healing, and many of them became Guardians of the Stones. My mother's maiden name was Portola."

Shocked, I could only stare at her. "You mean to tell me you're related to Grandmama Portola, Esmeralda, and Amalia?" I asked with disbelief.

"Yes, my dear. That is correct," she said. Her face broadened and transformed into a radiant smile.

It might have been my imagination, but I swear I saw a little of Grandmama in her smile. I looked over at Rodrigo, and he just shook his head in wonder, muttering something under his breath.

As we hurried along, the image of my little schoolhouse came to mind. A wave of gratitude washed over me—I would soon return to teaching the children of Zafra. Regardless of the century I found myself in, teaching had become an integral part of my identity. It had become my mission to educate, guide, and unite children, embracing their diversities, and by doing so, unite the people of Zafra.

I recognized the path Juanita was taking, and we arrived moments later at my former retreat, where I had painted the castle and crossed into Rodrigo's century for the first time. Anticipation bubbled within me. "This certainly looks familiar!" I blurted out.

Rodrigo looked at me, curiosity in his eyes. "Is this where you stumbled onto the stones and into my life?"

Smiling, I nodded. "Yes, this is the very spot."

Juanita moved between the towering stones, gesturing for us to kneel behind her. "Now, both of you," she instructed, "hold on tightly to each other and place your other hand firmly on my shoulder. Whatever happens, don't let go."

CHAPTER 118

Home Sweet Home

Slowly, I drifted back to consciousness, my head comfortably positioned on Rodrigo's lap beneath me and the familiar, gentle touch of his hand brushing hair from my face. I opened my eyes, disoriented yet hopeful.

"Are we home?" I whispered anxiously.

"Yes, my love," he replied, relief apparent in his eyes. "I checked a few minutes ago to be sure it was *our* castle and not that decrepit one in the future," he teased with a laugh. "Come, my dear—let's go home." His words wrapped around me like a warm blanket.

As we approached the castle, workers paused, eyes wide with astonishment, before one sprinted ahead to alert the rest of the household. When we reached the entrance, the entire staff stood waiting, their faces radiant with joy as they cheered and clapped. My heart swelled when I saw the people who had come to mean so much to me—Maria, Clara, Pedro, Amalia, Esmeralda, and Bruno. Their joyful welcome made me smile so widely my cheeks ached.

Rodrigo wrapped his arms around me, his voice a whisper in my ear. "Welcome home, Maryann."

Nearly eight months later, we welcomed a healthy baby boy into the world. We named him Adrián Diego Gutiérrez. Like his father, grandfather, and great-grandfather before him, he bore a small crescent-shaped birthmark behind his left ear.

CHAPTER 119

Where Has Maryann Gone?

Magdalena paced the cottage, her worry mounting. It was getting dark, and Maryann still had not returned from her walk. Brian called for the carriage, and moments later, they were on their way to the castle, the baby asleep in her mother's arms.

"Where to, sir?" the driver asked as they climbed aboard.

"The castle," Brian replied, his tone tense with anticipation.

When they arrived at the castle, Brian turned to the driver. "Would you mind waiting a few minutes? We shouldn't be long."

The driver nodded. "Take your time, sir."

Magdalena followed Brian to the castle's entrance with Sophia in her arms. He stopped short, catching his breath as he looked up. The castle stood tall, vibrant, and alive, with little sign of decay, as if generations of loving hands had watched over it. Brian's gaze caught on several children playing around a courtyard fountain, their laughter ringing through the air. Magdalena looked up at him, her face mirroring his discovery and amazement.

The door opened as they approached the grand entrance, revealing a young girl with auburn hair, green eyes, and freckles across her nose. She looked up at them with an open, curious grin, emphasizing her adorable dimples.

"Hello! May I help you?" she asked brightly.

Brian cleared his throat. "Is Francisco Gutiérrez here?"

The girl nodded. "Yes, he is. Come inside. I'll get my father," she said, leading them into the castle.

Inside, the space was alive with color and light. Fresh flowers adorned every table, and vibrant greenery thrived in each corner. Familiar paintings graced the walls, lovingly maintained, but Brian didn't see Maryann's painting of the castle. Suddenly, his eyes fell on a large portrait hanging prominently over the fireplace. He approached it, his heart both light and heavy with recognition of the couple depicted in the painting. Magdalena came to his side, softly squeezing his hand as they shared this poignant moment.

Just then, Francisco entered the room, joined by an attractive blond woman and an elderly man and woman. He extended his hand warmly and introduced himself. "Hello, I'm Francisco Gutiérrez, and this is my wife Denise, my father Miguel, and my aunt Juanita. I believe you've already met my daughter Miriam. Our other three children are playing outside."

Brian shook Francisco's hand, slowly shaking his head and trying not to look too baffled. Why didn't Francisco remember meeting him? Smiling confidently, he said, "I'm Brian Golding, and this is my wife, Magdalena, and our daughter, Sophia. We're visiting from Germany and hoped to see the castle before heading home."

"Of course," Francisco replied cordially. "My father and I will happily give you a quick tour."

Turning to Magdalena, Francisco added, "Would you like to join us, Mrs. Golding, or would you prefer to rest here with my wife and aunt?"

Magdalena glanced down at the sleeping baby in her arms. "Thank you, but I'll stay here and let Sophia sleep a bit longer."

Francisco nodded, then looked to Brian. "I noticed you admiring the portrait above the fireplace."

Brian somehow managed to choke out a reply. "Yes, it's a beautiful painting."

Francisco's face lit up with pride. "Those are my ancestors, Lord Rodrigo Gutiérrez, his wife, Lady Maryann LeMaster Gutiérrez, and their son, Adrián Diego Gutiérrez. Lady Maryann herself painted this in the seventeenth century. She was a woman well ahead of her time who spoke fluently in four languages:

Spanish, French, Romani, and English. She was also a gifted artist, musician, and archer."

Brian's hand shook with his heart hammering as he processed Francisco's words.

"Remarkably, she opened a small schoolhouse in the valley where she taught Romani and Spanish children side by side, uniting the communities in ways we still benefit from today." Francisco beamed with pride, adding, "Lady Maryann set a legacy of courage and compassion that Gutiérrez women still honor. Mr. Golding, would you like to start the tour?"

Brian blinked back the tears that threatened to spill. "Yes," he replied, his voice tight. "Lead the way."

Brian followed Francisco and his father but abruptly stopped when they reached the wall of ancestral portraits. Brian couldn't help but smile in wonder as he looked upon Maryann's smiling face next to Lord Rodrigo.

Francisco turned around and nodded when he saw which portraits had captured Brian's attention. He cleared his throat before declaring, "Lord Rodrigo changed the tradition of painting only the lord of each generation. Above all, he cherished his wife, Lady Maryann, and valued her as an equal partner, which began a new tradition of painting portraits of the lord and lady for each subsequent generation."

Brian furiously dabbed at his watering eyes, fearing he might lose control of his emotions at any moment. He was amazed by the perfection with which destiny had woven the final threads of Lord Rodrigo and Lady Maryann's story through time.

In the parlor, Magdalena and Juanita sat together on the love seat. Sophia slept soundly in Magdalena's arms while Denise prepared refreshments. Juanita reached over, gently clasping Magdalena's hand with a knowing look.

"I believe Lady Maryann saved the Gutiérrez family line and strengthened it in ways that spanned many generations. You know, my dear, though your journey has been long, I can also see a joyful future for you and your family."

A lump grew in Magdalena's throat as gratitude filled her. "Thank you for sharing this with me, Juanita. It feels as if I've restored something precious too."

Juanita chuckled, her eyes crinkling at the corners. "Lady Magdalena, you've done more than you know. Your path could have taken an entirely different direction. I am glad you chose the path you did. I only wish we had more time to share these stories."

After they said their goodbyes, the carriage returned down the mountain, and Brian's thoughts drifted to their incredible journey—across time and across generations. Once they reached the town, he suggested they pick up a few essentials at the Zafra market before returning to the cottage.

They'd nearly reached the market when Brian stopped in his tracks. A new sign hung above the entrance, bold and striking in red and green letters, written in English and Romani: *Welcome to Pilato's Family Market, Where We Offer Merchandise and Fine Gypsy Wares.*

A joyful grin tugged at Brian's lips as Magdalena leaned into him, with Sophia between them. The past and the present had come full circle, intertwined by love, heritage, and the enduring legacy of those who had come before them.

The End

About the Author

Deborah L. Gonzalez is a California native whose love for storytelling took root in her preteen years and never let go. Her creative spark first ignited through writing and blossomed further in her teens with a passion for dance—ranging from flamenco and modern to ballet and jazz—and music, where she played flute and piccolo in her high school band.

After earning her degree, Deborah spent over twenty years navigating the fast-paced world of civil litigation as a paralegal—all while raising four children with her husband, Mike, a talented musician and former city building inspector.

In 2018, the couple swapped urban life for the snowy pines of Prescott, Arizona, but after braving five-foot snowfalls, they traded winter for warmth in Evans, Georgia, where they now enjoy gentler seasons and Southern charm.

When she's not crafting imaginative tales, Deborah enjoys discovering the many parks and scenic trails in Georgia with Mike, always in search of their next adventure—or story.